The General's Wife

An American Revolutionary Tale

Regina Kammer

5th anniversary revised edition
Viridium Press

Copyright © 2013 by Regina Kammer
5th anniversary (2nd) revised edition based on a story originally published © 2009-2011 by Regina Kammer
Minor corrections © 2015 by Regina Kammer
Cover design: The Killion Group, Inc. 2015

Published by: Viridium Press, Friday Harbor, Washington
ISBN-13: 978-0-9910166-0-0 (paperback)
ISBN-10: 0991016602 (paperback)
ISBN-13: 978-0-9910166-1-7 (ebook)
ISBN-10: 0991016610 (ebook)

Acknowledgments

Thanks go out to my family and friends for their enthusiastic and continued support of my writing. Thanks to my beta readers Karysa and Sara, and my editor Barbara for all their insightful feedback. Thanks to Chris Baty for inspiring authors across the globe with National Novel Writing Month. Most of all, thanks to my husband for his encouragement, advice, patience, and love.

American Revolution erotic romance
by Regina Kammer

American Revolutionary Tales
Book 1:
The General's Wife: An American Revolutionary Tale

Book 2:
Winter Interlude: An American Revolutionary Novelette

Book 3 (Coming soon!):
The Viscount and the Veteran: An American Federalist Tale

Short story:
"On the Eighteenth of January, '78; or, A Night At Valley Forge"

CHAPTER ONE

New York, September 1777

From her usual perch on the second-story window seat, Clara looked out at the tops of the trees, their vibrant, fiery leaves accenting the scarlet coats of the British soldiers exercising in the yard below. She wrapped her woolen shawl more closely around her. Autumn had descended upon New York all at once one day in late September, a phenomenon so different from what she was used to back home in the Cotswolds. *Home.* She had to stop thinking of England as home. This was her new home now, her second autumn in these raw American colonies, and she would have to get used to it.

"Lady Strathmore"—well, she was finally used to that, after a little over a year. Papa had chosen the Viscount Jeremy Strathmore to be her husband, a highly regarded military man, a general who had fought with distinction and valor in the Seven

Years' War waged along the colonial frontier fourteen years before. He now led his troops in the new battle against American colonists obstinately demanding separation from the crown.

It certainly wasn't the marital match she had hoped for.

The general had returned to his estate in Gloucestershire in the summer of 1776, and he had made no secret of his mission. A man in his forties, he had said, needed to find a wife to produce an heir or two: a boy to inherit the title, and another in reserve because life was so unpredictable and dangerous in the colonies that one never knew who would survive.

The general's handsome features and commanding charisma made him the center of attention everywhere he went. He attended dance after dance, soirée after soirée, inflaming the passions of unmarried girls and flattering the egos of their mothers. His tall, lanky frame set him above the crowd, his scarlet uniform stood out against a sea of pastels, his shock of unpowdered gray hair unique amongst the wigs of the *ton*. All in attendance knew where he was and whom he was with at all times. Girls swooned under the gaze of his penetrating gray eyes and glared in jealous disappointment when he escorted another onto the dance floor. He danced with only the most beautiful of England's young noble ladies. Fewer still were privileged enough to walk with the attractive officer in a host's garden under cover of moonlight.

Then one night toward the end of the summer, the general noticed Clara. She had just turned eighteen, and Mama made sure she stood out, matching her dress to her eyes, daintily arranging her curls, pinching her cheeks pink. Mama's efforts ensured a great many young men set their sights on Clara, but the watchful gaze of her older brother, Oliver, and the political ambitions of their father kept all lesser suitors at bay.

As the general approached, Papa bent his head in her direction. "Now Clara, be a good girl. General Strathmore is a valuable ally."

"Yes, Papa."

And when the general was before her, she suddenly understood what all the fuss was about. His cool demeanor was intriguing, his presence magnetic. Her heart beat a little faster as her lungs tightened in their sudden need for air.

He nodded to Papa, "Lord Buckland," then turned to Oliver, "Lord Thornton."

"It is our pleasure, Lord Strathmore," Papa responded smoothly. "May I introduce my daughter, Lady Clara Hastings?"

Clara held out her hand.

The general tickled her fingers with his own, causing such a thrill to course through her she feared she would faint.

When General Strathmore asked Clara to dance, Papa and Oliver nodded approvingly. When he took her arm to promenade her to the center of the floor, she watched the puppy-dog gapes of would-be suitors turn to crushing disappointment. The general himself barely took his eyes off Clara even during the moments when he was paired with another in the set. His attention was flattering, befuddling, prickling her skin to gooseflesh while melting her insides with disconcerting desires.

The night of the Millington family ball, the final dance of the summer, changed everything. The general chose to partner only with Clara, making it quite clear what his intentions were. She had never danced so much in her life. Weary and flushed in the ballroom's heat, she begged for a break in the cool night air. The general brought her a glass of lemonade which she tried not to gulp down despite her nervousness and thirst. He then suggested they take a walk in the adjoining garden. Lost in pleasant chitchat, before long they found themselves very much alone amidst the tall boxwood shrubbery. He stopped near a bench, stripped off his gloves, and turned to her.

"I should like to kiss you, my lady," he said in a low sultry drawl.

New heat rushed to her face. "General Strathmore, sir?"

"I think, Clara, you know my intentions." His arms snaked about her waist and he drew her to him.

Her heart thumped wildly in her chest, racing with her quickening breaths. His hand at the back of her head held her steady as he took her in a savage kiss.

She had never been kissed before, had never known the wonderful sensations of a man's lips and tongue tasting her own, of his hands clasping her body to press her more fully against his masculine form. It was extraordinarily delightful, but it was ever so wrong.

Her hands flat on his chest, Clara tried to push him away. "Please, my lord, we are not engaged. This cannot be right."

He remained firm and unyielding, holding her just a little more tightly. "We don't need formalities to express our mutual passions, Clara, my love."

The seductive strains of his voice eased her into compliance. When he bent his head to kiss her again, she dared to cling to his shoulders, then, emboldened by his attentions, encircled her hands behind his neck.

"That's right, my sweet," he murmured against her mouth.

He lifted her up into his arms, took her to the garden bench, and laid her down. He covered her body with his own, enthralling her with kisses. He gently stroked her thigh as his lips trailed down her neck to her bosom.

Clara's senses spun in a fog of confusion and craving. This could not be proper conduct even for an engaged couple! She pushed him away again to no avail. Instead, he pressed his hips against hers, grinding her into the marble bench.

"Relax, my love. I will give you a night more memorable than your wedding night."

With that, he raised himself up to separate her legs, moving one to the other side of the bench until she was grossly splayed open. Her dress still covered her—for that she was thankful—but the general lay on top of her, crudely rubbing the stiffness in his crotch into the apex of her thighs.

"Please, sir, leave me be," Clara whispered harshly. She struggled once more against his resolute form.

He held her steady as he untucked the sheer, lace-trimmed neckerchief from her stomacher, then nudged her sleeves off her shoulders, freeing her breasts from her daringly low-cut neckline. Exposed to the cool air, her nipples tightened, the sensation sending a shock of need to pulse through her, a sudden yearning for his attention. He murmured admiration just before drawing a delicate peak into his mouth. The wet heat surprised her, thrilled her, distracting her so much she did not notice his hand moving up her stocking-clad leg to lift her skirts until he tickled the naked flesh near her mons, then proceeded with one finger to the dampness between her thighs.

Clara gasped.

"You are so very wet, my dear," he groaned. "I see you want me as much as I want you." His tongue continued to torment her aching nipples.

His fingers tantalized her, exploring the folds until he found a spot that sent her senses reeling. He massaged and pressed in an exquisite rhythm as she lay enraptured, lightheaded, wanting something but not quite certain what, knowing somehow it simply mustn't be this.

"Sir, this cannot be right." Her voice was breathy, quivering, annoyingly not conveying her fear.

"Ah, my dear, then why do you respond so willingly?"

His truth stung. She was rocking her hips against his fingers, his ministrations eliciting little moans between her panting breaths.

And then he took his hand away.

Grim reality untainted by wanton pleasures descended upon her. The general unbuttoned his breeches. Clara lifted her head just enough to see the enormous rod of his manhood spring from the open placket.

She tried to get up but he was too quick for her. In one movement, her voluminous silk skirts were at her waist, his hands pinned her arms above her head, and his prick was at her swollen, heated entrance.

In an instant, he slammed inside her, tearing apart her virginal barrier, covering her mouth with his own to swallow her shocked scream.

For a moment he remained motionless as his very presence stretched her, impossibly so. After the initial surprise subsided, he began moving in and out, each movement deeper, more urgent than the one before, a battering ram seeking full penetration.

Clara was too stunned, too clouded to resist. The general thrust and grunted over her. Yet through the pain there was a pleasure so elusive that it enticed her to join her seducer in the tempo of his violation.

"Yes, my dear, yes. You see now how man and woman were meant to be." He pushed further and faster, building to his own satisfaction.

Clara tried to match his pace, tried to grasp the summit her body was racing toward. But the general was too quick for her. With one final growl he emptied his seed inside her. A moment later, he unceremoniously grabbed a handkerchief from his coat and wiped his cock as he pulled out.

"Well, at least you really were a virgin." He folded the stained square of linen and pocketed it.

Clara lay on the bench, regret, anger, hatred washing over her. She was no longer pure. She was a fallen woman.

"Get up, my dear. We mustn't tarry too long in the garden. We might stir up rumors of impropriety." He glanced over at her. "And for heaven's sake do not cry. It is not the end of the world. I dare say you enjoyed it." He pulled her up and fussed with her hair. "I see your *coiffeuse* foresaw that you might be seduced tonight. Your hair fared remarkably well through the encounter."

After straightening out her neckerchief and skirts and checking the state of his own clothes, the general led Clara back into the ballroom. As she begged out of any more activity, the general took the opportunity to dance with a few more beauties that night. None of them, however, was invited into the garden. Once home, before going to bed, Clara washed the blood from between her legs, then vomited into the chamber pot.

A week later, Papa called her into his office. General Strathmore sat on the visitor's couch, its bright yellow upholstery attractively setting off the red of his military attire. With crossed legs and one arm draped along the back of the seat he appeared far too relaxed, perhaps triumphant. She turned her back to him as she stood before Papa's grand desk.

"General Strathmore has asked for your hand in marriage, Clara, and I have consented. It is a very good match for you." Papa stood up and embraced her, then held her at arm's length to look her up and down. "Ah, my child, I shall miss you."

"Miss me, Papa? I can visit any time." The Strathmore estate was not too far from their home near Cirencester.

Lord Strathmore coughed.

"A military wife must follow her husband. After your wedding, you will go to the American colonies. That is part of the arrangement, my dear."

Clara panicked. *Leave England? For a war zone?*

Papa patted her on the back. "And now I shall leave you two alone for a moment." He smiled. "Not too long. You and your mother have much to prepare." He kissed her forehead and left.

Clara heard the general get up and come toward her. She did not turn around. She stood her ground.

His hands were hot on her shoulders. He briefly and very gently wrapped his fingers around her neck as if in warning, then sought the soft skin of her breasts under her kerchief. He delicately and expertly squeezed her tender nipples.

Against her better judgment, Clara let out a little whimpering moan.

He chuckled. "Why should I choose to marry a whore who spreads her legs for any virile rake demanding satisfaction—" he began in his seductive bass tone as his lips brushed her neck.

Clara stiffened.

"—when instead I can have you whose virginity was certainly no pretense?"

Initial confusion curdled to comprehension. "Those girls … those girls you took into the gardens at dances … you did to them what you did to me, didn't you?"

He turned her around to face him. "You were the only one who struggled, my dear." He fixed the lace at her neckline. "If the others cared so little for their virtue that they were so willing to part with it, then none was worthy of being my wife." He tipped her chin up with his index finger and moved her head side to side as if inspecting her. "Although now I consider the matter with hindsight, perhaps not all of them had done such unseemly acts before. I certainly did not want some other man's cast-off, but I fear I may have made a few of my own."

"You monster," she hissed. "I won't marry you."

In one swift movement, the general pressed her against the desk and lifted her skirts, holding them in place just above her hips as he reached between her legs. Clara clenched her thighs shut, desperate to prevent him from discovering her body's betrayal of her reason, but his heavy boot between her delicately shod feet and his demanding fingers thwarted her defense.

He smirked when he found her heated and moist. He held her eyes as he stroked her slick plumpness, seeking and uncovering her excited nub ready for his insistent touch, raising a brow in victory as she descended into lustful oblivion.

"You, however, were delicious in your pathetic struggle to preserve the only item a woman may truly possess as her own. I shall delight in your embrace in our marriage bed if it will be as exhilarating as that every time. But, as I have already taken your innocence, there will be far less excitement now."

"You sicken me," Clara said hoarsely, her mouth dry from her agitated breaths. Her body began its carnal climb, reaching to grasp an elusive sensual summit.

But once again, the general took his hand away. "Of course I do." He let Clara's skirts fall, then sucked lasciviously on his dew-covered fingers before her. "In two days' time we shall be married by special license. Soon after that, we shall leave for America. There you will do your duty and provide me with two sons. I care not for any daughters, you may have ten of those. But you must provide me with two sons. Until you have done so, you will not be allowed to return home to England. I have written that into your marriage contract."

Clara gasped. *Two sons?* The earliest possible time she could see her family again, even if she were pregnant at that very moment, would be in two years.

She had little time to grieve. Five days later she was on a three-masted ship heading toward America. It was during those weeks at sea she realized she was not with child, and, as her husband rarely visited her in bed, she would not very readily become so. He spent a great deal of his leisure time gambling with the other officers on board. Frustrated that he had not been to her bed in over a week, one night she went to his room only to spy him thrusting into another officer's maidservant from behind. Betrayed and hurt, she closed the door quickly to avoid any confrontation. She had heard older married women gossiping at parties about such things, never thinking it would happen to her so soon after her wedding.

Once landed, chaos reigned. New York City had been burned and plundered and housing was scarce. Lord and Lady Strathmore would have to be located elsewhere. As most of Manhattan Island was a battleground, they were settled on Long Island. A month and a half later, the general received orders to head a little farther north to the recently captured Fort Washington, renamed Fort Knyphausen to honor the Tory victory. The general, however, did not want to expose his young wife to garrison life, especially not a garrison filled with Hessian soldiers. They were established near the village of Chesterton, a few hours' ride north along the Hudson River, in a farmstead confiscated from a Mr. and Mrs. Cuyler. They were positioned not far from the neutral buffer zone between the largely republican upper Hudson Valley and British-controlled territory to the south.

Thus they lived as protectors of the reclaimed New York colony. Clara hated the colonies, so far removed as she was from civilization. She was comfortable enough, yes, as she lived in what passed for an elegant house. It was new, stone and wood, but the ceilings were much too low. Although the general outfitted the rooms with mostly imported proper English furnishings, what was not imported was sham and common befitting simple gentry as the Cuylers were. The fireplace had a mantel painted to look like marble; the woodwork was skilled but never gilded. The food was rustic, the fashions austere, and the people unsophisticated.

The Americans—loyalists in Chesterton, certainly not English-hating rebels—were all charming and nice to her in pointed contrast to her husband's indifference. He had not allowed her to bring her own lady's maid or any other servants from Cirencester. Instead, he hired the entire household staff himself. They were in the middle of a war, he reminded her, and the colonies were filled with spies. Their staff was kept to a bare minimum.

Her new maid, Annabella, was spirited and the only person Clara knew who could be called a friend. When Annabella wasn't around chattering away about village life or her betrothed, Redmond, or Clara's hair and clothes, Clara was lonely. She tried to amuse herself with her husband's library—which was certainly insufficient as he left the most valuable books back in Gloucestershire—or some gentlewoman's expected task like embroidery. But what she really missed were the long talks with Mama or the ambling walks with Oliver. Her husband took no interest in her. Had he done so, it might have lessened the pain she felt being away from her true home and family. The general's neglect only served to heighten her despair and remind her that it would be a long time before she could return to England. She desperately wanted to be pregnant, especially pregnant with the requisite sons.

The general visited her bed once a week, on Wednesday nights, but there was never the emotion of their first encounter, never the tension, desire, or even the fear. His actions were perfunctory, a chore he had to perform. They both wore their nightdresses, never revealing their bodies. Try as she might,

Clara could not charm her husband into her bed on a night other than Wednesday, and not just a few times he was unable to perform due to exhaustion or drink.

Then, quite unexpectedly, one Monday night, the general went to Clara of his own craving. He had won a little money at the gaming table, had joked and relaxed earlier with his friends, and smelled like tobacco and Madeira. He was in a playful and seductive mood. That night the general took off her nightgown and his own and, for the first time, touched her naked body. His lips and tongue covered each nipple in worshipful kisses, then trailed to her belly. Before he entered her, potently erect, his fingers played in the curls of her mons, dipping lower to spread the honeyed slickness to the sensitive nub, a feeling so rare and intense her body jerked and she let out a little cry. He calmed her with soothing words, then melded her mouth with his as he penetrated her slowly, letting her experience every inch in her eager, aroused state. For one night, their lovemaking was exhilarating, exhausting, and it was never to be such again.

That was the night, she was absolutely certain, she became pregnant.

When she told her husband, he merely thanked her with a casual air. She, however, was elated. She considered how far along she must be and counted the days, the weeks, the months the baby was inside her, and how many months she had left. She prayed to God it would be a boy, and secretly hoped it would be twins.

Clara spread her hand across the slight swell of her belly and looked down onto the yard. The reds and golds of the leaves were a reminder of summer turning into fall, of time marching forward. For once in this horrible backwater of a place, she was happy. Every day her child grew stronger, and every day brought her closer to home.

CHAPTER TWO

Annabella gaped at her lover as he pointed to the hayloft with a quirk of his brow. "Not there either, Redmond," she complained, her hands on her hips.

Redmond laughed and pulled her to him, a twinkle in his blue-green eyes. "I can think of no place more secluded to enjoy your luscious body, my sweet." He greedily kissed her mouth.

For a second, she complied, until the whinny of a horse reminded her where they were. She shook herself free. "I will not go into a hayloft and mess my hair and dress. Lady Strathmore and I will be going to Chesterton this afternoon and I will not look like a harlot."

Redmond grabbed her at the waist, securing her easily as he tantalized the sensitive skin of her neck with a slow stroke of his tongue.

"I will not lie with you in a horse stall nor a hayloft." This time her protest was a bit more subdued. If it weren't for the fact that she would not have time to bed her betrothed *and* fix her hair and dress before doing her duty for her mistress, Annabella would have lain with Redmond anywhere, in any position, damn the hay and smells.

"I have brought a very large, well-shaken, comfortable blanket for you, my love," Redmond said, his mouth now at her cleavage. "And you may be on top. Your dress will not get mussed."

He did not wait for an answer but grabbed the aforementioned blanket hanging over a stall partition and proceeded up the ladder to the hayloft.

"Oh, damnation!" Annabella muttered before following him.

By the time she reached the top, he was already lying on the blanket, his hands laced behind his head, his desire apparent from the bulge at his crotch, his lips spread in a devilishly inviting smile.

It was precisely that look that had captured her heart six months ago.

Before she met him, Annabella was just beginning to realize she had something men wanted, and that she wanted something from them in return. From their whispers and entreaties, she discovered her auburn hair, blossoming womanly figure, and new-found coquettishness gave her a certain power with the men in the village, and especially with the soldiers quartered there. And then she caught the attention of General Strathmore. He had come to the village to hire his household staff, his eyes betraying an ulterior motive the moment he espied her. He asked her intimate questions and she responded willingly, ensnared by his seductive charisma. She admitted she was a virgin, and he immediately paid her mother a handsome sum to live in the Strathmore home as the lady's maid.

It was the general himself who gave Annabella her first kiss and taught her how to provide particular pleasures to a man with her mouth and tongue.

Annabella quickly realized she could get whatever she wanted from a man if she promised him a kiss or allowed him a grope or especially if she offered the services of her newly acquired oral skills. She could also withdraw her attentions to punish the men who worked for the Strathmore house. Annabella held sway over the footmen, butler, and boy-of-all-work—who was really a man at eighteen. Never, though, did she part with her virginity.

Then she met Redmond Moncrief. He was a groom in the Strathmore stables, strong and charming, with chiseled good looks and sandy blond hair, a little older than she—and at first not very interested. Redmond knew the general amused himself with Annabella and grumbled to her that he wanted no part of an illicit affair. Annabella flirted for a bit, then grew indifferent after his unwavering rebuffs. There were plenty of other men to play with.

But Redmond's very presence weighed heavily. He was always, simply, *there*—saddling horses for the general and his men or harnessing a team to the coach for Lady Strathmore, laughing heartily, complimenting freely. She grew very fond of him, and his smiles let her know he responded in kind. One afternoon he announced he utterly burned for her and could no longer resist her, which was just fine as she couldn't stop thinking about him.

His kiss was genuine, affecting, so different from all the others. It was not a kiss to satisfy a man's curiosity as to what it was like to taste her full lips, but a kiss meant to be as pleasurable for her as it was for him. She learned from him that a man may kiss a woman in other ways, a kiss that would keep her virtue intact, but imparted unimaginable pleasure.

But it wasn't enough. It didn't take long for her to give in to their mutually pressing desires. It happened in the utter darkness, in the dead of night, amongst a grove of trees far away from the main house. Redmond promised Annabella he would marry her as soon as the general decided he no longer needed her services.

They had to keep their relationship secret, although Annabella accidentally told Lady Strathmore. With that admission, Annabella found herself in the middle of a little intrigue. Lord Strathmore must not know about her and Redmond, and Lady Strathmore must not know about her and the general. For a girl of seventeen it was all very exciting.

And now, here she was with Redmond in the hayloft. She had gone to tell him to prepare the coach when they both realized they were alone in the stable. Nowadays, they took every opportunity they could get, sometimes making love more than once a day, sometimes not for several days.

This time, it had been at least a day since their last amorous encounter and she was on edge.

"I see you're ready for me, love," whispered Annabella sweetly. As she crawled to him in the hayloft, her thighs chafed and squeezed her sex, already swollen and wet. She immediately set about unbuttoning his fly, swiftly and expertly, licking her lips as his thick eager cock sprang forth proudly once set free. No words passed between them as she pulled up her skirts and straddled him, holding the head of his prick at her entrance. She teased him, wetting the glans with her own slickness, then taking in just the plum tip. She nipped him with her now-expert muscles, clenching and releasing, watching ecstasy spread across his face as he closed his eyes and lolled his head on the blanket.

But time was not their friend. Their encounters always had to be brief. Redmond gave her a chastising look and grabbed her thighs as the signal to stop her playfulness. She bent over him and gently kissed his lips in response. Then, in one motion, she engulfed his enormous hardness and sucked his tongue into her mouth.

He encircled her with his strong arms, holding her steadily against him as he thrust into her from below, deeply, resolutely, a man in need of release. His ragged exhales matched his rhythm, while she gripped him with a syncopated beat until her first orgasm overtook her. His would soon follow, but he slowed his pace as he often did, generously allowing her to have as much sensual indulgence as possible.

Annabella buried her head in his shoulder to muffle her puffs and pants. She had learned not to scream, to not make any noise whatsoever, even as wave after wave of wanton orgiastic joy thrilled her. She knew Redmond's cues, knew the excited pace of his breathing and the lost look in his eyes that precipitated his crisis. He was there now.

He let go of her, letting her sit up and take control, even while he continued thrusting. He nodded to her, his twisted expression reflecting the strain of holding out to the last possible moment.

She rolled to his side then held his cock to the blanket as he came in abundant spurts. He allowed himself to exhale audibly.

Annabella kissed his heated cheek. "I must be off to my lady, my sweet. I'll see you when you bring the coach around." She smoothed down her skirts and descended the hayloft ladder, unable to contain the smile on her face.

"...and tell Bridgers I want to talk to him. I have word that he is in Chesterton for a few days."

Clara overheard her husband speaking to his aide-de-camp as she took tea and tried to read poetry in the parlor. The sound of his name, *Bridgers*, sent a rush of warmth to roil her core, making it very difficult to concentrate on Oliver Goldsmith's lamentation on English village life. Mr. Paul Bridgers was not the handsomest man she had ever met, but he was certainly the most alluring. He was solidly built, somewhere between her age and her husband's—perhaps thirty—and just a little taller than she, which meant when standing face to face, Clara could look deeply into his lovely, light brown, almost golden eyes. Of course, she almost never gathered up the nerve to look into his eyes. When she was around him, her insides twisted and flipped, she grew overly hot, stammered half the time, and, when she did glance up at his face while speaking to him, had to quickly look down or away so he wouldn't notice the utter turmoil she was in. Afterward, when they had parted company, regret and displeasure would nag at her, and she would relive every word of their encounter in her head, only then imagining what she should have said. She sometimes thought about him at night alone in her bed, thoughts a woman should only ever have about her husband. Then, if she saw him the next day, embarrassment would overtake her, afraid he could tell what she had been thinking the night before.

A trip to Chesterton did not always present the chance to see Mr. Bridgers as he lived a little farther north, in the neutral zone. But his work warranted regular visits to the village. He was a sutler who supplied the British army, his myriad and far-reaching connections making him uniquely qualified to procure almost anything of necessity, or even of desire. There were rumors that he worked both sides of the war, as well as talk that his supplies were not simply of the material kind but encompassed transactions of a more venal nature. His indispensability, however, kept him inviolable, and General Strathmore, if he knew of any nefarious dealings, kept his opinions to himself.

Once Clara knew Mr. Bridgers would be in Chesterton, she made certain to venture out.

As she climbed into the Strathmore coach with Annabella the next morning, a twinge of self-consciousness pulsed through her. The staff would know there was really no reason for the lady of the house to go into town. She had offered to pick up the few items the cook forgot to have delivered, and had said she needed to visit the seamstress anyway for the fitting of a new riding habit that would accommodate her increasing middle. Yet, the seamstress could come to the house and a boy could be sent for the groceries. Perhaps, she hoped at least, the staff would see that the errands afforded her the rare opportunity to be useful, to relieve the tedious bouts of ennui, to remove herself from her husband's weighty disregard.

And even without the prospect of meeting Mr. Bridgers, Clara liked going into Chesterton. The villagers were gracious, and most knew Annabella, so it usually meant, besides the requisite gossiping, learning news of the war. If the war ended soon, she could return home. Surely, her husband would not want to remain stationed in the colonies forever?

She looked out the window as the coach pulled into the bustling yet rustic shopping street near the dressmaker's, staring absently as a man cutting a dashing figure in a green frock coat waved at the driver.

Mr. Bridgers.

She jerked back against the cushioned leather bench, desperately hoping he had not seen her staring at him. The carriage halted and she struggled against the compulsion to look out the window again. She allowed herself a peek. Mr. Bridgers waited while the footman prepared the coach step, a light breeze coaxing tendrils of brown hair to dance against his temples. The footman opened the door, but it was Mr. Bridgers who offered his hand to help her out. Luckily both their hands were gloved, as she was sure she would burn at his very touch.

His warm smile liquefied everything inside her. She had to remember to exhale in his presence. When she did, it came out as a humming sigh. "Mr. Bridgers," she said in too high a pitch. "How lovely to see you."

"I saw your crest on the coach and wanted to say hello, my lady."

Clara flushed.

His eyes followed her as she stepped down to the ground beside him. For an endless minute, they gazed at each other, their gloved hands still touching, dreams buzzing about in her head as she beheld a glimmer in his eye betraying something more than simple kindness behind his smile. Clara licked her lips.

Annabella stuck her head out of the coach door. "Mr. Bridgers!" she exclaimed. "As the footman has disappeared, will you do me the honor?"

Mr. Bridgers gallantly held out his hand for Annabella. Clara was envious of her maid's ability to be chatty and personable around him. But, then again, without Annabella's presence it would be unseemly for Clara to be seen talking to him about anything not strictly business. And, as only her husband handled their business matters, she would never have a chance to speak with Mr. Bridgers without the guardianship of Annabella. It was, as always, Annabella who opened the conversation.

"What are you doing in town, Mr. Bridgers?"

"Oh, this and that, Miss Rogers," he said evasively.

Annabella beamed at his use of her surname.

"And yourselves? What brings you to Chesterton on this rather chilly day?" Mr. Bridgers addressed Clara, although he probably knew who would answer.

"Lady Strathmore is in need of attending to at the seamstress's shop." Annabella grinned, then leaned in as if telling a secret. "You see, she is with child."

Clara flashed a stern look at her maid. Annabella knew such things should not be discussed in polite company. Her rebuke, however, dissolved to abashment as Mr. Bridgers turned his attention to her again. For just the briefest of moments, she saw disappointment flit across his face, but it was gone so quickly she could not be sure.

He took both her hands in his, his grasp warm and secure. "Then I am to congratulate you, my lady," he said graciously, holding her gaze with his own, a gaze so penetrating she could feel the joy dancing in the amber flecks.

"Thank you," she responded demurely, trying very hard to control the flush suffusing her skin.

He placed her arm around his. "I'll walk with you to the dressmaker's, my lady."

Her hand curved over his well-muscled arm, her fingers itching to stroke and explore, their compulsion provoking fantasies of his arms around her, while his closeness stoked the simmering heat below her belly. She steadied herself against him with their first step, shifting her weight, only to discover a luscious dampness between her thighs. She looked away, certain he could tell.

"Yes, thank you, that would be lovely," she managed.

They walked and chatted about the village, about the war, about how Clara hoped for a son, although she did not reveal why. Mr. Bridgers asked Annabella discreetly about Redmond. Annabella merely blushed and said he was very well, thank you.

The walk to the dressmaker's front door took all of five minutes, but for Clara it was five minutes of agonizing heaven.

"This is where I must leave you, my lady." Mr. Bridgers turned to her once again and took her hand in his as a gentleman might. But, instead of offering a simple bow, he brought her fingers to his lips, then kissed them softly, delicately, the warmth of his breath permeating the soft leather of her glove.

The simmering exploded through Clara's entire body, shooting sparks through every nerve. For one blissful moment this man she admired—no, *desired*—was touching her in the most intimate way an acquaintance may touch a lady in public. She was utterly unused to such romantic gallantries. It was the most sensually thrilling experience of her life.

Then Mr. Bridgers bowed and continued on his way, crossing the street. Clara finally exhaled.

Annabella took her lady's arm with a little whimper of delight as they turned to enter the dressmaker's shop. "He likes you," she said clandestinely.

"Who?" Clara hissed.

"Why, Mr. Bridgers!"

"Don't be silly, Annabella. Of course Mr. Bridgers is fond of me. He works for my husband. He has to maintain a certain level of civility amongst his clientele."

"No, I mean, he, well, seems to enjoy your company as a man might enjoy a woman's company." Annabella squeezed Clara's arm. "You know, like Redmond enjoys my company."

Clara knew she should reprimand her maid. But Annabella was neither a flatterer nor a schemer. She was far too guileless. She was telling Clara the truth of the situation as she saw it. Still, it would be improper to acknowledge that such an attraction might exist. "Don't be foolish, Annabella. You know only my husband enjoys my company."

"Of course, my lady," Annabella replied quietly.

The maid's observation, however, incited her fantasies, making it very difficult to stand still for her fitting … making it very difficult to concentrate on anything. Mr. Bridgers would be occupying every second of her dreams that night.

Paul Bridgers watched surreptitiously behind the Strathmore carriage as Annabella and her lady entered the dressmaker's shop. His stones throbbed from restraint. With her soft honey-brown hair framing an angelic face set with piercing emerald eyes, Lady Clara Strathmore was the most beautiful woman he had ever met, probably had ever even seen, and that included all the whores who had ever worked at his brothel. He ached to have her in his arms, to hear her moan underneath him in his bed. Every encounter meant his dreams that night would be filled with her, with the two of them tumbling together in a lover's embrace, her cries of ecstasy filling the night and the void in his heart.

But he had not expected Lady Strathmore to become pregnant with the general's child. He had presumed—hoped, he had to admit—she would be widowed at her very young age and desperately in need of male companionship. General Strathmore did not realize the prize he held in his home, did not deserve such a charming, kind, beautiful soul as she. General Strathmore did not deserve much of anything, really.

Paul sighed. He would be in need of one of his girls' oral expertise that night. Constance would be good. Yes, Constance, who looked quite a bit like a blond Annabella. He chuckled to himself. So artless, so buoyant, so buxom. Annabella would make a very good whore, indeed.

Over supper that evening, her husband dictated Clara's future—or, rather, the future of his unborn child.

"I just spoke with Colonel Phillips. You'll have to be moved somewhere much safer than here," he said, jabbing into his chicken. "Somewhere with much better medical care."

Clara was a bit taken aback by the pronouncement. She had just gotten used to living in the inelegant farmhouse, had just gotten to know some of the locals, and already was being sent away. "Really, sir, I don't think that's necessary," she replied.

"You'll do as I say, madam," he responded sharply. "You will go to Manhattan Island for your confinement. You may take that girl of yours—"

"Annabella."

"—and I'll make arrangements for you to stay with one of the other officers' wives. You are to prepare yourself so you can leave at a moment's notice."

Clara continued eating the now tasteless food. At least she was allowed to take Annabella. But the idea of living in someone else's house and giving birth to her son amongst strangers dismayed and even frightened her.

She wanted to distract the frenetic worrying of her brain with talk of poetry or politics. The classicism of Alexander Pope or even the presumed tactics of General Washington would take her mind off her husband's settled future for her. She glanced up at the man sitting across the table. He appeared to be in no mood to discuss anything, much less the "intellectual nonsense"—as he was wont to call it at times—that she needed at the moment.

The rest of the meal was spent in silence, as it often was.

CHAPTER THREE

Annabella waited in the corridor, knowing her master would call for her, then peered through the crack between the parlor doors. General Strathmore stretched out his long legs in front of the fire, enjoying his after-dinner port alone. He regarded his black leather Hessian boots for a moment in the dim light.

"Jenkins!"

The frail, bony servant appeared almost immediately. "Sir?"

"Get me that girl, my wife's maid."

Annabella swallowed hard.

"Yes, sir." Jenkins bowed and left.

After she was bidden, Annabella entered the parlor reluctantly. While it was much warmer than her tiny closet of a room in the lean-to off the kitchen, she knew what her master would demand.

"You called for me, sir?" she said meekly.

The general sipped at his port. "Yes, my dear. Come closer."

Annabella did so.

"Don't be shy."

She moved forward until she stood between his opened legs, her skirts brushing against his thighs.

The general reached out and grabbed her limbs through her skirts, squeezing the tense muscles above her knees. "Take off my boots, girl."

Annabella knelt down and proceeded to do as she was told, pulling off each polished Hessian revealing Lord Strathmore's masculine stocking-clad calves. When she finished setting each boot next to the chair, she remained on her knees.

"You may unbutton my breeches now."

Annabella dared not look the general in the eye. She was here to service the man, not to seduce him. She did as asked and unbuttoned the placket of his trousers, then folded down the fabric.

"And my drawers."

She did the same for the undergarment, revealing the general's magnificent prick. Even in its semi-hard state it was long and thick, resembling a ruby-topped ivory scepter befitting a military leader.

"Now suck me."

Annabella enjoyed sucking Redmond when she got the chance. He was playful, appreciative. The general, however, was different. He was demanding, forceful, unconcerned for her comfort. He sought only his own satisfaction. Still, she loved it. His commanding presence roiled her senses, leaving her wanting more of his wickedness.

She took the bulbous head between her lips, rolling the prepuce back and forth with her tongue. In a moment he was fully erect, smooth and hard to the touch, the purplish-red glans glistening from her ministrations. She released him to lick the shaft, wetting the skin before taking the length of him into her mouth.

The general groaned his approval.

He was huge, too long for only her mouth, so she had to use both her hands. She would really rather have him somewhere else, and imagined taking him between her legs. It made the experience more diverting, especially if she were in a position to squeeze the tops of her thighs together, as she was now.

She sucked the swollen glans while grasping the bottom of the thick shaft with her small hands, bobbing her head up and down, languidly at first. She knew he did not like to come too quickly.

"Take me deeper."

Annabella released her hands and adjusted her position. Slowly she took his cock as far as she could, until it touched the back of her throat.

"Deeper, girl."

She inhaled so as not to gag and swallowed as much of him as possible.

"Yes," he murmured.

When she had to take all of him, she could only do the act gradually, but that never satisfied the general. She knew what would happen next.

His hand pressed down on the back of her head insistently every time she swallowed the tip. He grew more and more forceful with each stroke, increasing the pace of the action. She had learned to breathe when she could, to relax the back of her throat, to let him take control. He would come soon, anyway. Her very presence meant he had not been pleasured in at least a day.

His frantic moaning resonated in her ears as his palm held her head steady. The prefatory emission oozed its salty essence on her tongue. Tears welled in her eyes as he rammed the back of her throat with his potent rod, shoving his hips against her. She sucked harder. Popping sounds filled the air whenever the tip left her lips, becoming the meter to his familiar rumbling growl indicating it would be over soon.

With a husky cry, the general stopped the upward thrust of his body. He continued to hold onto her, trapping her head between his pelvis and his hand as he spewed hot semen into her mouth. Annabella quickly swallowed. Lord Strathmore hated stains on his breeches.

The general grabbed a handful of her hair and pulled her off him. She pitched backwards, her legs splayed open, her skirts above her thighs. The general looked at her knowingly and laughed.

"Does my prick excite you that much, girl? You are as wet as a whore in heat."

Annabella flushed and pushed her skirts down.

"Someday, I'll have you for my own. I suppose it ought to be soon as you'll accompany my wife during her confinement."

Unsure if she was meant to say anything at all, Annabella kept silent.

"Come here," he commanded.

She stood up and went to her master. His hand snaked up her skirts seeking the glistening jewel he had just seen. When he found it, he played in her folds briefly before rubbing her clitoris with the most delicate of touches. For an instant, Annabella worried that he might probe further, discovering she was no longer a virgin. But he merely massaged her pleasure spot until she instinctively began to move against his finger.

Then suddenly, he took the finger away.

"I won't sully your virtue tonight," he said, wiping his fingers on a handkerchief. "I suppose girls of your class know how to gratify themselves. I will leave that chore to you." He casually buttoned up his flies. "You may go."

Annabella was frantic, in need of her own release. Encounters with her master always left her unsatisfied, as only his pleasure mattered. In her bed that night, she fingered herself slowly, imagining it was not Redmond licking her but General Strathmore. She wanted the general's tongue to excite her, longed for his massive cock inside her. She stroked herself frenetically, concentrating on the slick nub of pleasure, infuriatingly losing her grip. Spreading herself with the fingers of her left hand, her right hand worked harder, until her ravenous body reached its peak.

Exhausted, she fell asleep with both her hands between her legs.

"Manhattan Island? I don't want you going to Manhattan, love. I want you here." Redmond linked his fingers on top of his head and stared up at the stable rafters. "There's a whole damned no-man's land between here and the patriots up north. And a blasted doctor in Chesterton. I don't see why you just can't stay here." He let out a sigh of exasperation.

Annabella blinked. "'Patriots'?" He had never referred to the rebels as such.

"What?" he replied distractedly, his blue-green eyes flashing with annoyance.

"Patriots. You said patriots. Aren't they the enemy?"

"Damn, woman! Anyone who wants to reduce the king's bloody taxes is a patriot in my mind," he snapped.

Annabella stared at him in hurt and confusion. His expression quickly softened. He wrapped his arms around her waist and pulled her close. "Sweetheart, I'm sorry. I'm upset. It seems like I've only just gotten to know you and now you're being taken away." He kissed her forehead. "Maybe I can convince Lord Strathmore to at least let me drive your coach."

Annabella encircled his neck with her hands and pulled herself up to brush her lips against his.

"Damnation, you shouldn't do that—"

She giggled and drew her tongue along his plump lower lip.

"Your mouth is an instrument of the devil—"

Which didn't stop him from giving in to her demanding kiss.

"I've got work to do, love." He pecked her nose. "Although, at the moment, I can't quite remember precisely what it is."

Annabella pulled back a little. "Redmond," she said quietly. "We're alone. I'm not sure, but I think General Strathmore is in Chesterton with some Hessian officers, going over military plans and such." She pressed her body more closely against his. "At least that's what my lady says."

Redmond was dubious. "Then they must have walked. No one asked for horses this morning."

"Then only the horses will see us, love." She slid her hand down to cup his utterly hard prick.

"Oh, damn. Christ and damnation, you minx." He looked around for a secluded spot.

A listless old mare occupied one of the stalls. He raised a brow at her. She nodded. It would do just fine.

"Just a quick fuck then, sweet."

Lifting Annabella up by the haunches so her legs wrapped around him, Redmond carried her over to the back wall of the old mare's stall. She suppressed a squeal against his shoulder as he unbuttoned his breeches, then pushed her skirts farther up her thighs. He embedded himself fully inside her in one thrust, relief washing over his face to mirror her own satisfaction. He gazed at her lovingly, needfully, and slowly began his lover's motion.

"I had no idea I was running a whorehouse." General Strathmore's voice was forceful and deep, a tremor of distaste betraying his contempt.

Annabella pushed Redmond away and frantically flattened down her skirts while he furiously worked on buttoning his breeches.

"Seize him," the general snarled.

Five Hessian officers came forward, each one a wall of a man, clearly chosen for his role because of height, strength, and, apparently, virile good looks. They were dressed casually, with unbuttoned waistcoats and shaved heads bare of wigs and hats, their thigh-high jackboots polished to gleaming. Two grabbed Redmond by the arms, the half-buttoned flaps of his breeches and drawers hanging open, and dragged him to the workbench in the center of the stable.

Annabella shrank back against the wall and timidly looked up at the general. He was livid. Three of the Hessians stood behind him awaiting their orders, ogling her lustfully. Rumor had it that the general would fulfill any desire to those who were loyal to him, and the Hessians were fiercely loyal.

"Tie my groom to a chair," the general barked. "And bring the girl to the worktable."

The officers carried her across the stable floor. She watched in anguish as Redmond struggled futilely against the German soldiers tying his legs and arms. He flinched as one of the Hessians reached to button his fly.

"That won't be necessary," the general said curtly. "Leave it open."

Annabella stood terrified as two of the officers gripped her shoulders, one on each side. Without an order, they did not dare touch her indelicately, but looked as if that were the foremost thought on their minds.

"You, girl," the general spat, "live in my house as my property, for me to do with as I wish. You may not make your own choices about your life. And yet, it appears that you have." He circled around behind her and unfastened her neckerchief. He slowly pulled the lace-trimmed fabric across her flushed skin, then threw it to the ground. "I paid good money for your virtue. I've taught you particular skills for my own indulgence." He leaned in. "*My* own indulgence." His breath was hot on her neck. He reached around and untied the sash of her working short gown then slipped the garment off. She stood half-dressed before the group of rapacious military men, her breasts barely contained by her shift and stays. Instinctively, she covered her chest with her arms.

"Don't you touch her!" growled Redmond.

"Silence!" the general bellowed. "Restrain that man's mouth," he commanded. He returned his attention to Annabella. He drew a finger down her neck and traced her collarbone gently, as if he were seducing her in private. "Take your hands away, my dear." His tone was equally seductive.

Annabella quivered, unsure whether out of fear or anticipation.

"Take your hands away or I will have one of these men do it for you."

Annabella complied instantly.

"Good." Still behind her, General Strathmore pulled back the neckline and shoulders of her shift, then reached over her to free her breasts from beneath her stays. He turned to one of the hungry-looking officers. "Suck her."

Annabella gasped.

The Hessian carried out the command with alacrity, sucking in each nipple in its turn, then pushing her breasts together to facilitate his endeavor. His efforts were frenetic, seeking his own pleasure, certainly not hers.

"Touch him," the general ordered softly in Annabella's ear.

She did not need to ask where. She reached out to the German's crotch, feeling his huge erection hot against her small hand, finding it very difficult to mask her lewd delight at the attention being paid to her breasts.

"Apparently it doesn't matter who you fuck, my dear," her master said derisively. "Would you like to fuck this man?" he said, gathering up her wool skirts to her hips. He reached his hand between her legs, parted her swollen sex, and stroked her languidly.

Annabella was wet and aroused—whether from her earlier encounter with Redmond or from what was happening to her at that moment, she did not know. And the general was exciting her even more.

"It appears that you want to fuck someone," he said, inserting two very slick fingers inside her, then slowly moving them in and out. "The Hessian soldiers have joined our cause with far fewer women than the British. Their appetites often go unappeased for great lengths of time." The general quickened his finger thrusts. "They are as ready to fuck as they are to fight at a moment's notice."

Annabella closed her eyes to heighten the sensation. General Strathmore was pleasuring her. It was what she had fantasized about for months. Against her better judgment, she moaned.

"Ha!" the general laughed. He ripped his fingers away. "Put her on the table," he commanded.

She flailed as three of the Hessians lifted her onto the hard wooden surface. Seeming to know precisely what to do, they laid her down. Two each held an arm, while the third shoved up her skirts and opened her legs to expose her now-glistening pink flesh for all the men in the room to see.

Redmond struggled against his restraints.

"Hush, my boy," scolded the general. "We're only going to give her what she wants." He looked down at Redmond's erection jutting forth from his opened placket. "I think you'll enjoy the show, as well." He turned to the Hessians. "Take out your pricks," he commanded.

Each soldier obeyed gladly.

The general once again dipped his fingers in Annabella's sticky wetness, tantalizing her, watching her with a quirked brow, knowing his expert touch was driving her into the abyss of lust. He pinched her clit, and she jerked and cried out in shock and delight. He massaged the nub slowly, a smile spreading across his face as she further dissolved into wantonness. She pressed her hips against his fingers demanding more, needing his attention just a little bit longer—

Suddenly, he took his hand away.

She exhaled her distress.

"Beg for it," he said.

She knew he enjoyed being in control, but he had never been so cruel. "Please," she began hoarsely. "Please, sir. I want you to pleasure me."

"Will you do anything?"

Oh, God. "I don't know what you mean, sir."

"Say 'yes' and you'll find out."

Annabella looked around at the seven men in the room, at the seven engorged pricks. Even Redmond's. The general's huge member pressed against his still-fastened breeches. The sight sparked a thrill that ignited her lascivious fantasies, setting them ablaze and out of control.

"Yes," she answered with an unexpected tone that expressed her eagerness all too clearly.

Redmond's horrified expression almost killed her, but she had no time to think before the general grabbed her by the ankle and turned her ninety degrees on the worktable so her body lay on the shorter width. Her head now hung off the side.

Responding to General Strathmore's orders, one of the Hessians positioned himself at her head and pushed his prick in her mouth.

Another entered her cunt.

As one corps the men moved in and out of her orifices, sometimes in unison, sometimes varying their speed and thrusts. The general's fingers continued playing with her sensitized clitoris.

Annabella tried to accommodate the impossibly huge cock in her mouth without spitting and gagging. The Hessian cared very little for her needs, only adjusting the depth of his thrusts according to his own whim. He reached out for her breasts, now fully exposed as they spilled from her undergarments, squeezing the inflamed peaks in rhythm to his panting breaths. She writhed on the table under the double ecstasy of the general's finger and the other officer's abundant manhood. She tasted a drop of musky emission and knew the soldier at her mouth was about to come. She prepared herself.

"Next man!"

With military precision the men executed the general's orders. There was now a new man at each of her gaping holes eager to do his duty. From what she could tell, the three remaining Germans were masturbating. Not one had come yet, and the general was not letting her come either. He masterfully toyed with her clit, as she clipped the cock in her cunt edging toward abandon. Her climax was imminent. She thrust harder against her tormentor's hand.

"Next man!"

Annabella could have screamed in frustration, but the cock in her mouth was too quick. She was penetrated below by a most lusciously thick tool. She eagerly squeezed it in appreciation.

"You two. Work on him."

She quickly counted. One of the Hessians was in her mouth, two more stood on either side of him pumping their enormous pricks. Someone was fucking her—was it the general? It was a fantasy come true, a fantasy she so wanted to indulge in, except she worried about Redmond. Two of the Hessians were unaccounted for.

Annabella spit out the man at her mouth and lifted her head, seeking purchase to raise herself on her elbows. The general smiled amusedly as he penetrated her. Two of the Hessians were at Redmond's chair. She scrambled to get off the table but the Hessians at her side grabbed her arms. The general pushed his cock inside her as far as it would go, then leaned in and held her by the throat.

"I think she wants to watch," he said to no one in particular.

"Don't you dare hurt him!" she choked, tears filling her eyes.

"On the contrary, girl. No one is going to hurt your young man. In fact, he may find what is done to him quite pleasurable." The general pulled out to play with her wetness again, this time drawing the moisture to the puckered hole of her arse. He eased a finger inside the tight orifice.

Annabella gasped and lurched, trying to dislodge the general's finger, only succeeding in tightening her muscles around him. His invading digit burned inside her as it slid slowly in and out.

"Ah. Apparently your lover has left this virginity intact. Good." The general pulled out of her arse to once again play in her swollen cunt, this time wetting another finger alongside. His left hand grabbed her chin, forcing her to look him in the eye. Then he calmly pushed his two wet fingers inside her anus, stretching her. "You'll find it much more enjoyable if you relax, my dear." He pushed and pulled his two fingers in Annabella's arse, while his thumb worked once more on her frustrated clit.

Mouth agape, panting, she stared at him during the sensual assault, gradually feeling the tight ring of muscles inside her loosen. She ever so slightly began to move her hips in encouragement.

"That's right. Let me pleasure you." Still delicately working her excited clit with his thumb, the general removed his fingers from her arse and took hold of his still-stiff shaft with his left hand. After two quick shoves in her dripping cunt, he positioned his prodigious prick at the tighter hole.

"No!" Annabella croaked, her voice ragged.

The general said nothing. He spit on his cock, then with excruciating deliberateness pushed his way into her arse while applying more pressure on her engorged nub. It was heaven and hell all at once.

Redmond rocked in his chair, his expression racked with hate. One of the Hessians at his side held him solidly by the shoulders while the other grabbed his cock and began masturbating him despite his struggles.

Annabella wanted to scream for them to stop, but the wondrously lewd assault on her own body was too overwhelming. If she couldn't see what they were doing to Redmond, she would be able to endure the experience. She tried to lie back on the table.

"Remain as you are," the general commanded.

In support of the general's order, one of the Hessian officers held her steady as she straightened her arms. With his hand at the back of her head, the German turned her to witness the violation of Redmond, then released her to take his place by the groom's chair. Four of the Hessians jerked themselves as one furiously frigged Redmond.

The general's eyes bore into her as she watched Redmond's face and body exhibit all the tell-tale signs of building toward climax. Unwittingly, she was surging toward the same culmination. The general, this time, did not stop stimulating her. His thrusts were stronger, deeper. The pain had turned into delirious ecstasy long ago.

The four Hessians pumped furiously at their machines while one did the same to Redmond. Her betrothed was lost to her. His eyes were closed, his expression screwed in a fight between submission and control. As if on cue, two of the officers exploded at once, spurting their creamy fluid onto Redmond's upturned face.

Annabella was at her peak. She tried to hold on, to challenge the general's dominance, but he was truly her master. She screamed her orgasm, desperately pressing her body against the general's prick and thumb. General Strathmore shot his hot seed inside her bowels with a sharp groan.

Redmond came a second later.

"She's all yours, gentlemen," the general said viciously as he stepped away and took out a handkerchief.

The Hessian who had violated Redmond took the general's place between her legs, ramming her neglected cunt. The other two Germans matched his rhythm with their hands, vigorously masturbating their now dangerously engorged pricks.

At the last possible moment the Hessian inside her pulled out. All three men erupted at once, milky jets streaming against her thighs.

"General Strathmore, sir?" The voice at the stable door was tentative but firm.

The general looked up from fastening his breeches. "Ah, yes, Lieutenant Hawkins. What can I do for you?"

Lieutenant Hawkins surveyed the room casually, as if he had witnessed such lurid scenes before. "A dispatch, sir. From Colonel Woods. About your wife." He said this last with just a touch of derision.

"Thank you, lieutenant. I will see you in my office presently." The general turned to Annabella. "You will like Colonel and Mrs. Woods, my dear, when you reside with them in Manhattan. The colonel is much like myself."

Annabella sensed the lieutenant's gaze from across the room. He knew who she was, would know her mistress would be utterly appalled by such abuse, and might be able to help Redmond. She turned to him with a pleading expression. He merely pursed his lips and walked away.

That night, Redmond crammed his few belongings in a knapsack, vowing to avenge his assault and Annabella's rape. He desperately hoped her too-easy submission had been an act of appeasement, but could not erase her expression of utter abandon under General Strathmore's touch. She needed to learn who her true lord and master was.

He braced himself against the biting midnight air and slunk away into the surrounding woods.

CHAPTER FOUR

Captain Samuel Taylor woke to a familiar arm draped across his hip, a warm hand wrapped around his morning erection. Nestled against him was the soft, plump form of Prudence, the whore he had enjoyed the night before. He turned to the sleeping man on his other side. First Lieutenant Patrick Hamilton had his own whore sprawled over his nude body and yet somehow had managed to free up his hand to grab Sam's prick.

"Let me go, Pat," Sam whispered softly in his junior officer's ear. "Or there'll be the devil to pay. Besides, I have to pee." Not getting a reaction, he extracted himself from the mass of bodies on the bed and went to the chamber pot to piss a healthy stream.

Prudence squirmed sleepily and rolled onto her stomach. He smiled at her as he fumbled for his clothes among the various garments strewn about the room.

"You not coming back to bed, love?" she asked.

Sam held a shirt against his chest and decided it was his.

"You get a morning fuck for your money."

He tossed the shirt aside and jumped on the bed. "Then what are we waiting for?"

She squealed as he tugged her on top to knead her abundant breasts.

The mattress bounced under their enthusiastic tumbling, eliciting an annoyed grunt from Pat. "Christ, Sam," he said, pushing Sam with his feet. "You'll wake Chastity."

"Chas needs to get up anyway for your morning fuck, lieutenant," remarked Prudence.

"Isn't that always extra?" Pat yawned.

"Mr. Bridgers likes the two of you patriot boys. You get it for free." Prudence threaded her fingers through Sam's chest hair, then licked a nipple. He encouraged her with a sigh. She knew how to rouse a man first thing in the morning.

Chastity finally stirred from her slumber. "Ugh, I feel awful," she whined, grabbing her belly and curling up, revealing a spot of blood on the sheets.

"Chas! You started your courses!" Prudence waved at the red stain.

Chastity groaned, then turned over to kiss Pat. "Sorry, love. You'll have to settle for a suck." She drew a finger across the stubble of his face. "At least we know you're not a father this month."

Pat nipped at Chastity's finger. "You're not supposed to know about that."

"Connie and I don't keep secrets, lieutenant." She tugged on his earlobe with her teeth. "We're like sisters. She said you would have married her but for the war."

"And Mr. Bridgers doesn't want children in his whorehouse," added Prudence.

Sam glanced sidelong at Pat. That the incident still stung was reflected in the twinge of regret that flickered across Pat's face. After the pregnancy had been ended they never spoke of it again.

"We have to leave soon anyway, girls." Sam twisted his fingers through Prudence's blond locks. "You know, the British are mere miles away."

"What about a quick one, then?" said Chastity. "I mean a suck in my condition. I bet I can suck off Pat quicker than you can do Sam, Pru!"

"Ha!" Sam laughed. "And the losing man—he who spends the quickest—has to pay for both whores. What say you, Pat?"

"Agreed," said Patrick, with a smirk "I forget, captain, how many times did you come last night?"

Sam smirked back. Pat had apparently noticed he had passed most of the night pleasuring Prudence before attending to his own needs. Pat knew his urges far too well. Sam was practically bursting.

Still, he would have to teach his lieutenant a lesson in overconfidence.

Chastity scrambled between Pat's legs and quickly took his semi-erect prick in her mouth.

"Hey! Whose side are you on, Chas!" Pat complained.

Chastity hummed a laugh with her mouth now full of Pat's engorged cock. Prudence made quick work of Sam, too, sucking and licking him to full-stand, teasing his stones with nimble fingers. Before long, the girls pumped away with their mouths, glancing and giggling at each other.

Sam indulged himself with a quick peek at Pat. He rarely got a chance to watch his descent into ecstasy. His eyes were closed, his mouth agape, smiling, his satisfied groans matched the rhythm of Chastity's bobs. The arousing display was intensified by Prudence's efforts below. He had to restrain the urge to smooth his palm over Pat's flexing abdomen, to cup his rough cheek as he plundered his mouth.

Prudence slid Sam's cock to the back of her throat, doing something devilish with her tongue, something Pat never did to him. He groaned as she clipped the glans, stroked her hair in appreciation, wanting so desperately to simply give in. But pride reared its ugly head. With Pru's professional skills, he would be the losing man if he did not do something quickly.

He grabbed her shoulders and dragged her with him as he scooted alongside Pat until the hair of Pat's arm tickled his own. He sucked his middle finger, wetting it thoroughly, then nudged his hand under Pat's butt.

"Hey!" Pat's eyes flew open, and realization quickly ensued. He pushed Chastity's head back down while lifting his hips just enough. Sam found his puckered hole and slowly inserted his wet digit. Pat relaxed for his invasion, keeping silent as Sam delved deeper, the secrecy of their mutual craving heightening the sensual tension.

Sam leaned in and pressed his lips against Pat's ear. "Don't you wish it were my prick fucking you … slowly … in your tight arse?" He exhaled a teasing moan. "You know how big I am … I fill you, I stretch you … and you love it. You love how your arse burns when I tear you open…"

A grin spread across Pat's face as he growled a husky groan, resonating within Sam from their point of connection. Sam sucked in a breath to maintain his own control.

"You love it when I reach around to take your hard cock in my grip … pumping you … steadily … forcefully … as only a man knows how to pleasure another."

"Damn you, damn, damn, damn," Pat muttered, his head lolling on the pillow.

Sam quickened his thrusts as Pat flexed around him. "I'm frigging you hard ... harder, faster ... my cock so deep inside you ... my stones slap against yours. Your stones tighten ... you're gonna spend. God, I'm gonna spend too ... I'm gonna spend my scorching hot seed in your arse."

Pat grabbed Chastity's head and pushed her into his crotch as he thrust up, blaspheming loudly as he came down her throat. Her swallows beat a metrical accent under his continued grunting moans. Sam massaged until every bit of spunk was expelled.

Pat realized his defeat. "No fair!" he cried.

Sam laughed and pulled out surreptitiously. He lay back and gave in to Prudence's expertise, coming quickly in her mouth. She held him inside her, gulping until she had savored every drop.

A sharp knock on the door sounded the alarm before it was opened. Paul Bridgers poked his head through. "Sorry, boys, I gotta kick you out," he said. "Sentry's just come in warning that General Strathmore is approaching with some men. I think he's got Hessians."

"And a good morning to you too, Bridgers," Sam said teasingly. He retrieved his brown linen shirt from where he had thrown it earlier and pulled it over his head. "And don't leave the door open. Come on in and have a seat."

Bridgers sank into a slipper chair in the corner of the room, looking less like a brothel master and more like an older brother come to check on his errant siblings. The uncertainty of war made a man find family where he could. Especially if one's own family did not share one's republican sympathies.

Bridgers furrowed his brow. "Sorry, Pat, I have to use Connie for the general," he said glumly. "She knows his tastes already. She's used to it."

Pat pursed his lips as he buttoned his breeches. Sam flashed him a sympathetic glance. The general could be rough, but Constance was well-trained. "Yeah," Pat sighed. "I understand."

"Look, as long as he follows my rules, she'll be safe."

"Mr. Bridgers," Chastity said smoothing down her shift. "I started my courses. I need a towel."

"I'll get you one, sweet," Bridgers soothed. "Come here." He patted his lap and she happily bounded over to him.

Sam sat opposite them on the edge of the bed fastening his spatterdashes. "We're camping about a day's ride from here, Bridgers. We'll stay there until you can get the supplies to us. Unless you think that imprudent." He stood up and winked at Prudence. "That's what you should really be named, my dear." He wrapped his arms around her waist, then kissed her willing mouth, tasting his own musky flavor on her lips. "If it weren't for the war I could enjoy your charms all day."

"And if it weren't for the war, Pru would be a farmer's wife with half a dozen fine strapping sons, and you would be a lawyer in some big city," Bridgers commented scornfully. "I'll see what I can do for you, Sam. Now you boys get out of here quickly."

From behind the glazed lights surrounding the front door of the brothel, Paul watched as General Strathmore and his party arrived in the yard. There were five of them: the general, plus two Hessians he had never met, and two British officers—a colonel and a lieutenant colonel—he only knew by sight.

The patriots had left long ago, but not without a few tears from Constance as she said her goodbyes to Pat after her own client had departed. Paul knew he shouldn't even offer Connie's services to Strathmore. She was far too good for the likes of him. The general owed a substantial purse of money from his last visit, and the only reason Paul even let him build up credit was the fact that the British army paid on time for his legitimate services.

And Strathmore's presence at the brothel was a potent reminder that the general was cheating on his beautiful, innocent wife. The man was a swine.

He sucked in his breath to compose himself and opened the front door. "General Strathmore, what a pleasant surprise."

"Bridgers," the general grunted his greeting before dismounting his ride.

Paul snapped at his grooms to take care of their guests' horses.

"My wife is pregnant," the general began. "I'm here with a few friends to celebrate the happy occasion."

"Congratulations, my lord," said Paul, masking his disgust.

The general ignored the felicitations. "I'll want the usual."

"Of course. The building is ready as we speak."

"And that same girl."

Paul nodded.

"It's a shame you're not closer, Bridgers," the general said, removing his gloves. "I'm sending my wife to Manhattan Island for her confinement and she's taking that whore of a maid with her. You should set up shop in Chesterton."

"It is rather costly to run a brothel, my lord," Paul insinuated shrewdly. "I would lose several regular clients if I moved. I certainly could not afford to keep two houses open."

The fatter colonel chuckled and patted the general on the back. "Sounds like you owe him money, Strathmore," he said.

A consummate strategist, the general ignored the bait of unpleasant topics. "How are those supplies from the northeast coming along, Bridgers?"

"The republicans want textiles and iron in return for unobstructed passage of your goods."

The general sighed loudly. "I'll allow it," he said, not without a little annoyance. "Give them some rum as well while you're at it. That might placate them for the next time. And my wine?" General Strathmore had ordered French wine as a gift for another officer.

"It should be arriving directly in Chesterton next week. I'll have my man deliver it to your house."

"Give it to Lieutenant Hawkins, he's the only honest man I know. I'll be at Knyphausen."

"As you wish, sir."

The Hessians and British officers were clearly impatient to do what they came to the brothel to do. Constance was already waiting in what was a former smithy on the property now set up as a space for clients who had a taste for restraint and discipline.

Paul bowed and gestured toward the outbuilding. "Now, if you are ready, please follow me, gentlemen."

The yellow light of the autumn sunrise streamed through the window of the brothel's bathing room. Constance could barely stand in the tub as Paul washed the blood from her bruised and beaten body. Chastity had to hold her by the arms to steady her as Connie was unable to sit or even lie down. It was heartbreaking enough to have to tend the welts and wounds that marred the previously perfect flesh, but to see tears streaming down Chastity's face wrenched his soul. All his girls had a deep affection for each other, but these two were like sisters.

The general and his men had been particularly brutal the day before. It was unlike anything Paul had ever seen during his years in the whoring business. He hated himself for not intervening when he had first heard her screams but tried to placate his nerves with a reminder that he had, as he always did, gone over the rules with Strathmore and that Constance had screamed before. Usually the more corrupt clients expected—if not demanded—it. After a while, the screams had, as per usual, stopped, signaling the descent into a new depravity by the general and his entourage.

Sometime before dawn, General Strathmore and his companions had left unnoticed and without paying. Concerned by the eerie silence from the building, Paul dared to investigate only to discover Constance still tied up, covered in blood and semen, and barely conscious. It was the last straw. If Patrick Hamilton had been there he would have hunted down the officers and killed them all, probably with his bare hands so as not to waste precious bullets. But Paul was a trading man, a negotiating man, and would have to do something according to his own nature.

"I'm shutting down, Chas," he sighed. "I'm sending all you girls up the Hudson as soon as Connie is ready to ride in a coach." He tried to control his voice against the sorrow and anger raging within. His girls had seen him upset before, but this was so very different. He didn't want to scare her.

"Yes, Mr. Bridgers," was all she said.

CHAPTER FIVE

Clara dressed herself on the morning she was to leave for Manhattan, which wasn't such a bad thing. Annabella had been morose ever since Redmond had disappeared, attending to her duties in the most subdued fashion, sometimes with tear-dampened lashes. Clara didn't want her maid to see the spot of blood on her shift from the day before, anyway, or the stains on her nightgown when she woke up. She had no idea what to expect while with child, but she was pretty sure her courses were supposed to stop. Perhaps that was not true for all women. Still, she felt fine. It was the first morning without nausea. But Annabella would have probably called for the doctor.

She also did not want Annabella to know about her stays, so she slipped her arms through the shoulder straps and settled it around her. The less handling of the garment the better and Annabella should only have to deal with the laces. Alone at night during the last week, Clara had stripped out some of the whalebone stiffeners and replaced them with several pieces of her jewelry, carefully replacing the linen lining. The work had been tedious, and the garment was heavy. It was worth it, though. In the event she was left widowed and alone on Manhattan she wanted some sort of currency to purchase passage back to England.

Annabella came in a little later than usual to help her finish dressing. She apologized for her tardiness with a sniffle, and immediately went to work brushing Clara's bright yellow Brunswick and petticoat. It was an unnecessary act. The suit was brand new. "The coach is ready, my lady, whenever we are." Annabella's fingers trembled as she laced up Clara's stays. Something new had unsettled the girl.

"Thank you, Annabella." Clara turned so her maid could button her jacket and fuss with the ruffle of her habit shirt. "I'm sorry Redmond won't be driving us," she said quietly, searching Annabella's big brown eyes.

That brought fresh tears.

Clara clutched Annabella's shoulders. "Forgive me. I didn't mean to bring up—"

"Oh, my lady! It's not that." She timidly shrugged Clara off then moved behind her. "I thought maybe the general would hire a driver from town," she sobbed quietly, smoothing and straightening the back pleats. "But we are to be driven by one of the Hessian soldiers." She came back around to the front, one hand wiping a tear as the other brushed unseen lint from the quilted silk. "I ... I ... the Hessians look at me with a sort of hunger in their eyes, if you understand my meaning."

Clara flushed at the insinuation. "I'm afraid I can do nothing." She gently tucked an auburn curl behind Annabella's ear. "My husband is very particular in his ways." And would never listen to her anyway.

"He's to sleep with us at the inn tonight. In the same room." Annabella absently tugged and toyed with the flounce of Clara's sleeves.

"Where did you hear this?"

Annabella sniffled. "He told me. He took too much pleasure in telling me."

"Don't worry. I'll have a talk with the innkeeper when we get there. Surely the wife of General Strathmore should not sleep in the same room as one of his soldiers." At least an innkeeper would listen.

"Thank you, my lady."

The morning was cold and clear. In the coach, Clara and Annabella sat bundled up side by side in matching black hooded cloaks, woolen blankets across their laps. They said little as each was mired in her own misery, and each stared out the windows watching her world as she knew it fade away into the distance with every turn of the wheels.

Suddenly, the coach ground to a halt, pitching the women forward before sending them tumbling back against the seat. Above, the Hessian growled curses in German. Banging and clamoring on the roof brought more cursing, then grunts and growls as the whole vehicle rocked from side to side. Clara and Annabella exchanged horrified glances. Highwaymen? Clara had heard of highwaymen back home but not in the colonies. She braced herself against the seat and gripped Annabella's trembling hand.

The door crashed open. A cloaked man stepped inside brandishing a pistol, his brown eyes flashing beneath a hooded mask. He said nothing, but motioned with his weapon for Annabella to move to the opposite bench. He kept the pistol aimed at Annabella as he sat next to Clara and wrapped his arm tightly around her waist.

Terror ripped through her, but she dared not move, dared not threaten the life within. Her belly cramped from the tension of restraint. Panic ensued, dizzying her, overtaking her sense to breathe, until her lungs protested. She tried desperately to calm herself, taking small breaths, hoping the cramps would dissipate. A commotion outside jolted her attention out the window. Two hooded men, big in their own right but not as big as the Hessian driver, had the German between them, dragging him into the woods. The soldier fought back fiercely, almost freeing himself, but the men beat him to the ground, holding him prostrate with their feet. The larger of the two men took out a pistol. With one shot to the head, the Hessian lay motionless.

Clara gasped in horror as Annabella stifled a scream. Despite living in a war zone, neither had seen a man killed before.

Clara struggled against her captor. He held her more closely, too closely, his breath hot and heavy in her ear, the heat of his body penetrating hers. She relented. She had to, for the baby's sake.

The two men outside donned heavy black cloaks and returned to the coach. The shorter one climbed up top to take the reins, the larger one—the killer—came inside. He took the seat opposite Clara and her captor, grabbing Annabella's wrists in one thick hand, subduing her. The coach lurched forward. But they did not continue on their intended path. They turned in the opposite direction, away from Manhattan, to the north.

Clara's captor held her firmly, one arm around her waist, the other around her shoulders, ensuring their bodies moved together as the coach swayed and bounced. His grip was almost an embrace, touching her carefully, delicately, as if he knew of her condition.

Not so the man opposite. He grappled roughly with Annabella until she was enveloped underneath his voluminous cloak, then pulled his arms through the sleeves and inside their private tent. He forced her legs open amidst her struggles and cries, subduing her with a harsh utterance in her ear. She surrendered, slackening against his body, letting him manhandle her, screwing her eyes shut against the assault, her whimpers quickly turning to agitated breaths.

Alarm coursed through Clara. She renewed her struggles, but her captor gripped her more tightly. "Unhand her, you brute," she hissed, her voice shaking.

Her captor clamped his hand on her mouth to silence her. All she could do was stare with abhorrence at the monster opposite. From under his hood his eyes pierced hers with loathing. His eyes ... a striking shade of blue-green. Only one man had such color eyes.

Her breath hitched in her throat.

Redmond. It was Redmond who ravished Annabella.

She tried to look away, but could not, thoroughly transfixed by the lascivious scene, Annabella's expression a mirror to the pleasure elicited by her lover, a pleasure Clara barely knew herself. At Clara's side, the heat rose in her captor's body, radiating through her. He shifted in his seat, the movement exposing the wet fullness of her sex. His breathing was ragged, an aural accompaniment to Annabella's moans. Unwittingly, Clara's breaths synced with his, their chests rising and falling in unison, as if they too were joined intimately.

Annabella's yelp of ecstasy shot right to Clara's core.

She flushed in chagrin, hyper-aware of the closeness of the coach, and that her captor sat aroused at her side. He removed his hand from her mouth, brushing her cheek reverently before he resumed his grip of her shoulder, as if a caress after love-making.

Clara shuddered in shame.

* * * * *

They drove all day. Clara's body cramped with the tension of trying not to lean against the man holding her, to not renew their unexpected intimacy. They did not even stop for relief and she feared the dampness on her under-petticoat was not just sweat. It was thoroughly barbaric.

As dusk turned to night, they pulled into the drive of what was apparently the kidnapper's intended destination, a well-maintained two-story wooden house, rather elegant with six-over-nine pane windows. A still-masked Redmond carried Annabella to the front door, while the driver carried her traveling box. Clara and her captor waited in the coach in silence. With the end of their journey imminent, his muscles relaxed as his breathing evened, so she took the opportunity to shift slightly to relieve her discomfort.

The driver returned and took his position. As they drove away, Clara saw a candle flicker in an upstairs window. Annabella and Redmond would be having a reunion of sorts.

Minutes later, the carriage stopped before a small cottage with a steeply pitched roof and large chimney. In case she had the urge to run, which she certainly did not, her captor flashed his gun as she was helped out of the coach by the driver. Once on the ground, her kidnapper picked her up and carried her in his arms. Before them, the driver opened the door to the little house, then went about lighting candles. Clara's captor put her down and motioned with his gun for her to sit in a wingback. She did so immediately, then surveyed the tiny space. One wall was almost entirely taken up by an enormous hearth, well-used, with a black pot hung inside. The driver knelt to start a fire. Along the walls were shelves and cupboards. The room was obviously a kitchen, but one with a large bed placed in a corner.

The fire lit, both men stepped outside for a minute and conversed in low tones. Her captor stepped back inside, keeping his eyes on her. The driver returned shortly, carrying her traveling box, then left. As her captor locked the door, the coach pulled away, the crunch of wheels on gravel and the jangling of harness and axle disappearing into the distance, leaving only the crackle of the growing fire to fill the void.

Clara's gut clenched. She had never been left alone with a man other than her husband or brother. It was unseemly, more so given the scene they had witnessed earlier that day.

He stood at the hearth with his back to her and removed his cloak and hood. He let out a heavy exhalation. "I am so sorry to have frightened you, Lady Strathmore."

Mr. Bridgers?

Clara balked at the familiar voice, then jumped up when he turned around. Disheveled from his hooded mask, bedraggled from the ride, his brow twisted in remorse, he was still the handsome, gallant object of her fantasies.

Her fantasies. She had just been in his arms for the better part of the day. Confusion agitated her senses, mixed with a bit of relief and excitement. For some unknown reason, Mr. Bridgers had abducted her, Redmond had abducted Annabella, and both men were now alone with their respective captives. She had entertained many imaginary scenarios of being alone with Mr. Bridgers, but this one was playing out too roughly for her tastes. A man had been murdered, for God's sake.

"Mr. Bridgers, please, what is going on? What is this place?"

He sighed as he hung up his garments near the door. "Until a few days ago it was a very profitable brothel." He sounded disappointed.

"A brothel?" She never imagined such an establishment would resemble the estate of a gentleman farmer.

"Annabella and Redmond are in the main house. This is the kitchen." He peered inside the pot next to the fire, then swung it over the flames. "I had it built separately as clients do not always like the smell of food while they are, uh, being diverted."

Clara eyed him incredulously. "You? This is your property?" *A brothel?* "I had no idea." Her back twinged in pain. She sat down.

"And as for what is going on, I have had it with your husband, to put it bluntly. He owes me quite a sum of money."

"My husband?" Clara said vacantly. "He owes you money for supplies?"

"No."

It took but a moment for the information to sink in. "My husband would never go to a brothel."

Mr. Bridgers said nothing.

Clara stared at him. "No," she said hoarsely, shaking her head.

"I will tell you one thing, my lady. Over the last year the general has never come to the house on a Wednesday."

Her hand flew to her mouth as tears welled in her eyes. "Oh, God!"

"I'm so sorry to have to be the one to tell you this," he said, genuinely apologetic. He drew in a long breath. "One of my girls has certain specialties which General Strathmore enjoys. She's my best girl."

"What do you mean by 'specialties'?" She wasn't sure she wanted to know.

"She's very good at oral copulation and enjoys participating in erotic flogging."

She gaped as tears trickled down her cheeks. "Pardon?"

The color rose in his cheeks. "Uh, she pleasures his prick with her mouth until he spends his seed. After that he is aroused again by controlling her. Usually she is tied up and he whips her."

Such a thing sounded preposterous. "No," she said, her voice a whisper. "That can't possibly be."

"I regret to tell you it is true. Several days ago, he came in with four other officers, two colonels and two Hessians. They wanted Constance—that's her name—they wanted her services. After they left she was barely alive." He cleared his throat. "My lady, your husband not only owes me a thousand guineas for our services here, he almost killed my best girl. He is a rake, a scoundrel, a liar, and a cheat, and I intend to disabuse him of the notion that he can continue to treat others in such a horrendous manner."

The room spun slightly as she tried to comprehend all that she had heard, suddenly remembering Annabella's confession that morning of her fears regarding the Hessian driver. The general was a blackguard and, it seemed, surrounded himself with the same. "He cares naught for me, you know."

"Yes, my lady, I do know that," he concurred. "It is unfortunate and, for that, he does not deserve you. However, he does care about the child you carry."

"Yes, of course," she said sullenly.

"In a few days Redmond will release Annabella with a ransom note. Ethan—my boy-of-all-work Ethan Pitt was the driver in this whole affair—will leave her somewhere near Chesterton. Annabella will not be told that I am behind the scheme, nor will she know where she has been kept. If Strathmore tortures her she can reveal nothing."

"Torture! My husband would not torture her!" she blurted.

"Pardon me, my lady, but you do not know what General Strathmore is capable of."

Apparently Clara did not know anything about her husband, and it was beginning to sound like she was better off being the captive of Mr. Bridgers. Yet, something did not seem right about the plan. "But if my husband comes here as frequently as you say he does, might he not appear unexpectedly?"

Mr. Bridgers nodded. "I've sent word out that we have shut down for some renovation work needed before the snows come. We've done that before, so it will not seem so unusual."

The fire popped and crackled against the stillness of the night.

"The house looked empty. Are the—" *what did one call them?* "—girls there now?" Clara flushed just saying the word.

He inhaled deeply. "I've got a friend with a house farther up the Hudson River. They've been sent there and they'll all continue to work. Except for Constance. She'll be well-looked after, though." He leaned on the mantel and stared into the fire.

"And Redmond? What is his part in this plan?"

"He came here looking for work last week sometime. He also holds quite a grudge against the general." He quickly glanced in her direction, then returned to contemplating the flames. "Your husband has been abusing Annabella."

"Oh, God." She knew she had married a brute, but that was unconscionable. She sank farther in her chair. Her back complained.

"That Hessian, your driver, he was involved in the abuse." He caught her eye. "Perhaps you can see it was easy for Redmond to kill the man."

The web of plots and plans, of deceit and violence, was terribly unsettling. Could she trust Mr. Bridgers? She had to. She couldn't trust her husband, as if she ever did. The room stopped spinning but instead grew warm, too warm, flushing her skin with prickling heat. She was still wearing her heavy cloak. "Mr. Bridgers," she said quietly, "are we to stay here? Will there be more traveling? May I remove my cloak?"

Mr. Bridgers started. "Oh, my lady, I am sorry. Yes, please."

She shook out her cloak and went to hang it next to his.

"And you must be half-starved." He went to a cupboard on the wall opposite the hearth, the wall containing the bed. "We have a meat pie already baked for tonight," he said over his shoulder. "I hope you don't—"

He did not finish his sentence. He stared at her with a noticeably panicked expression.

"Mr. Bridgers?"

He ran to her and took her hands. "My lady … your gown … there's blood."

Clara grabbed her skirts and twisted around to look. Near her buttocks and thighs against the bright yellow of the silk was a large red stain, the edges dried brown. It was much worse than the spots she had seen that morning. "Oh, God!"

She fell to her knees.

"Lady Strathmore," Paul said, gently shaking her by the arms.

She did not respond. She wobbled on her knees as she clutched at her skirt.

"Lady Strathmore," he tried again. "My lady … look at me, please." He cupped her face, forcing her to look up at him. "I fear you are losing your child."

She sank down farther, covering her face with her hands. "Oh, God, no, no, no."

Paul glanced around the room frantically. He usually kept supplies in every room in order to presuppose his clients' every need. *There must be towels. Yes … the lower cupboard to the left of the hearth … near the door … easy to replenish.*

He grabbed the towels from the cupboard, went to the bed, and flung back the covers. He laid the towels on the bed three thick and doubled. He turned toward Lady Strathmore. She would have to get out of her clothes. Into a nightdress, maybe. No. Better to have her remain in her already soiled shift. *Christ!* He hadn't thought this far ahead.

She's not one of the whores. She is simply not going to do this in my presence.

He knelt down beside her. "Lady Strathmore, I need you to listen to me. I am going to turn my back while I make you a tea—a tea to relieve your pain—and I need you to—" Paul inhaled deeply "—I need you to take off your clothes, I mean only to your shift. You have another, do you not?"

She roused herself. "Yes, yes. In my box." She took his arm as he helped her stand.

They stood for a moment facing each other, her forehead furrowed with anxiety or fear. Probably both.

"I'll need help with my stays," she said.

"I'll unlace them. I've done it before." The second he said it, Paul cringed. He quickly went to the cupboards near the hearth, searching the stock of herbs for the right remedies, pulling down the needed jars, gathering cups and spoons, mumbling the ingredients. The sounds of her undressing were unusually loud, and he tried to make as much noise as possible. He checked the kettle. The water was boiling, so he swung the pot out, perhaps with too much enthusiasm, splashing a bit on the brick floor.

"I need your help now."

Her voice was plaintive, her need for him arousing. Paul tamped down his desires and turned slowly. Her back was to him. She had stripped to her under-petticoat. If she hadn't been still half-dressed as such, Paul was not sure what he would have done. He unlaced her stays, trying desperately to keep his trembling hands from touching her body. The temptation was driving him insane.

"All finished, my lady," he said with an unexpected sultry tone. The words did not come out as he intended.

"Thank you," was all she said.

"When you are ready, my lady, please lie on the bed over the towels and draw up the covers." He turned his back to her once again to attend to the teas.

He prepared three tonics: willow bark to relieve cramps, valerian to do the same and help her sleep, and bitter wormwood with honey to quicken the release of the fetus. He knew the recipes for relief by heart. How many times had he done this for his girls? Relief for menstrual cramps was to be expected, but too many of the girls lost count of their days, or forgot to take carota seeds after intercourse, or forgot to use a pessary. Too many times Paul had had to end an unplanned pregnancy.

One by one he brought the brews to Lady Strathmore, making sure she had a bit of meat pie between each drink. She might experience a slight fever, he told her. Eventually, she fell asleep amidst tears and sweat. Paul stripped off his jacket and shoes and climbed into bed with her, pulling her to him but unsure for whose comfort the tender act was meant to be.

CHAPTER SIX

"I should be so mad at you." Redmond paced the length of the second-floor bedroom, his arms tight at his sides, hands balled into fists, restraining the urge to hit something, anything.

"Redmond, love, please understand, I had to do it. They might have hurt you more if I hadn't given in." Annabella sat on the edge of the bed wringing her hands. "They could have killed you," she said hoarsely.

He had spent the better part of the week cursing her, wanting to punish her, playing out scenarios in his head. Exerting his control over her in the coach only served to rile him up. She had given in far too easily to a man who, at the time, was a stranger to her. And now, after she had attempted a tender reunion, they had spent the last half hour arguing about her conduct with the general and the Hessian officers.

He was starving. He couldn't continue arguing with her on an empty stomach. Besides, finally alone with her, the very first time without the risk of someone walking in on them, he simply could not stay mad at her.

And that just made him mad at himself.

He leaned against the mantel and ran his hand through his hair in exasperation. "Christ, Annabella. What should I think?"

She stroked his back tentatively. "That I love you. That I would do anything for you."

He softened at her caress.

"Redmond, sweet, I have been sick with worry for the last week. And now you're here with me. Please forgive whatever it is I have done. I just want to be with you right now."

His stomach rumbled.

She giggled. "I'm hungry, too. Is there anything to eat?"

"We stocked food in an old kitchen downstairs." He turned to face her. She looked up at him, earnestness mixed with trepidation. He lifted her chin and pecked her lips. "C'mon."

They had never shared a meal together, and the simple act of eating cold pies and cider inspired talk of living a normal life as man and wife. She flirted and giggled and made him laugh, and he quickly forgot his anger. But he could not forget why they were there in the first place. She didn't ask. She probably thought she had been kidnapped just to be with him.

Annabella pushed back from the table and gazed at him with a tilt of her head and a raised brow. "Redmond," she said, licking her lips. "We've never been alone like this before. Shouldn't we make the most of it?"

She was right, and anything he had to say to her could wait for morning. He smiled a devious smile. "Let's go back upstairs," he said, taking her hand.

The fire had died in the bedroom, but it was still cozy. He threw another log on the grate and pulled up an old wingback by the hearth. He sat down.

"Take off your clothes," he commanded.

Annabella hesitated and shot him a questioning look.

"Perhaps you did not hear the first time," he growled. "Take off your clothes, woman."

She sucked in a lip and proceeded to untie her kerchief, then pulled it off languidly, holding his gaze until his eyes dipped to her bared cleavage.

He swallowed hard, waiting for the next bit of clothing to come off.

But she stood there with a smirk, rebelling against his imperious tone.

Shit. His cock stirred. He would have to let her have her little game. He toyed with the buttons of his waistcoat.

It worked.

She began to untie the laces of her short fitted jacket, and with each tug, he freed one of his own fastenings. She slowed her pace and he stopped. Her garment was far more complicated. He couldn't let her win.

Her jacket undone, Annabella turned her back to him. She lifted the jacket over her head, then twisted to look over her shoulder. His waistcoat was now completely unbuttoned, and he gripped the arms of the chair to keep himself from molesting the little minx.

She smiled and turned back to face him, clutching her jacket to her chest. Slowly, she pulled the garment away from her body, then dangled it out in front of her before dropping it on the floor.

Redmond licked his lips and stared at the tops of her breasts, billowing out from beneath her stays, yet still covered by her shift. She smiled provocatively as her hands went behind her to worry the button at the waistband of her quilted over-petticoat. He locked her gaze with his as he unfastened the three buttons at the waistband of his breeches, and when she pushed her heavy skirt over her hips and down to the floor, he proceeded to the buttons of his fall front.

She stepped out of her skirt and kicked the garment along the wooden boards.

She drew her hands from the top of her stays down the front of her body to land at the waist of her woolen under-petticoat. She grasped the linen tie. Redmond readied his fingers at the buttons of his drawers, then hesitated. He lifted a brow at her. She would have to go first.

She scowled, then pulled the end of the bow and untied the string. With a sway in her hips, she shuffled the garment down, then once again stepped out and pushed the skirt across the floor.

She didn't have much else to take off. Behind her, the firelight danced, leaving the front in shadow. His cock complained.

She loosened the top of her shift, exposing a little bit more of her pale fleshy bosom. She strolled seductively over to him.

He stared up at her as she nudged open his thighs to stand between his legs. She lifted her left foot onto the worn padded arm of his chair. Redmond reached out to touch her leg, now so close within his grasp. She stilled his hand, then smiled as he instead freed his erect cock from his drawers and began stroking himself lazily.

Annabella unbuckled her shoe and returned her foot to the floor, then switched legs to unbuckle the other. She stepped backwards and slipped off both shoes, wiggling her stocking-covered toes.

Once again she turned her back to him and reached around to unlace her stays, untying and then loosening the strings at a maddeningly slow pace. She pulled the stiff garment over her head and held it out at arm's length before dropping it to the floor. It made a soft thud when it landed.

Redmond had never seen her in such a state of undress. The flickering light cast by the fire and candles cast shadows across her body, concealing and revealing her form under the sheer cotton shift. She swayed her hips in a soft undulating movement while languorously gathering up the fabric along her sides as if she were going to lift the final piece of clothing off her body. It took every ounce of self-control to remain seated and not throw her to the floor and slam inside her cunt.

She let go of her shift and looked back at him, biting her lower lip.

"You're a saucy one, aren't you?" he said. "You're the devil's mistress. Come here." He motioned for her to resume her position between his legs.

"No, love," she said as she sauntered over to him. "I'm *your* woman." She looked down at him, beaming. "Yours."

He reached up and untied the strings at her sleeves and loosened the openings, tickling the skin of her arms. He pulled the drawstring at her neckline, untying the bow. He took a sleeve in each of his hands and tugged the shift off one shoulder, then the other. With a final yank the filmy garment fell to the floor and pooled at her feet.

His eyes drifted up and down her body, taking in every soft curve. "Damnation," he whispered reverently. "You're a sight to behold."

Her generous white bosoms capped by tender rosy peaks jutted forth buoyantly as if floating on air. Redmond cupped a hand on the side of each breast, taking time to brush his thumbs against her aroused nipples as he weighed the demi-globes in his palms. He traced his hands down her figure, curving in where her body nipped in a little at the waist, then out at the swelling of her belly. He stopped at her fleshy hips, caressed them gently, then glided around to grab her plump buttocks. He kneaded the luscious pillowy cheeks before drawing his hands down the backs of her thighs, eliciting a sighing mewl. He stopped at her garters and fumbled to untie them. "I want to see all of you," he said, pushing down her stockings.

Annabella stepped back slightly and one by one stripped off the last of her clothing, revealing her shapely calves. She now stood before him utterly nude. He gawked, stunned, and grabbed his erection. With a glimmer of wickedness in her eyes, she posed this way and that, her hands playfully hiding bits of flesh or presenting her attributes for his approval. Redmond laughed in delight while stroking his engorged prick.

"Come to me. Be with me." He held out a hand.

Annabella touched his fingers before kneeling down between his legs. Her hands rubbed his thighs, still confined in tight breeches, and reached around underneath to cup his buttocks. She dipped her head and licked his cock teasingly before gently taking him into her mouth.

Redmond groaned. "Oh, God, woman." He reveled in the familiar feeling, heightening it by stroking her nude shoulders and back. He pushed his hips against her mouth. She quickened her pace. He was in heaven, he was…

He grabbed her hair to pull her off him, tearing her cap off in the process. "No! Damn it! Don't make me spend yet." He nodded toward the bed. "We have a bed, love, a proper bed with a mattress and sheets. I want to make love to you there. And I want to finally be able to wake up next to you in the morning."

Annabella took his hand and he stood up. She giggled at his undone breeches and drawers.

"Damn," he said. He had no patience to strip slowly for his beloved and tore off his clothes, tossing jacket, waistcoat, cravat, shirt—everything in a pile on the floor. In a minute he stood stark naked before her.

Annabella watched, stunned, her eyes wide and mouth open. "I … I never knew you had so much hair." She swallowed. "You're perfect."

In two steps Redmond crossed the floor, picked her up amidst her joyous squeals, and threw her on the bed. For a second he hovered over her, his prick poised at her entrance, aching to be inside her.

"You liked it when he fucked you in the arse, didn't you?"

She stared at him, a mixture of confusion and desire in her eyes. Tears formed on her lashes.

Damn. That was not the way to put it. "Love," he began gently, "if I poke you in the arse, I can spend inside you." He pecked her nose. "Darling, I don't want to have to pull out."

"Then don't. I want to make love to you the proper way, in a proper bed." She held his face in her hands, stroking his cheeks. "Spend inside me. Please, Redmond. I want you to. I want your child."

In an instant he was inside her, plunging deep, a man possessed. He grunted and growled, and she laughed and moaned. He came too soon, she too often. Minutes later he was up her again, this time taking it more slowly.

They made love the entire night, tumbling like newlyweds. Alone in a vacant house with no one around, they made all the damn noise they wanted. When exhaustion finally descended in the hours after midnight, Redmond wrapped his arms around his Annabella, protecting her as they slept.

He would tell her what she needed to do in the morning.

Clara awoke with a start. She had been dreaming the most delicious dream. Mr. Bridgers was lying with her on the bed, holding her, caressing her breasts, whispering naughty words in her ear. She stretched against him with a moaning sigh.

But something about it wasn't just a dream.

She was actually curled up against him as he leaned against the headboard. Even more indecently, she was lying between his legs. She stiffened.

"You're awake," he said, stroking her hair lightly.

"Mr. Bridgers?" She sat up, clutching the covers around her. "What is going on?"

He chuckled and got off the bed. He was fully clothed except for his jacket and shoes, although his waistcoat was unbuttoned, his cravat loosened, and he needed a shave. "Don't worry. I did not take advantage of the situation. But you were crying quite a bit and I thought you could use some comfort." He looked at her more seriously. "I had to change the towels several times over the last two days."

"Two days!"

"You've had a more serious fever than I expected," he said quietly. "I think, though, it may be a few more days before the child is finally gone."

Her son. A twinge of grief passed through her, but she wasn't sure if it was because she had lost the general's son or because it would be that much longer before she could return home to England.

"I'm sorry, my lady. Please accept my condolences."

Three rhythmic raps sounded on the door.

"Ah. That's Ethan with some supplies."

Mr. Bridgers went to the door to retrieve a crate. She recognized Ethan from having seen him in Chesterton. The boy did not come in, but nodded to Clara through the window before he left.

"I think you will find yourself quite hungry in a short while," Mr. Bridgers said as he placed the crate on the table. "I'll make some stew for today."

She glanced around the space and saw her box against the wall opposite the bed, seemingly so far away. There was no privacy at all in the one-room building. She couldn't see getting up to retrieve her clothes as she was only in her shift. Not only that, the garment was disgustingly filthy, reflecting the state of her own skin covered in dried blood and sweat. She would have to take a bath.

"Mr. Bridgers?"

He looked up from chopping vegetables on the center table. "Yes, my lady?"

"Would it be at all possible for me to have a bath?"

He seemed a little taken aback by the question.

"Or, perhaps, I could just have some warm water and a sponge and towel?" Clara had never actually had a bath without the assistance of a maid, but she was sure she knew how it must be done.

Mr. Bridgers glanced at the wooden laundry bucket at the bedside filled with bloody towels. "There's no bathing tub, my lady. You'll have to take a sponge bath. I'll go pump some water and heat it up. It will be a few moments."

"Thank you, Mr. Bridgers."

He made a slight bow and went out the door.

Clara sat on the bed waiting, surveying the room once again. Then she spied the chamber pot. Mr. Bridgers had said she was in a fever for two days. She must have had to relieve herself during that time, but had absolutely no recollection of how that might have been accomplished. She stared at the commode in wonder.

Mr. Bridgers returned carrying two buckets of water. He stood in the doorway for a moment, watching her. She looked at him, distressed.

"I helped you, my lady."

The distress turned to horror.

"As, I am sure," he said gently, putting down the pails of water, "you would have done for a very ill friend." He exited out the door again, returning with an empty laundry bucket.

Relief now crept through Clara. He was right, of course. "I'm sorry, Mr. Bridgers," she said. "I'm afraid I'm still in shock over all that has happened." She watched him pour boiling water from the kettle and cold water from a pail into the large wooden basin he had placed in front of the fire. He set a sponge, a small cake of soap, and a clean dry towel on the kitchen table.

"I'll be outside, my lady. Please let me know when you are finished." He closed the door behind him.

Clara got up from the bed and stripped off her shift. She was humbled by Mr. Bridgers's concern for her modesty and moved by his caring for her. And not only for her. He had been quite upset about what had happened to the girl in the brothel.

As she washed, Clara was reminded of another time when she had had to wash blood from her body: the night of the Millington ball when the general had taken her virginity in the garden. That night when he had danced with her and then suggested they take a walk, she had considered herself not in love, of course, but smitten perhaps. By the end of the night she knew precisely what he was. He was a cruel man and their marriage was a sham. She was only the means by which he would obtain an heir. She did not want to go back to the man. Perhaps Paul could get his ransom and then help her escape home to England.

Paul. For the first time, she had thought of him as "Paul" and not as "Mr. Bridgers". *Paul.* She loved spending time with him, would love to call him by his first name, hoped that they would have such intimacy. She laughed softly to herself. He had already seen her practically naked with just her shift, and had helped her piddle. How much more intimacy could there be?

The kind that she had dreamed of just that morning. She always got a funny, glowing feeling inside her when she saw him during her trips to town. In fact, she could say she hoped to see him so she would get that feeling. It was quite pleasant. And she never felt it with her husband. She only felt it with Paul.

She smiled as she dried herself, then padded over to her traveling box to see what Annabella had packed for her to wear.

Even as he snatched a glimpse through the window, Paul knew he shouldn't look. He had seen women in various states of undress every day for the last several years and had never felt the compulsion to look at any of them. But Clara was different. She was beautiful and … something else. It was a mixture of endearing innocence and unconscious sensuality, and it drove him to madness. The last couple of days, seeing her in nothing but a sheer piece of cotton, having her need him, having to touch her in response to that need, had sent him out of doors to frig himself several times. He didn't know how long he could sustain the fiction that she was nothing more to him than a pawn in a game with her husband.

He had never put curtains in the kitchen building. There was no reason to, and the light inside was much better without them. He struggled not to peer through the tiny panes. He busied himself with everyday tasks. There was wood to be brought from the shed and fresh water to be pumped.

"Mr. Bridgers?"

Her voice calling to him from a crack in the door woke him as if from a dream. He went inside the kitchen immediately.

"Yes, my lady?"

She stood near the fire almost entirely dressed except for the lack of a bodice. Instead, her stays hung loose over her clean shift. Her hair was brushed and fell in soft honey-brown waves down her back.

"I need help with my stays," she said demurely. "I can't lace them myself."

She cast him a chaste pleading look that sent a flutter from his stomach straight to his groin. "Yes, of course," he said. She turned back around when he approached, drawing her hair to one side. *This is impossible. I have to tell her.* He pulled the laces taut and tied the ends in a bow.

"Thank you," she said, her back still to him. "Now can you hand me my Brunswick on the chair there?"

Paul picked up the exquisitely made silk jacket and reached around to hold it out to her. His arm brushed her shoulder. The flutter in his groin flared with heat.

"I want to thank you so much for everything you have done for me while I was ill," she said as she worked on the buttons. "I am so grateful. I don't know what would have happened if I had lost my child in my husband's house. I fear he would have done something horrible to me."

He stood frozen, saying nothing.

She turned around to face him. "Paul?"

They were so close, practically nose-to-nose, he could see the concern in her eyes. "Clara, I can't do this anymore—" He stopped. "You called me 'Paul'."

She smiled. "And you called me 'Clara'." She quickly turned her head and looked down, trying to hide her adorable blush.

He lifted her chin gently until she faced him again. "Don't look away. You don't know how beautiful you are at this moment." He dipped his head and touched his lips to hers.

In a flash, his senses exploded, the world as he knew it crumbled away. For a man who had performed or witnessed every erotic act the human body was capable of, this simple kiss was unexpectedly, devastatingly sensual. Her lips were the warmest, the most tender, the most luscious lips he had ever touched with his own.

She held back in her innocence, not knowing what to do, and he showed her. He tasted and teased her lips, gradually parting them with his velvety tip to play with hers. She was hesitant, tentative, until instinct overtook modesty. She sucked his tongue into her mouth with a hunger and passion that had lain dormant, merely awaiting the right lover to awaken her.

They finally parted for want of air, panting, still touching.

"Paul," she said in almost a whisper. "I want to repay you. You've done so much for me." She took his hand and held it to her breast.

He felt weak, his head spun out of control, his cock strained against his trousers. He wanted her desperately. But, she had just lost a child and he knew she would not be ready to accommodate him for several weeks. He held her face in his hands and pressed his forehead to hers. "My lady ... Clara ... God, you don't know what you are saying. Please. You are in no condition. You must wait after what you have just been through. Please know I do desire you. By God, I want you. But we have to wait. And for your well-being, I am willing to wait."

Clara kissed his palm. "There must be something I can do for you?" she said with unaffected naiveté.

He almost fell on his knees before her. "Not just yet. Please. I cannot take pleasure from you without giving it back." He pulled her into his arms. "You don't know how long I have wanted you." He kissed her hair. "Clara, darling. I want this to be right, to be wonderful for both of us." He drew in a long breath, then held her at arm's length. "Let's take this slowly, love. You haven't had a proper meal for two days. Come." He led her to the table and sat her down. "I'll show you how to make a stew."

Annabella could tell something was preoccupying Redmond. It was probably because he wasn't telling her the truth of their situation. But he would tell her—of course he would. He had played the part of devoted husband very well the last week.

They lay in bed huddled under the quilt, his strong arm around her shoulders. She nuzzled against his robust chest, letting the soft hair tickle her nose, breathing in the scent of his strength. She glided her hand down, feeling every bump and ridge of his muscled torso, skirting his groin to reach his massive thighs and absently tug on the fine hairs there. He pulled her closer and kissed her, his other arm enveloping her, protecting her from some unknown foe.

"Annabella, love, there's something I have to tell you."

"Yes, my sweet." She threaded her fingers through the hair on his stomach.

"We can't stay here."

She sighed into him. "I had figured that part out. Where are we going to go?"

Redmond inhaled deeply. "I'm going to join the patriots."

"What?" She raised herself up on her elbows. "No, love, no. Please. You can't. You'll be killed." Her head swirled and ached at the possibility.

His beautiful blue-green eyes gazed at her with remorse. "Sweet, it gets worse. The other man in the coach when we kidnapped you, he's holding Lady Strathmore hostage—"

She gasped.

"General Strathmore owes this man a thousand quid and he's demanding the general pay up in return for his wife." He drew her back down to lie on his thick chest, his heart thumping in her ear. "It's known she's with child. That's the reason why the general will pay."

Annabella lay silently for a moment, soaking in his warmth, his strength. "What is it that I need to do, Redmond?"

"You need to take the ransom note back to General Strathmore."

Tears welled in her eyes. He was asking the impossible. Go back to General Strathmore? And his Hessian officers? "Please, love, don't ask that of me. I would rather join the patriots."

"And I would rather you were coming with me."

He kissed her forehead. She looked up at him to see his lashes wet with tears. He had never cried before her. The sharing of such a deep emotion brought her closer to him, forever binding them together.

Annabella sucked in a steadying breath. "I'll do it, love, for you. But you have to promise you'll come find me and take me home with you. Wherever that might be."

"I love you, Annabella." He hugged her tightly. "I love you with all my soul."

CHAPTER SEVEN

Over the course of a fortnight, Paul grew to know Clara far more intimately than he had thought would ever be possible. Because of her condition, he had tried to go slowly. The first week had been torture, with languid kisses and semi-clothed embraces, Clara asking pointed questions about what his girls did in the brothel. Eventually, the temptation of her young, supple body and her eagerness to explore a new-found enthusiasm for carnal indulgence was just too overwhelming. At nineteen, her form was exquisite. Firm breasts—each a perfect handful, as white as a dove's wings and tipped by blooming pink buds—swelled gracefully above her taut belly. Her skin was soft, unblemished, lusciously inviting. Initially, he was embarrassed by his bulky shape, his own belly paunched from good living, and the mass of dark hair trailing from his chest to his groin snaking around to cover his butt. But Clara reveled in his body, exploring him as much as, if not more than, he explored her. At night they lay naked, clinging to each other, caressing, kissing, he struggling against unfulfilled needs.

He did what he could for her, helping her discover her body, touching what he allowed himself to touch to release pent-up desires. Clara's response was astounding. Simply drawing a nipple in his mouth, tantalizing the erect tip, could bring her to climax. His whores had never delighted in their bodies so much. For them the act of love was a display of skill, not so much an enjoyment of pleasure.

The eroticism of their lives lived so closely in the little outbuilding was simply too much. He finally broke down and frigged himself in her presence. Clara watched in amazement as his hand raced, his muscles tensed, and he cried out as jets of warm milky fluid spurted onto his belly. She pleaded with him to show her how to make him come, and at first he refused. But, with pouting looks and cloying words, she persisted, and he relented.

He taught her how to suck him, where he most enjoyed her touch, how to take all of him into her throat. And, after the first time when she choked in surprise and spat out his seed into the chamber pot, he taught her how to swallow.

She was a quick learner.

"That's right ... yes, oh, yes ... aahh."

She knelt before him, naked, gripping his thighs. He brushed back her hair to get a view of her perfect breasts.

"Now inhale and take me in deeper."

She smoothed her palms along his hips to grab hold of his butt cheeks, then drew his cock in as far as it would go, fluttering her throat around the tip. He groaned as she pulled back, gliding her tongue along the sensitive underside and tantalizing his prepuce. Hers was by far the most luscious oral pleasure he had ever received, and he wished it could last forever.

But she had figured out exactly how to bring him to climax before he was ready.

She increased her pace, sucking him harder, drawing him all the way in then teasing the glans with the tip of her tongue. It was agonizing ecstasy.

He grabbed a fistful of her hair. "Oh, God, Clara … not yet, love … please…"

She giggled, the vibrations taunting him more.

"I'm … not … ready!"

She held onto his hips as he jerked up and came in her mouth. She kept him inside her to swallow every drop.

Paul sighed in exasperation and release. If Lady Clara Strathmore had not been the noble-born wife of a British general, she would have made a great whore.

"Lie with me, love. I think we've waited long enough for your pleasure," he said.

Clara giggled and stretched alongside him, her eyes wide in anticipation.

"I want you this way." Paul pulled her body to lie diagonally across the mattress. "Now lift your hips." She did so and he placed a pillow underneath her and gently pressed his palm on her belly. "Relax." He glided his hands along her thighs, massaging her muscles, then gently pushed her knees open. He settled himself on the mattress, his head between her legs. His finger dallied in her soft brown curls before touching the skin.

She was wonderfully wet and swollen.

He spread her open carefully, pink and perfect, her little white nub of pleasure peeking out.

"Have you ever been licked?"

"Licked?" She asked as if it were the most curious idea in the world.

"A man's tongue between your legs?"

"I've never heard of such a thing." Her voice held a trace of wonder.

Inwardly he groaned. No man had ever tasted her sweet flesh. The mere thought of being the first to pleasure her made him hard again. He ground his groin into the mattress as he slowly drew his tongue through her slit.

Clara jumped at his touch, crying out in surprise. He gently urged her body back down against the pillow, soothing her with honeyed words until she relaxed.

And then he proceeded to tease and taunt her with his tongue.

She gasped, but did not flinch, instead rolled her hips, undulating rhythmically against his mouth, her cries and moans accenting every upward thrust. He swirled his tongue around her clit and flicked his gaze up to watch her descend into lubriciousness.

He worked the erect nub tirelessly, willing her toward climax.

Her belly tightened, her breaths quickened. She was there.

She tugged on his hair. "Paul, I need you. Inside me." Her voice was soft and pleading.

But he couldn't, it was still too soon. He rubbed himself more furiously onto the mattress, as his delicate licks turned into frenetic laps. He sucked in her clit, the engorged nub hard against the tip of his tongue, then released her only to begin again. Her entrance fluttered provocatively, tightening and relaxing, tempting him to be inside her, to feel her gripping his prick. He slid his tongue around the throbbing hole, wanting desperately to plunge in and taste all of her. She thrashed against the sheets, calling out his name, pressing her hips against him with more demanding force. He sucked her in once more, then gently nipped her lusting pearl of pleasure.

She seized a pillow to scream into it as she slammed her crotch into his face. A second later, she was silent, her face still covered, her chest rising and falling rapidly with her breaths.

Paul hauled his body alongside hers, satiated despite his nagging erection. He took the pillow from her face to grin down at her. She looked up at him, panting, smiling.

"I didn't know it was supposed to be like that," she said breathlessly.

Paul leaned on an elbow and kissed her cheek. "It isn't always like that, my lady." He touched her nose with a fingertip. "You appear to have quite a responsive body." His hand meandered along her belly, her waist, finally cupping a perfect breast. "And quite an appetite."

She licked her lips. "I want to taste."

Paul bent down and kissed her mouth. She sucked his lips and tongue a bit too eagerly.

He laughed as he pulled away gently. "Easy, love." He pulled up the covers. "Let's get some rest."

He sighed. He couldn't wait to fuck her.

The fire had died, but the warmth of their bodies huddled under the blankets was all Clara needed against the chill of the late autumn night. She had slept only a little as thoughts of the last few weeks busied about in her head.

Making love to Paul was the most revelatory experience she had had in her life. During the few times she and her husband had engaged in relations, something was always missing. That something was her own pleasure. It was a pity the general had not thought to explore her carnally. He would have been pleasantly surprised, and might have found he had no need of whores. Her capacity for sensual delight was boundless.

But could she have satisfied all his desires? What were those desires exactly? And why did Constance almost end up dead? Paul had said there were five men with Constance, that she had been bound and flogged. Could she herself have been able to bear such torturous abuse? Did not a wife have a duty to gratify her husband? And would her own husband have abused her to such a horrific extent?

A chill crept up her spine and she pulled the blanket more tightly around her shoulders. "Paul? Are you awake?"

He groaned sleepily against her shoulder. "What is it, my love?"

"Why did my husband want to hurt Constance?"

He tensed at her side, then let out a heavy exhale. "I truly don't know." He lay in silence for a moment, then raised himself on an elbow. "Every man has a unique way in which he expresses desire and wishes to experience fulfillment." He drew his fingers along her arm, sending tingling shivers to tighten her nipples. "To produce an erotic culmination, some men like to be dominated by a woman, to submit to her commands. Others like to dominate a woman and have her submit to his will." He rested his warm palm on her belly.

Could she make a man submit to her will? "Which type of man are you?"

Paul chuckled. "The sexual needs of men are complex. I did not mean to imply that there are only the two types. There are, perhaps, endless varieties of letches."

"So, you like something else, then?" She would do whatever it was.

"Well, I am a bit like yourself in that I achieve gratification through a great many experiences. Like what we have already enjoyed together." He kissed the tip of her nose. "But, since you inquired, I do derive pleasure from having a woman submit to my erotic desires while she is restrained."

A thrill stirred in her belly under his hand. She tilted her hips hoping he would proceed further.

"However, I absolutely do not gain pleasure from hurting women. That is something that seems to be unique to your husband." He thinned his lips, momentarily lost in thought. "I never truly felt comfortable leaving Constance alone with Strathmore."

Clara reached up and stroked his cheek, masculine and rough. "Paul, I want to know what my husband did to her. I want to see where it happened. I want to experience what it is he likes to do to women."

Paul looked at her with concern. "Clara, do you know what you are asking?"

"I mean to say, not the hurting part. But, I do want to experience what this 'letch,' as you call it, is." He had ignited her imagination since their very first kiss. Her curiosity was as insatiable as her body.

He pulled her close. "I'll see what I can do. I need to be certain that we are not seen or heard on the property. It might be best if we do it at night."

In the dark, where no one could be witness to whatever wickedness lay in store to thrill her.

Clara tasted the stew and, much to her surprise, found it to her liking. She lit the oil lamp and placed it at the center of the kitchen table, then snorted in amazement. Paul had taught her so much, every day filled with learning even the simple tasks only servants had ever done for her. She was hungry to learn anything and everything he was willing to show her, not just carnal pleasures.

He came through the door just in time for dinner.

"I see you've been busy," he beamed.

"Sit."

He plopped on the bench as she put his bowl on the table before him. He breathed in the scent of the steam, then shoveled a spoonful into his mouth.

He beamed again.

Clara exhaled with a measure of pride and relief and joined him at the dinner table.

"I needed to make sure Redmond and Annabella hadn't left yet," he said, chewing. "I don't want any surprises coming from General Strath—, uh, your husband," he added soberly. "Once Annabella delivers the ransom note, we'll have to be on constant watch."

"Does Annabella know what is expected of her?"

"I talked to Redmond. She's not happy, but she'll do it."

Annabella was tremendously brave. And tremendously in love with her betrothed. "I can only imagine it will be difficult for her to leave Redmond now that she's found him."

Paul pursed his lips. "Yes, well, I've given them two days' time. Ethan will make sure things go as planned." He resumed eating.

And if things went well, perhaps Annabella and Redmond would be reunited after the war. Whenever that would be.

"Clara, love," Paul started. He pushed his empty bowl aside. "I've set things up for us, for tonight. For what you said you wanted."

Clara gulped. *Constance.*

He met her gaze. "Tonight you will encounter several new experiences which I think you are ready for. But one thing that you might find strange is a change in my character. What we will be doing is a sort of performance, at least between you and me." He sighed. "Your husband, I fear, does not act."

"A performance? Like acting on a stage?" Excitement fluttered in her core. Only a certain type of woman did such things. Women like herself led horribly boring lives.

"Yes, of a sort." His forehead wrinkled in concern. "Love, it will be very different for you. If you feel something is wrong, if you experience pain you're not willing to experience, you need to let me know. Especially after what your body has just been through." He stretched out his hand for her to take. She lay her palm against his and his thick fingers enveloped her with their strength. "Ever since your husband began engaging my girls for his particular letch, I had to lay down some unique rules for him. I've not needed to use this for any other client, just him." He drew in a long breath. "I've found it useful to choose a word to say so the one restrained can let the other know there is a problem."

"A word?"

"An unusual word. One that you might not say in the course of love-making."

"Oh." That covered quite a bit of the English language. Or perhaps it wouldn't be English? Incantations in a foreign tongue? It was all so intriguing. "Who chooses this word?"

Paul chuckled at her enthusiasm. "I will for tonight. The word will be 'patriot'."

"'Patriot'?" Clara giggled. "Yes, I can say that. I think."

He grew stern again. "You only say it when you feel you are in danger, you understand that?"

She nodded. "Yes, right. I understand."

"And if you are unable to say that word—"

What? "Why would that be?"

He drew in a breath and squeezed her hand. "I won't touch upon that at the moment, but if you are unable to speak, you must let me know without using words. I suggest that you stomp three times with your right foot."

The scenario was becoming completely and utterly fantastical. And wondrously exciting. "Yes, I will do that."

A log popped in the fire, shooting sparks to land on the floor of the hearth. Paul turned to look out the window.

Clara followed his gaze. Through the trees the hazy grays of dusk were turning to the dark shades of night.

He stood and turned off the lamp. "Get your wrap, my lady, and I shall show you a new pleasure."

Yes, oh yes. Clara grabbed her cloak and his hand.

They crossed the grounds behind the kitchen in the direction of the house, but off to the left. A low, unassuming building of stone and brick lay ahead in the darkness. It looked like a blacksmith's shop.

"This is a smithy's when not needed for other purposes," Paul explained as he led her inside. He bolted the door behind them.

The workshop seemed much larger on the inside, with wooden beams below the ceiling spanning the length of the space. The pale stone walls were whitened with ash, and against one wall stood a large brick hearth blackened by smoke. The particular shape of the hearth, smaller than the kitchen's and with a shelf, was the only hint of the building's usual use. There were no tools of an ironmonger. Instead there were devices and contraptions of metal and wood that reeked of iniquity, as if she were a prisoner in the black tower of the Castle of Otranto. Clara shuddered.

Paul took off her cloak and kissed her mouth, deeply, reassuringly. "Love," he said. "This is when the performance begins."

She nodded.

"Take off your clothes."

"I—"

"Take off your clothes in silence."

It was said in a commanding, biting tone tinged with chastisement. The flutter of excitement stirred again, surprising her.

She slowly stripped, even her stays, another skill he had taught her. Paul did not watch, but instead busied himself with lighting the fire.

Once nude, she wrapped her arms across her nipples contracting from the cold. He came forward, now divested of his jacket and waistcoat, the placket of his shirt unbuttoned, sleeves rolled up, his expression cast with determination and a touch of lust.

With gentle force he unwrapped her arms and placed them at her sides, then slowly drew a finger from her neck to her mons. "You are so lovely tonight," he growled with a dark sensuality.

"I—"

He placed a finger to her lips. "No words."

He was harsh. His face, his demeanor had changed, his eyes no longer their comforting light brown, but a foreboding black.

He took her by the wrist and led her to a spot just before the forge and signaled for her to stay still. She looked down to see chains and manacles on the floor, contraptions Paul proceeded to place around her ankles. She remained silent as he did so, the shock of the cold, bare metal rippling goose bumps across her flesh.

He reached up to pull down similar devices hanging from the wooden beams. Horror ripped through her at the realization of what was to come. Frozen by fear and the floor constraints, she remained still as he placed the metal bindings on each of her wrists.

She stood spread-eagle in the middle of the room, the fire warming her back. Paul circled her, slowly, as if she were his prey, teasing her with tender touches, fleeting across her flesh, anywhere and everywhere. She stared straight ahead, unsure if she was meant to look at him, flinching when he tickled, struggling to remain silent. He stopped behind her, his breath hot and hungry. He kissed her neck as he drew his nails from her thighs, over her buttocks, to the middle of her back, shooting chills to tingle the tips of her fingers.

He pressed his heated skin against her back. He was shirtless. The tingles speared her toes.

He cupped her breasts, kneading her nipples delicately, a tenderness in juxtaposition to the milieu. She forgot herself, relaxed against him, and let out a sigh.

He pulled back as the dangerous sound hovered. Mortified, she bit her lip in shame, waiting for chastisement, hoping for chastisement, and unsure from where such a desire sprang.

He came around to face her and quirked a brow in reproof. But instead of offering a reprimand, he pressed against her, the hair of his chest tickling her, his cock through his breeches rampant against her hip. He lowered his head and took an erect nipple in his mouth.

She jostled against the cold iron, trying to keep silent, thrashing against his thrilling tongue, his sucking lips. His hands snaked around her, holding her firm so he could assault her further. She stifled moans but could not steady her ragged breathing.

And then he bit her sensitized nipple.

She cried out. Or rather, she screamed. Never had she felt such pain, yet never had she felt such pleasure. She wanted more, yet wanted him to stop. The strain on her arms was enervating, yet she had never felt so alive.

"I told you to be silent," he rasped, menacingly.

He left her side, left her alone to feel the flush of shame suffuse her skin.

Behind her, he tinkered near the smithy's workbench. He returned carrying what looked to be a knot of rags between two strips of cloth. She shot him an inquisitive look.

"Open your mouth," he said firmly.

She sucked in air.

"Open your mouth and say nothing." He moved behind her.

Curiosity turned to alarm as he placed the knot in her mouth and tied the two strips of cloth at the back of her head. Her jaw ached until she relaxed around the gag, her tongue hitting the knot, tasting the essence of those who came before, acrid and salty. Her own saliva flowed uncontrollably to mingle her distinct flavor into the mix.

This is what it meant to be unable to speak, to protest, to scream. Like Constance.

Alarm turned to fear.

Clara tried to remain calm against the turmoil of emotions welling within. As Paul pulled away, his hands trailed possessively across her body.

The fear pulsed with desire.

He went to the same place near the smithy's workbench again, this time making a racket with his fumbling around, exaggerating the clank and scrape of metal against metal. He returned carrying a large pair of iron scissors.

Clara froze.

He rested the blades ever so lightly between her breasts. Slowly, deliberately, he drew the sharp tips in a line from her chest to her pubis, never scratching the skin, but coming so incredibly close. She held her breath, afraid any movement would cause his hand to falter and the blades to nick her. An image of Constance being brutalized flashed in her mind.

He stopped at the thatch of hair at her mons, barely an inch above her clitoris. Light-headed, she breathed in puffs trying to remain still against the sharp iron. With one hand he dug in the tips just a hairsbreadth, almost enough to cut, while the other hand grabbed, then tugged at her pubic hair, her slickened sex sliding with a delicious friction at the jolt.

Paul pulled the wiry strands of her motte straight, then gradually, methodically, cut off a lock. He held it up for her to see before throwing it into the forge. It burned, acrid and exciting. Clara closed her eyes, puffing rapidly in anticipation of another cut. The next snip was quick but much closer to the skin. Once again, the lock was tossed into the fire.

The slickness pooled, on the verge of trickling down her legs. Paul tickled the inside of her thigh. He knew.

He walked to a corner of the room and retrieved something hanging on the wall, then returned, toying with the item reverently. A well-used horsewhip.

Arousal dissipated. Constance had been left for dead, covered in welts.

Instinct and self-preservation fought with curiosity. She could signal the end with a stomp of her foot. But Paul would never intentionally hurt her.

With one flick of a wrist, he unfurled the long braid of leather and snapped the air. Clara jumped.

He came to her again, caressing her bottom with one hand as he pressed the whip's hardened handle of hide against her belly. He drew it down her thigh, ever so lightly brushing her clitoris with his thumb, then rubbed the handle against the soft flesh between her legs.

"I could fuck you," he said, his lips against her ear. "I could fuck you in your cunt." He thrust the handle against her wetness, preventing penetration with his fist. "And fuck you in your arse." His fingers at her butt tauntingly circled her puckered hole. "At the same time."

God, yes. Her insides melted in a molten mass with the threat of sensual invasion. Anything. She wanted him to do anything to her.

He stepped away several paces and dallied with the whip, slapping the ground casually before slicing the air with determination, each crack coming closer and closer to her body. Panic tore through her and she smothered her instinct to flinch, not knowing where the leather would lick next. When he finally nicked her abdomen, it did not hurt so much as surprise her. It was the second flick that cut, eliciting a muffled cry. She looked at him with fear. He turned his back to her, ignoring her transgression, and she exhaled in relief.

The third lash was unexpected, and unexpectedly painful.

Tears dripped down Clara's cheeks, soaking into the knotted cloth, blurring Paul's hardened expression as he approached her. One hand still gripping the handle of the whip, he leaned in against her body, his face near hers, his eyes holding hers as his free hand grabbed her crotch, firmly pulling at the remaining pubic hair. A smile flickered across his lips as his hand uncurled to let the middle finger play between her folds. She was dripping wet, yearning for gratification. He stroked her, holding her gaze, teasing her clitoris, smug in his mastery, growling praise as her body weakened against the metal bindings. She closed her eyes, letting the waves of satisfaction eddy through her.

Suddenly he stopped. She looked around to see him once more at the smithy's workbench retrieving another object. He stalked toward her carrying a very large manacle attached to a thick chain. Behind him dragged a solid iron ball scraping along the bricks. He stood before her and worked the clamp, opening and shutting the ring. With the ring opened he approached her, his hands at the level of her neck.

Clara jerked back futilely, then watched in horror as he calmly placed the ring around her neck and clamped it shut. The chain hung heavy and icy down her back, the ball at her feet.

"That is so you do not run away," he said quietly, his low bass tone resonating darkly in her core.

He bent down and unlocked the shackles on her ankles, holding each leg tightly as if to prevent her from kicking him. He then stood and worked on her wrist cuffs. Stiff and cold from lack of blood, each arm fell limply to her sides.

He moved behind her to what looked like a tall piece of furniture draped with cloth. He stripped the wrapping away, revealing a most unusual table. The top was tilted so that the edge closest to her was lower than the edge further away, and was covered in padded leather. Even more strange was an oval hole situated nearer the higher edge, with a ring-shaped pillow around it.

Paul stood by the table and motioned for Clara to come to him. The ball and chain were heavy as she dragged them across the floor, the screech and clang of metal piercing the hollow space. He merely watched, a smirk tugging on his lips, amused by her utter abasement. She flushed in shame.

"Well done," he praised, and positioned her so she was facing the table. He pushed her legs apart to shackle them to the legs of the table. Only when he had secured her did he then unfasten the neck collar, throwing it loudly onto the floor.

He stood behind her and wrapped an arm around her waist. "Bend forward and lie against the padded board," he instructed, holding her as she did so. Her face almost matched the ring pillow and, after he made a few adjustments, she was able to press her face against the cushion and see out the hole. His hands wandered about her, adjusting, stroking, caressing, helping her relax into her new position. He took each of her arms in turn and positioned them over her shoulders where he tied them, this time with buckles and leather straps, yielding and soft compared to the metal cuffs.

Paul pressed the length of his body against hers, his chest hot against her back, his arms stretched along hers to hold her hands, his erection insistent at the cleft of her buttocks. He ground himself into her, licked along one shoulder to the top of her spine, then teased and tickled her neck. His warmth penetrated her, his tenderness relaxed her. And then he bit her. Hard. Clara screamed into the gag.

He left her. A cold draft bristled against her skin, stinging the sore muscle of her ravaged neck. She twisted, trying to see if there was blood, but instead glimpsed Paul taking off the rest of his clothes. He was completely aroused. His cock sprang forth urgently as he unbuttoned his drawers.

He returned and gently urged her head back into place. A moment later, a nutty scent filled the air. His fingers reached under her, between her legs, to fondle her wet cleft. He stroked her, trailing the sticky moisture to the tight hole of her arse, where his finger remained poised. A warm oily liquid flowed over his finger and he penetrated her, moving in and out of the crinkled aperture, each time adding new oil, until he slid in with slippery ease.

He pushed in further, too far, and she recoiled. He cooed in sympathy, coaching her to relax around him, massaging inside as he continued to breach the unwelcoming passage. She evened her breaths as he instructed, consciously releasing the tension until the pain became pleasure.

And then he introduced a second finger. She clenched in shock.

"Shh, shh, my love. Let go."

With each exhale she breathed out the pain. And when he pushed in a third finger, she was ready for him.

"You are so tight," he groaned. "I assure you it will only hurt a little." He pressed his cock against her thigh. He was hard as stone and oily like her bum.

Clara's breath faltered. Such an act was forbidden, a sin against God. Once more she tensed around his fingers, tucking her hips under to protect herself, trying to turn to face him to tell him "no".

He reached around to her clitoris and stroked it expertly. "Of course it is forbidden," he said, reading her thoughts. "That is what makes it so exciting. That's why it feels so very wonderful."

She weakened under his touch, her qualms bled out. She craved having him inside her in that shameful way.

"But I want to hear the sounds of your rapture when I claim your virginity." While one hand still pleasured her, his other untied the gag in her mouth and peeled it off.

Her jaw ached in its freedom, slackening with each excited puff as he tormented her clit. She groaned heavily when his prick nudged her nether hole. He pushed deeper, slowly, stretching her as she had never been stretched before, until the stretching threatened to tear her apart and she screamed.

He purred reassurances as he pressed further into the dark passage, all the while teasing her tender nub. He felt so huge, so impossibly thick and long inside her, and yet her body responded, expanding for him, accommodating him. After a minute that seemed like an eternity, he paused. He had filled her. She exhaled.

Suddenly, he delved even further, thrusting cruelly through her burning muscles tensing and clenching to prevent his advance. Yet he persisted, ignoring her whimpers, her thrashing body, until he breeched the tight ring buried within.

Paul remained inside her, unmoving. He curved over her, his pliant flesh melting into the contours of her spine, his chest rising and falling in cadence to the excited breaths in her ear.

"You're mine," he whispered. His lips trailed kisses down her back, cooling her heated skin. His finger at her clit caressed her slowly, gently. "You belong to me."

There was a desperate edge to his voice, masking an emotion, a sentiment that seeped into her with every thump of his heart.

He began the movement of love, pulling out and pushing in slowly as her body accommodated to him until she accepted it as the pleasure it was. Her hips rocked in rhythm with his, her moaning sighs the melody to his sonorous grunts. He pumped faster, pushing impossibly deeper with each thrust. Her climax reared, then wavered and dissipated from the pain. He sensed it. He rubbed his finger frantically on her clit, pressing determinedly, not letting her go, willing her toward orgasm. She screamed at the peak, letting loose a flood of warm liquid to drench his teasing hand. Her cunt clenched in satisfaction, tightening the other hole around his cock. He barked a cry of ecstasy and hovered a moment, deeply embedded, letting her squeeze him, then emptied his hot seed inside her with a growl.

Paul curved over her once again, their panting breaths merging in unison as they both recovered from their exertions. He reached up and one by one unbuckled the straps around her wrists.

"Move slowly, my love, you may feel a little stiff," he said.

Clara let out a long exhale and pressed her body back against his as she brought her arms to her side. "Are you *you* again?"

He chuckled as he pulled back. "Yes, the act is finished." He unhinged the manacles at her feet. "How do you feel?"

Finally free, she turned to face him. He enveloped her in his arms.

She sighed. "I feel exquisite. Sated. It was so … so very … intimate."

"Good." He kissed her hair. "That is how it is meant to be."

She breathed in his masculine strength. "But that's not how it was for her."

He stiffened, then held her more closely. "No. There was no intimacy. Only cruelty."

None of the elation. Only the horror. "Paul, I never want to see my husband again." She snuggled against the hair of his chest, finding comfort. "Ever." She couldn't be trusted to not kill the general in his sleep.

CHAPTER EIGHT

Annabella tried to stop crying. Several hours earlier, Ethan had had to physically pull her away from Redmond. Redmond had cried, too. She had never seen him cry so much before, both of them terrified they would never see each other again.

When they had handed her the ransom note, Annabella had merely glanced at it. She couldn't read, but she did recognize the name of "Lady Clara Strathmore" because her lady had taught her a little bit about letters using their names. But as kind as her lady had been to her in the past, Annabella no longer cared much about her or her unborn child. She only wanted to be with Redmond. She placed her palm on her belly, hoping and praying she was carrying his son.

Ethan drove her in the coach for hours. They had to leave in the middle of the night so she would arrive in the Chesterton area by morning, and they had to drive a little ways out of the way to mask their actual path. Ethan would have to leave her alone with the carriage while it was still dark so he could make his escape. Redmond had taught her a few months ago how to handle a horse, and as long as the roads were good, she would be able to manage. If not, she would just have to leave the coach and its horses and walk.

The carriage stopped. Ethan scrambled off the roof to the ground. Annabella wiped her tears on her cloak. Redmond had told her to be strong.

"This is where I leave you, miss." Ethan opened the door to help her out. "Sorry, but dawn is just about to break and I got myself a long ways back. Do you need help getting to the seat up front?"

"No. Just hold the reins while I get there."

The horses were calm but Ethan held the reins anyway, then gave them to Annabella when she was settled in the driver's seat. He doffed his hat and fled away into the lifting darkness.

Annabella urged the horses slowly. She was absolutely in no hurry to see General Strathmore and his officers. Besides, this close to Chesterton, someone would hear her and, as the general's coach was well-known in these parts, she was bound to stick out. People must have been aware by now that she and Lady Strathmore had never arrived at their intended destination. Maybe there was even a reward for their return.

Dawn broke and she plodded along through the early morning mist. Finally she saw someone up ahead, in fact several someones all dressed in red coats. She reined in the horses to stop and braced herself.

A fine-looking officer approached her on horseback. He looked at her queerly, then recognition washed over his face.

"You're Lady Strathmore's maid, aren't you?" he said gently, with a note of astonishment.

"Yes, sir." Annabella wasn't sure if she should offer an explanation for their disappearance. She decided she would wait. She had strict instructions to deliver the ransom note directly into General Strathmore's hands and no one else's and didn't want the petty politics of officers getting in her way.

The officer scanned her up and down, then rode around the coach peering into the windows.

"Where is Lady Strathmore?" he asked when he came back around.

"I have instructions to only speak with General Strathmore about the whereabouts of my lady," she replied.

He looked at her rather intensely for a moment. "Well, then," he finally said, "I'll have to take you to the general." He motioned for one of his men. "Take my horse, cadet," he said as he dismounted. "I will drive the coach with the girl."

"Yes, lieutenant."

The lieutenant climbed into the driver's seat next to her. He flashed a smile. She had seen him before.

"And what is your name, miss?"

"Annabella, sir. I'm Annabella Rogers."

"Nice to make your acquaintance, Miss Rogers. I am Lieutenant Sebastian Hawkins with General Strathmore's regiment." He flicked the reins and the horses proceeded to trot.

Hawkins. Where had she heard that before? She glanced at him again. Her heart fell. He had seen the assault by the general and his Hessian officers, but hadn't bothered to help her or Redmond. She looked away, her gut roiling as she hoped, *prayed,* he was not anything like those other soldiers.

"How is your health? I mean, what happened to you, were you treated well?" He seemed concerned, as he should have been in the stable.

"Yes, sir. Thank you. I am fine, sir," she said softly. She did not want to tell him she felt simultaneously sick and famished.

They rode in silence the rest of the way. She grew more relaxed at the lieutenant's side as he acted the perfect gentleman. Until General Strathmore's residence came into view. She stifled a cry from her throat, but could not stop the tears from trickling down her cheeks. She quickly wiped them away with her sleeve.

He leaned in. "I'll stay with you, Miss Rogers," he said quietly. "I won't let you be alone with him."

Annabella snapped her head toward his, only to find their faces very close. He had a pleasant countenance, sweet and gentle. His gray-blue eyes surveyed her face as his tongue flicked over his plump lower lip, then he smiled and set his attention back to driving. He didn't wear a wig under his hat, and his wild sandy brown hair had been somewhat tamed in a queue down his back. He wasn't as thick and masculine as her Redmond, but he did cut a fine figure in his military uniform.

He looked honest enough. Perhaps she could trust him.

The moment she had recognized him, Sebastian had felt Annabella tense at his side. The memory of her pleading face in the stable that day over a month ago still stung his heart with regret. But clearly, by the time he had arrived, the deed had already been done. Plus, the general's Hessians were a notoriously cruel bunch, and would certainly have forced him to participate, or worse. If the girl had been a common whore perhaps he would not have felt so much guilt. Now that she sat next to him, he saw how young she was, how lovely, how utterly frightened she was. Maybe a little hungry and tired, too.

He parked the coach alongside the general's house and helped her down from the driver's seat, holding on to her waist as she jumped off. When she landed, he continued to hold her, not wanting to let go. Her auburn hair peeked out from under the hood of her cloak. Something compelled him to pull her hood back and arrange her hair, tucking it under her lacy cap. She regarded him curiously.

"Come," he said, patting her briefly on the shoulder before offering his arm. He led her into the house and, when he knocked on the general's office door, he kept one hand tightly wrapped around her upper arm.

"General Strathmore, sir?"

"Hawkins?" came the familiar bass voice. "Enter."

The general had been reviewing maps and plans over breakfast. When he saw Annabella his expression changed from contemplative to angry. He looked at Hawkins for an answer.

"We found her with the coach just on the main road, sir. She was alone." He kept a firm grip on Annabella's arm as the general walked around her.

Strathmore leaned in to her ear, far too intimately. "Where is your lady? My wife?"

Annabella closed her eyes. "I do not know, sir."

"It has been practically a month since you left. What have you been doing all that time, girl?"

"I was held in a house. I was left there alone. My lady was taken somewhere else." She looked up at the general. "I swear, sir, I do not know where they took her."

"And who is 'they'?"

"Men. I don't know who they were." Her expression lay somewhere between fear and guilt.

"Soldiers?"

"No, not soldiers."

"Accents? British? Colonists? Come on girl, speak up!"

"They were Americans, sir. They had accents like mine. There were three of them and they wore black hoods over their heads so I could not see their faces." She looked down at her feet. "Please sir, believe me, that is all I know." She looked back up at the general, now perched on the edge of his desk. "I was given a note for you, sir." She reached under her clothes.

Instinctively, Sebastian grabbed her, turning her body toward him. If this was a ruse to kill the general, Sebastian was well-trained to act. In the tussle, Annabella dropped a folded piece of paper. She lifted her eyes to him. He tried to convey his mortification and apologies. She bent down to pick up the note and handed it to General Strathmore.

He scanned it, then, grunting and growling, read it a second time. "I don't recognize the hand." The general looked sharply at Annabella. "Who wrote this note, girl?"

"Please, sir. I do not know, sir." She was trembling.

He eyed her intently again. "What sort of house were you held in?"

"A big house, sir."

"Big? How big? Two stories like this house?"

"I think there were two stories, sir."

One side of the general's mouth curled sinisterly. "Good, good," he muttered. He waved his hand toward the door. "You may leave me now, Hawkins. The girl may still have some usefulness left in her."

Sebastian saw terror flit across the girl's face. This was precisely the situation he had wanted to avoid.

"No," the general said, reconsidering. "I have too much work to do here now. Take her to Colonel Fritzlar. His men will know what to do with her."

Sebastian was not going to deliver her into the hands of the Hessians. "General Strathmore, sir?"

"Yes, lieutenant?" he grumbled.

"My men and I need a maid-of-all-work."

The general looked up from his papers, glancing over at Annabella and then back at Sebastian. "Go on, take her. I'm sure your men will find a use for her."

Sebastian led Annabella out of the house as calmly as he could. Once outside, he breathed a sigh of relief.

"Thank you, sir. I don't know how to repay you."

"Not in the way you're thinking, miss," Sebastian snapped. He shook sense back into his head. "I apologize. Look, I really could use a maid. I run a very disciplined barrack, so you will not have to fear for your safety. Unless you wish to go back home. You're from Chesterton, aren't you?"

"My mother sold me to General Strathmore, sir. I don't think she wants me back."

"Sold you! That's impossible!" Sebastian looked down at her. She probably had no idea what really transpired between her mother and the general. She did not seem like she wanted to return home, though. He glanced around the yard. The coach was still there. The Strathmore groom had disappeared a long time ago and his duties were never reassigned. Sebastian's cadet was positioned nearby with the lieutenant's horse.

"Do you have anything in the coach?" he asked.

"Only my box, sir."

Sebastian called for his ensign and motioned for him to dismount. "This is Miss Rogers. She will be joining our staff. Please fetch her box from the coach and bring it to the barrack. I will need your horse as well."

"Yes, sir."

Sebastian turned to Annabella. "You will ride behind me." She looked so relieved and yet still so fragile. "Don't worry, miss, you'll be fine." He tried his best to sound reassuring.

* * * * *

"And I would love you all the day,
Every night would kiss and play,
If with me you'd fondly stray
Over the hills, and far away."

Clara had a tendency to sing songs Paul had never heard. And quote poetry, too. It all sounded like Shakespeare to him since he had read so little of the stuff. He didn't read novels either, as she clearly did. Really, the only works anybody ever read these days were political tracts against monarchy and for independence.

Clara's silliness and frivolity accentuated the fact that she was only nineteen years old and had been pulled from her carefree noble life and thrust into a war zone. Paul loved her innocence, her playfulness. He truly loved her, but he knew there could never be anything lasting between them. He had simply seen too much of life to ever recapture such an ingenuous state.

It was morning and they lay in bed, casually fondling and cuddling, naked despite autumn's chill. Annabella had left the night before. Redmond was most likely already with the patriots up north. It wouldn't be long before Clara would have to be returned to her husband. Paul had demanded quite a bit of money for her with the stipulation that the general should pay a portion as a sign of good will. It was that portion which would cover the general's debt to the brothel, and then some. But, after he got that first payment, did he really have to let Clara go? He nuzzled against her shoulder.

She turned her face to his and kissed his lips, lightly, tenderly. The heat rose in his body, pumping more blood to his half-hard cock. He moved over her to frantically feast on her mouth, then pulled back. She was flushed, her face suffused with wanton desire. His needy cock twitched.

"Love," he began softly, trying to find the right words. "I think we have waited long enough. I want to make love to you. Properly." He was surprised by his own bashfulness.

She stared at him with wide eyes. "Yes, please, Paul. Yes."

Her plaintive tone humbled him. Suddenly, he was a boy again experiencing his first carnal union, except this time he would know precisely what to do. His fingers found her wet and aroused, but she had to be more than ready for him. He did not want to hurt her.

He kissed her mouth succulently as he massaged her clit. "This is for you, sweet. Let me pleasure you."

His motions were languorous, punctuated with provocative teases to rouse her only to pull back when she least expected it. She giggled at his game and pecked at his lips lovingly.

His stroked her silky folds, finally daring to touch the entrance to her feminine passage. He slowly inserted a finger. She held his eyes as he did so, biting her lower lip, then nodding in assent. His thumb worked her excited nub as he slid in a second finger. She closed her eyes, lost in the sensual indulgence of his touch, her neck and shoulders arching against the pillow. She cried out as her libidinous muscles clenched around his fingers, pulsing, wanting more, inviting him inside her.

He was achingly rampant. He moved to lie between her legs. His cock in his palm, he slid it through her wetness, then aimed precisely. He took his time as he pushed in, luxuriating in her squeezing palpitations. When he was fully seated inside her, he let himself relish in the thrill of her body before continuing with his lover's motions.

She was tight, unused, so he moved cautiously, kissing her, whispering encouragements, until their bodies undulated as one. He pulled back a little to gaze at her. Tears filled her eyes and trickled down the sides of her face to the pillow.

A sharp stab of remorse pierced his heart. He stopped. "Love? Am I hurting you?"

She sniffled and wiped her tears. "No, no. Paul, it's wonderful." She cupped his cheek with her palm. "Sweet, it has never been this good for me before." She smiled reassuringly, her expression a mixture of joy and lust.

He resumed his rhythmic tempo, slowly increasing his pace, her pulsating passage gripping him. She held his gaze until her head fell back and her body jerked and arched in climax. Her slick muscles grabbed him, demanding more, clenching intensely. Her head thrashed against the pillow, her nails dug into his shoulders, and she let out an orgiastic wail to the heavens.

He was at the precipice of desire, wanting so much to remain at the point just before the peak, but he would not be able to hold on much longer. She herself was lost in ecstasy, her writhing body continuing to grasp him with such determined force that he had to follow. He pushed his limits, thrusting inside her until his body began its release, then, at the last possible moment, he pulled out with a howling cry and shot his seed onto her belly.

He collapsed beside her, panting and laughing, more satiated and drained than he had ever been from the act. She smiled, staring at the wood beams of the ceiling, slowing her breaths. She lifted her head and looked at her belly, tentatively touching the milky fluid pooled there and just beginning to drip down her sides.

"Why did you not stay inside me?" she asked with genuine naiveté.

He propped himself on his elbow and played with the damp brown curls that framed her face. "To prevent you from becoming with child." His fingers wandered capriciously over her rosy skin. "Although, as your husband does not know you are no longer pregnant, I suppose the precaution was unnecessary." He pecked her lips. "Imagine my son growing up as a viscount's heir." He pulled a corner of the comforter over and dabbed at her stomach.

Clara searched his eyes. "Paul, do you love me?"

He had been expecting the question. Of course he did, but not in the schoolgirl way she loved him. "I worship you, my lady," he said trailing kisses across her skin. "I desire you. I want to pleasure you. That is all I know of love."

She feigned disappointment. "Your brothel has jaded you against such a divine sentiment." She giggled as he grabbed her by the waist and playfully nibbled on her neck.

"Your husband would love what a little whore I have made of you."

She tensed. "Paul," she whispered as if someone could hear. "I don't want to go back to him. I can't go back to him." She sighed. "When we married he made a stipulation. I could not return home to England until I bore him two sons. Sons, mind you. It had to be male children. So I'm stuck here and won't be able to return home to my family for years. I hate this place. I hate the American colonies. And I hate the war." Her eyes dewed with tears. "I want to go back home to England." She held his face in her hands. "And I want *you* to come with me."

Paul inhaled deeply, gathering his thoughts. "Clara, I cannot go back to England. There is nothing for me there." He took her hand and kissed the palm. "My life is here in these colonies. Here I am somebody important, I'm successful, and I can do what I want. Over there, I am merely the son of a cobbler."

"Where are you from originally?"

"A small village near Birmingham—you've never heard of it, trust me," he said when she raised her eyebrows inquisitively.

"Like I said, my father was a cobbler, my mother's folk were tenant farmers. I just didn't have the farming or shoe-making blood." He drew a finger between her breasts to her belly button. "I wanted adventure." He gave her a little smack on the hip. "When I was fifteen, I went to Liverpool to make my fortune, as they say. There I worked on the docks, eventually taking a job aboard a slave ship. Brutal business, that is. The way they treat those people. Like animals. I thought another company would be better, but they're all the same. After two different runs with two different companies I stayed on in the colonies and found my way up here. I realized that everywhere I went there were whores. Men just need women. So I figured that would be a good business. I had learned a bit about bindings and shackles and such aboard the ships, so I gave my whorehouse a little bit of a difference. But, I treat my girls well and they stay with me."

She looked at him in silent amazement and wonder.

"Clara, what do you have waiting for you back home?"

"My mother, my father—he's an earl. My friends. And my brother." Her voice quavered. "We're very close."

"If you go home you will have deserted your husband. I'm sure he will seek redress."

"My husband is an adulterer—"

"As are you, love," he reminded gently.

"So cannot we be divorced?" she huffed. "What about your American laws? Is it possible to divorce here?"

Paul sighed. "I really don't know the answer to that." He chuckled. Sam Taylor had studied law before the war. "But I do know someone who might know the answer to that question." He twisted a lock of her silky honey-brown hair around his finger. *Sam.* Now there was a man well-suited to this intelligent, beautiful, young woman.

"Why should a foolish marriage vow,
Which long ago was made,
Oblige us to each other now,
When passion is decayed?"

"That's not Shakespeare is it?"

"No, silly," she said, laughing. "It's Dryden."

Yes, Sam would be perfect. "Clara, you must realize that returning to England is very difficult, given the war. It would not be easy for an English girl to gain passage on an American or French ship. And, if you tried to get aboard an English vessel, they would simply hold you and alert your husband. Plus, even if you did get on board any ship, you would be faced with the possibility of a battle at sea or a pirate attack. It is simply too dangerous."

"We could bribe the crew of an English ship."

"With what money? That would have to be quite a sum for a ship's captain to double-cross your husband."

She hesitated for just a second. "Before I left to go to Manhattan Island, I sewed some of my jewelry in my stays. I had thought that if I were widowed, I would have something to barter for passage back to England."

Paul sighed. Clara was from an aristocratic family, and most likely her jewels were worth quite a sum.

"And there's my ring." She tugged off the gold band from her fourth finger. "My wedding ring must be worth something."

He took the proffered ring. It was simple, plain, not the sort of thing a wealthy man gives to a woman he loves. Nondescript so as to be almost untraceable. "Let me think about this, love." He put the ring on the bedside table. "You should know that Annabella left last night to deliver the ransom note. It won't be long until we receive the first payment. We'll head to patriot territory then."

She giggled. "'Patriot'."

Paul pulled her close. When the time came, it would be very difficult to let her go.

CHAPTER NINE

Paul threw off the covers. It was far too warm for a late October morning, although it seemed they had overslept. The room was too bright for dawn. Next to him, Clara lay sound asleep but had also tossed back the counterpane. Only as his body roused from its usual drowsiness did he realize the kitchen smelled like smoke. He looked out the window. The brothel was in flames.

Strathmore.

"Clara, Clara," he said shaking her, his voice urgent. "You have to get up now, love. You have to get dressed. We have to leave."

"What?" she said sleepily. Once she saw the eerie light coming through the window she sat up with a jolt.

She dressed as quickly as a woman with a complicated wardrobe could. Paul was dressed in a flash. He strapped his knife belt around his waist, then grabbed his pistol and cartridge box.

Clara sidled up next to him as he peered out the window, his pistol at the ready. The brothel was fully engulfed, flames licking through a ghost of its structure. "Shouldn't we leave?" she said anxiously.

"Not yet. We should make sure it's safe."

"Paul, the fire is quite close—"

"Ethan has been staying in the house. That boy is far too responsible and capable to let a fire get out of control like this. Something is very wrong." He fell silent as he scanned the scene before him. "Just as I thought," he said gruffly. "Soldiers. British soldiers."

He pulled Clara away from the window and against the door. He watched as two soldiers passed the kitchen building and walked toward the blacksmith's shop. He took the belt with the knife and sheath from around his waist and handed it to her.

"Wear this, love, and wait here." As Clara buckled the knife at her waist under the drape of her overskirt, Paul opened the door slowly, stepped outside, then closed the door behind him. He walked to the corner of the building, then around the next corner, always looking around to make sure the enemy was not hiding. He returned inside, took her hand in his, and hurried away, closing the door behind them as if the little outbuilding had not been disturbed by occupants.

They went past the herb garden, behind the building, toward the woods. Paul's plan was to head west for a few miles, then head up north to patriot-controlled territory. Any soldiers who followed them would be surrounded and probably killed.

A blood-curdling scream in the distance stopped him cold.

He urged Clara behind a tree and surveyed his property to find the source of the cry, hoping, praying desperately it was not

Ethan. With a soothing word, he left Clara where she was and, from the cover of the woods, searched the scene before him.

And then he saw Ethan.

He was bound and shackled to a hitching post along the side of the big house, the heavy chain attached to the iron ball hung down his back. The sight was sickening, the work of a madman. Ethan would only be free once the post burned, but would be killed by the smoke and flames well before then. Paul had to save him.

He ran back to Clara.

"Love, it's Ethan. I have to go." He grabbed her hand and looked deeply in her eyes. "Stay here, right here, and watch me. Once I am no longer in your sight, start to count to three hundred. Count steadily. If I am not back in view by then, I want you to run. Head this direction." He pointed into the woods. "It's west. Keep walking until you think it is noontime. Then go to your right. You'll be heading north. You want to try to get to Fort Revolution. When you get there, talk to Captain Samuel Taylor. Tell him you know me. Tell him you want to go home, but you need to wait for me. I will find you there."

Her wide eyes stared at him, utterly terrified. "Yes, Paul," was all she said.

He stroked her hair. "I love you." He kissed her quickly, then ran out into the clearing.

Clara watched until she could no longer see Paul, craning her neck until the last possible moment. She began counting, maintaining an even rhythm, something she had learned from the dancing and music lessons young girls of her class were required to take.

At two hundred a shot rang out.

She jumped and glanced around, then continued to count, trying to remain steady, to not hurry, to give Paul a chance to come back to her. By the time she reached two-hundred-and-ninety she slowed considerably. At three hundred she stood on the tips of her toes straining to look in the direction he had gone, but there was nothing. She wanted to simply stay put, in the hope he would eventually return. But he was right. It was simply too dangerous to stay amidst burning buildings and marauding British soldiers.

She ran in the direction he had told her, holding her skirts, trying not to trip, the sounds of her huffing breath and pounding heart deafening, drowning out the crunch of her steps on dry leaves. Running was not something her body was used to, and she quickly tired. She pressed on, driven by fear, by hope, by her love for Paul. Cold sunlight peeked through the canopy above, and when she thought the sun was retreating back to below the horizon on its low autumn arc, she turned right, praying that it was indeed the northern direction she was meant to go.

She continued doggedly, stopping once to drink her fill from a creek, then stopping again later to pee. Only after she had relieved herself did she realize how hungry she was. She glanced at a bush laden with berries, suddenly remembering a casual conversation with Paul about edible and poisonous plants, and decided that water would have to sustain her.

Dusk fell, heightening the eerie silence of the forest, bringing a little flurry of panic. She was surprised that she had seen absolutely no one. How far could she possibly be from the fort Paul had mentioned? And what was she supposed to do once night descended? She was lucky to have brought her cloak of black wool. She could wrap herself up and hide in the night, against a tree or rock perhaps, get some sleep, and start afresh in the morning. She had never in her life been so exhausted.

She walked until her legs complained and the darkness was simply too overwhelming, then found a bush, cleared out a patch along the bottom, and curled up. Sleep came quickly.

"What do we have here? A hedge whore?"

Clara awoke with a start and to a horse's nostrils snorting moistly against her face. It was morning, although how early she did not know. She looked up to see two men mounted on horses, British soldiers, not the Americans she had expected, their waistcoats unbuttoned, neckcloths loosened. She sat up and pulled her cloak more tightly around her, determined to not speak so they would not know who she was from her accent.

"I suspect we have here a common strumpet on an unfortunate adventure," slurred the fatter soldier.

The two men laughed at their little joke, then dismounted unsteadily, one landing on his backside after his foot did not find the ground in time. They approached her. She backed up against the bush with nowhere else to go. One on either side, they lifted her up to standing.

"These colonies produce the most delicious morsels of laced mutton, do they not?" Fat One said, his breath reeking of spirits, his nose and cheeks shiny and flushed.

"Quite," said his skinny, sandy-haired cohort with a burp.

Clara did not recognize the men, but the laces on their cuffs indicated they belonged to the regiment beholden to her husband, and their dress denoted their ranks. The fat one was a colonel, the other a lieutenant colonel.

Her lungs tightened. Paul had said two colonels were with her husband when he brutalized Constance.

She glanced around. The officers were alone. They must have been sent by her husband to find her. Yet they had no idea they had already captured their prize.

Sandy Hair circled behind her, reached up to her neck to untie her cloak. Clara's hand instinctively shot up to stop him.

"Be still, my little pug. You know what we want and you know how to give it to us."

A chill of terror stilled her as Sandy Hair stripped her of her cloak, then began stroking her unbound hair with shaking, clammy fingers. She fought back tears.

"You must be well-kept to dress in silks," said the fat colonel.

She hadn't thought that might give her away. All of her clothes were well-made of expensive European fabrics. Everything packed in her box was of fine stuff. She prayed they would not suspect her of anything more than having a rich patron.

"That's quite a gallant who could array you in such fine frocks, my girl," Fat One continued. "Who is he? General Washington? Benjamin Franklin?"

Sandy Hair chuckled. "Or maybe it's the whoremaster Bridgers. His wines were rather expensive. He must have paid Satan to get them here from France."

The two men laughed.

Her heart clenched. They knew Paul. They knew he had whores. It must have been they who set fire to the brothel.

Fat One went back to his horse to search in his saddlebag. "Bollocks! Last one." He returned carrying a bottle of wine, then, mimicking a grotesque butler, displayed the label to Clara. She immediately recognized it as a very expensive and rare vintage, something her husband had taught her, never having realized that Paul was the one who had supplied such scarce luxuries. She tried to keep her reaction neutral.

"Would you like some, my little moll?" drawled the lesser officer still pawing at her hair. "It's very good. I'm sure even your blasted gallant hasn't offered you such a treasure." He emitted a gravelly and malodorous belch.

Clara froze. They were expecting an answer. She had no idea how to feign an American accent, so she figured she would simply try a new voice.

"No, thank you," she said with a clumsy inflection and timbre unlike her own.

Luckily, they did not really care what her answer was, and practically ignored her. They had no reason to suspect she was the wife of General Strathmore alone in the middle of nowhere. They began to drink the wine, passing the bottle back and forth between them, laughing and talking of things that did not concern her, pacing aimlessly, until they closed in on her, Fat One in front, Sandy Hair at her back. Fat One grabbed her waist. She flinched with a shudder, but he continued to draw his hands up to cup her breasts as she stood stock-still, too scared to stop him. Suddenly, Sandy Hair shoved her forward. Clara held out her hands as if to catch herself, instead falling onto Fat One. He gripped her wrists tightly and forced her down as Sandy Hair held her ankles. Together they brought her to the ground on her hands and knees.

She struggled to get away, but they held fast, laughing at her.

Sandy Hair pressed his knees on her calves and into the rough ground, then tossed up her skirts from behind. She struggled again, only to have her legs cruelly pressed against the rocky dirt. "Give me a swig of that," Sandy Hair said to his companion. He drank liberally, gulping noisily, belching after popping the bottle from his lips. His free hand roamed over her buttocks before he forced his thumb into her split. She winced at the intrusion and her stomach churned.

"You're a professional, sweet. I expect you to be ready." He spread her cheeks and spit on her twice, the second time missing his mark considerably.

Clara screwed her eyes shut, squeezing out tears, praying the act would be over as soon as possible. He fumbled behind her, probably to unbutton his breeches, but taking far too long for such a simple act. Finally, he pressed his fist against her, smooshing something soft into her quim. She opened her eyes, only to see the fat colonel removing his flaccid penis from the fall of his breeches.

"Fuck. You do it," Sandy Hair said pushing her forward so her face fell onto the colonel's impotence.

"There's an idea. Why don't you give me a suck, molly?" Fat One waggled his limp member. "There's a good girl."

He pinched her nose. She gasped for air and he shoved his flabby cock in her mouth. Impulsively, she spit him out. The officers laughed.

"I see you've not been to France, doxy," said Fat One, withdrawing from her face. "Put her on her back. She'll know what to do."

Sandy Hair chuckled as he pushed Clara to the ground, manhandling her until she lay on her back and he straddled her face, pinning her shoulders to the dirt. She struggled for air only to breathe in the stench of his crotch. The colonel forced her legs open and tried unsuccessfully to shove himself inside her. He retreated to perform some exertion, then tried his assault again, still to no avail. He reached for the bottle of wine left on the ground and noisily finished it off.

Sandy Hair swayed above her, his eyes struggling to stay open. He fell forward and off her, rolling into an awkward position. Now free of his weight, Clara sat up. Fat One still knelt between her legs. He muttered an oath about the wine before tossing the bottle to the side, twisting his body as he did so. It was her only chance. She kicked, striking him on the upper arm, shocking both herself and the colonel. For the briefest of moments he stared at her strangely, his body teetering ever so slightly. With all her might, Clara struck with her left leg and then again with the right. Fat One swooned and fell over onto his back, his head hitting a rock with a hollow thud, his body motionless, contorted in an ugly form.

As if he were dead.

She remained on the ground paralyzed, the only sound her pounding heart until it was drowned by the meter of Sandy Hair's deep drink-induced slumber. She moved carefully, trying not to make any noise as she got up and wrapped her cloak around her. She turned in what she hoped was the right direction, sneaking away unnoticed, until her cloak betrayed her, catching on the empty wine bottle, sending it rolling with a clink against the hard ground.

A thick hand gripped her ankle, pitching her forward onto her knees.

"Where do you think you're going, whore?" Sandy Hair grappled her around the waist, turning her onto her back, crushing his weight on top of her. He twisted her hair in his fist and pressed his face into hers, the stink of his breath making her want to vomit. "You know what we do to cunts what don't cooperate?"

Clara turned her head as far as she could, only to have a view of Fat One's exposed crotch.

"We *make* 'em cooperate." Sandy Hair tightened his fist, pulling her head back. "If you'd've seen Bridgers's twat all bloody and crying, I reckon you'd spread your legs faster than a bunter for a guinea."

With all her might Clara shoved against him, pushing his chest with her shoulders and arms. Sandy Hair grabbed her wrists and bore down even harder, crushing her into the ground, his hip grinding something into her thigh.

The sheath of the knife.

A prickling chill spread through her body. She knew what she had to do. It was the only way out.

She sucked in a bolstering breath, then flailed against him, her arms, her legs twisting and kicking, roaring screams into his face, her frenzy surprising him long enough for her to heave up and scramble out from under him and onto her feet.

Her heart pounding in her head, her lungs burning for air, she reached under the drape of her overskirt and found the knife, unsheathing it with trembling hands. Sandy Hair endeavored to stand, faltering on his knees, his foot slipping on a rock, sending him tumbling face-first onto the ground. She had to do it while he was down.

She had never killed a man, of course, and had no idea how one might go about doing such a wretched thing. The thumping beats of her heart increased, echoing in her throat and ears, a pulsing rhythm to her frantic thoughts.

She put her hand over her left breast. In the heart. That was certain to kill a man.

Gathering courage and rage, she plunged in, kicking a stupefied Sandy Hair to turn him over, stabbing his chest, having to use both hands to wrench the knife out of the wound, stabbing again, and again, until he lay defeated beneath her.

The white of his shirt turned red as blood soaked the fabric.

Clara jolted backwards in revulsion, hitting Fat One's legs, eliciting a groan.

He wasn't dead.

She froze. She couldn't do it again.

Fat One twitched.

She *had* to do it again.

She clambered above the colonel, wielding the weapon in a daze, barely noticing how this time the knife felt lighter, the flesh softer, perhaps because the buzzing in her brain was deafening, her vision obscured with tears and sweat. Within minutes, Fat One lay motionless, blood covering his shirt, his waistcoat, his face frozen in twisted agony.

She stood over the officers, catching her breath, hate still boiling within. Her gaze fell to their crotches where limp penises spilled from unbuttoned plackets.

It would be like slicing salt pork for stew.

She reached out and grabbed Sandy Hair's genitals. The knife was sharp, it was too easy. Next, Fat One was swiftly unmanned.

Clara stumbled up to standing, wavering on buckling knees, disbelieving the sight before her, the blood on her knife the only evidence of the savagery she had just done. She gulped sobs of horror and relief as she washed the blade and her hands from Fat One's canteen, then dried the weapon on his breeches before sheathing it.

She glanced around, trying to get her bearings as to which way might be north. She studied the horses thoughtfully. She did not know how to ride unassisted. Besides, having such an animal might trace her to the murder of the officers which, even though it occurred in the lawless American colonies, was still a capital offense.

Still shaking, she tried to calm her nerves, to steady her breath so she could think clearly. Paul was out there somewhere. Wherever he was, he promised to meet her at the American fort. She had no choice but to press on in the direction she best guessed was north.

CHAPTER TEN

Captain Samuel Taylor sat atop his horse surveying the quiet woods, scratching the stubble on his cheeks, his gaze focused on the pale shafts of morning sunlight misting through the trees. He raked his fingers through his unbound hair, then grunted a chuckle. He really should be attending to those daily ablutions that made a man more presentable, such as fashioning a queue and shaving, but some days he just didn't feel like it. Especially a clear, cold, autumn morning like this, when a walk in the woods would be just the thing. He settled his tricorn firmly on his head. It was a damn shame he had a war to fight.

He and several men from his regiment stationed at Fort Revolution had set up camp in the area waiting for a delivery from Paul Bridgers. It had been a couple of weeks since they pitched their tents, a little longer than usual, but Sam wasn't worried just yet. The fighting hadn't yet reached their location.

And the intelligence brought back by his scouts and their civilian informants sounded more like a melodrama than a war.

A handful of redcoats had encroached in the area, not a whole regiment, just a few Brits, one account claiming they were officers. Additionally, two women, the wife of a British general and her maid, had been kidnapped by rogue Americans hoping to acquire a hefty ransom for their return. Sam figured all the bits of information were related, that the redcoats were searching for the women, so he decided his scouts should expand their perimeter.

One of them approached. "We found something, captain," announced Corporal Silas Ogden.

"Finally," Sam rolled his eyes and followed Silas on horseback.

They arrived at a gathering of patriots surrounding a young woman who clutched her black cloak tightly around her. Sam dismounted and passed through the group, his men parting before him.

"What do we have here?" he asked no one in particular. The girl looked frightened. He hoped his men had not done anything to harm her.

"She says she's Lady Strathmore, sir, the wife of General Strathmore," said Silas.

"The one being held for ransom?" Sam studied the girl. She fit the description of one of the women well enough: pretty, light brown hair, green eyes, a cloak of expensive cloth. If she were really the missing lady, she had somehow gotten free of her kidnappers, an adventure suggested by her dirty and disheveled appearance and the fact that she was apparently found wandering around in the woods alone. Yet, she was much younger than he had expected for the wife of a general. He gave her a questioning look but she did not accept the challenge, so he addressed her directly. "Why should I believe that you are Lady Strathmore?"

Her brow wrinkled in scorn. "Because I am," she replied succinctly in an imperious tone.

Sam sighed. "Right." He did not want to deal with the situation in front of his men. He would wait until later. "Corporal Mercer," he said to the most senior soldier standing guard over the girl, "please escort the lady to our camp, to my tent. I will be there presently."

"Yes, captain."

Sam once again took off his hat and raked his fingers through his unruly curls. They would have to remain alert for any British soldiers searching for their lady, as well as be on the lookout for the American kidnappers. And now he was part of the equation and could not help but wonder if there was something he could gain from the situation. Perhaps trade the young lady for some needed supplies? No, Paul would get those to him, he was certain. What about an exchange of prisoners of war?

"Captain?"

The familiar, always-welcome voice of First Lieutenant Patrick Hamilton broke Sam's reverie. Sam turned to his friend. "Yes, Pat?"

"You look lost in thought. Want to share?"

"You know about General Strathmore's career, right? How old do you think he might be?"

Pat thought for a moment. "He fought in the Seven Years' War against the French and the Indians. He was quite a rising star in the ranks. I think he was already a colonel or something back then. Maybe in his mid-forties? Why?"

"We have just found a young woman who is claiming to be his wife. She looks like she could be his daughter. I was just thinking she might not be telling the truth."

"He's also a viscount, I believe. Don't those titled men all need heirs? If it were you, you'd want a healthy, fertile nymph in your bed putting out a bevy of little lords-in-waiting, wouldn't you?"

Sam laughed. "I suppose you're right." He shook his head. "Still, I find all of that a little disturbing."

"Is she pretty?" asked Pat.

"She's somewhat unkempt at the moment, but yes, I would say she was ... rather beautiful, really."

Pat snorted. "And I'm sure General Strathmore married her for that quality, as well."

Sam saw one of his scouts approaching. "Pat, do me a favor—"

"You mean, 'Lieutenant Hamilton, follow my orders'," Pat reminded him.

"Yeah, yeah. Go to my tent and make sure the lady in question is being treated well. See if she needs anything. Food, water, whatever."

"The young, beautiful wife of General Strathmore is in your tent, captain?" Pat's tone dripped with insinuation.

"Oh, Christ! Stop! Just get out of here!" Sam poked him in the ribs in encouragement.

Corporal Andrew Ross approached on horseback, a little winded. "Captain Taylor, sir." The corporal's voice held a tremor. "There's two redcoats. Isaac—I mean Corporal Holmes, is with them. They're dead, sir."

Well, this was news. "Dead? How long?"

"I couldn't tell you really, sir. Blood's not too dried. Maybe a day or so."

Fresh blood? Sam mounted his horse. "Take me to them."

The corporal hesitated. "Sir, there's something else. Their bodies ... well, they've been mutilated in a particular way."

"Mutilated?"

Andrew cleared his throat. "Their, uh, manly parts have been cut off."

Sam blinked. "Oh." His men had not seen much battle action since the war began. They were fortress-bound sentries and scouts, not infantry or cavalry. Such a sight would be horrifying to a young man, a boy really, such as Corporal Ross. "Lead me until we can see Corporal Holmes. Then you turn around and go back to camp."

"Yes, sir. Thank you, sir."

The two men stirred their horses to a trot and rode for an hour or more, until Corporal Ross pulled up his reins.

"This is where I leave you, captain, sir. Isaac Holmes is over there, by that clump of bushes."

"Thank you, corporal," Sam said gently.

Andrew saluted and sped away.

Sam approached the area slowly, until he saw Corporal Holmes standing, scratching his head, and surveying the scene before him. He looked up at the sound of Sam's horse and saluted.

"Hullo there, captain."

"Hello, corporal," Sam said as he dismounted. "So, Isaac, what do we have here?" He approached the area Isaac was investigating behind the bushes and stopped in his tracks. Before him lay the bloody bodies of two British officers, their chests riddled with stab wounds, and their crotches indeed stained a deep red.

Isaac pointed his foot to an object by the fatter body. "I think that's his, uh, male part, captain."

Sam looked more closely. The object did indeed appear to be a penis, perhaps a little smaller than what he had seen in his life. "Have you done any investigation in the surrounding area?"

"We found two horses, which I presume were theirs," said the corporal. "Nothing else. No other sign of redcoats—" he paused as he gazed upon the particularly messy scene. "Er, I mean, lobsterbacks. We know of no one in the area working for us," he continued. "Unless it was Bridgers's men."

"Bridgers wouldn't dare do something this abhorrent," Sam said, looking around. "He's a businessman. He has too much at stake to be linked to this sort of attack." He glanced at the flaccid, bloody member and winced. "This looks almost like someone took revenge."

"Yeah," said Isaac. "I agree. And something about the dead men doesn't look right, like they were killed but not robbed. You know, in a time when supplies are short the dead are often robbed. Especially to just leave the horses. So it wasn't locals either. This *was* revenge."

Sam spied a bottle under the fatter soldier and retrieved it gingerly. He cursed to himself when he recognized the label as a wine Paul had recently acquired from his French sources, then glanced at the corporal. Isaac was busy checking out the boots on the other body. It was of course possible that the British officers had somehow acquired the same wine on their own, but he did not want to risk any implication of a connection to Paul Bridgers. The taint of murder would destroy the legitimate side of his business.

Isaac looked up. "What is it, captain?"

"Just an empty bottle of wine. The same stock the British supply to their officers. I thought it might be a clue."

Isaac simply nodded his acceptance of the explanation and said nothing. Sam breathed a sigh of relief.

"Captain, I hate to mention it, but, you know, shortages and such. Should we strip the bodies?" The corporal seemed both fascinated and somewhat sickened by the scene before him.

Sam surveyed the dead officers. Everything covered in blood would be difficult to wash out. "Just the boots and stockings. Buttons and hats. Anything metal. Accoutrements. The cuts and blood have rendered the other articles unwearable, really. Unless you think something can be salvaged." He looked over at Isaac. "You have the horses?"

"Yes, captain. And their tack. Weapons, too."

"Good. Then, after stripping these two, corporal, why don't you go on and return to camp? You've done enough work for today. I'll have a look around and join you later."

"Yes, captain."

Still holding the wine bottle, Sam watched from the corner of his eye as Isaac swiftly and thoroughly followed orders. Certain the corporal wouldn't notice, he placed the bottle in his saddlebag. He wasn't sure what he would do with it, maybe try to burn the label off. He just wanted to get it away from the bloody scene. He paced the perimeter looking for any other items of value or any incriminating evidence, but found nothing.

He continued to feign investigation as he heard Isaac mounting and riding away. He needed just a moment alone. Something very bad had happened and someone had committed murder. It wasn't the crime so much as the need for revenge, for justice, that fascinated him.

Sam breathed in the crisp morning air. *Well, war is war.* He mounted his horse and rode away, leaving the bodies for the British to find.

Clara tried to eat daintily, but she was absolutely, ravenously hungry. The officer who had inquired about her needs, Lieutenant Patrick Hamilton, had provided her with a substantial portion of food—salt pork with beans—probably the same ration the soldiers ate. He also gave her water, which she had finished long ago, and a tankard of cider. She thought briefly that the food might be poisoned, but hunger prevailed over reason. Lieutenant Hamilton sat at a mean table across from her in what she was told was the captain's tent. He made very little small talk, mostly about the food, all the while keeping a watchful eye on her movements.

"That cider is the very best in these parts, you won't find any better. Our own Mrs. Scott brews it. The captain makes sure the officers have it when we're at camp."

The cider was quite good. She hadn't had much of the stuff since arriving in the colonies, having been told it was common. But since living with Paul she had learned to like it, although she still hadn't learned to tolerate it very well and would get tipsy rather quickly, something Paul had found endearing.

Clara regarded the lieutenant as she took another sip of the tasty brew. He was a fine-featured young man, with soft hazel eyes and curly brown hair, and appeared almost dashing in his regimental attire. His voice was matter-of-fact, but he was clearly trying to convey calm reassurance that Clara had not fallen into the hands of rapacious thugs.

A tall, well-built man entered the tent, the same man Clara had met earlier.

The lieutenant stood up. "Captain," he greeted, saluting.

"Lieutenant, I see you have provided nourishment to our guest," said the captain, seating himself at the head of the table. "And how do you find our simple fare, my lady?"

The man whom everyone knew as "captain" was of the same height and build, and probably age, as Lieutenant Hamilton. He was, however, unshaven almost to the point of having a beard, with wild, unkempt hair. He was not wearing a military uniform, but instead the ragged clothing of a huntsman.

The man was practically a savage.

"The food is good, thank you," Clara managed to say between bites. She truly was grateful. She needed sustenance if she was to escape later.

"I am afraid I have failed to introduce myself properly. I am Captain Samuel Taylor of the 4th New York Regiment. We're camped here for the duration of our mission, which is almost at an end. Our permanent garrison is Fort Revolution. You, it seems, are now our guest."

Clara coughed and grabbed her cup to take a sip of water. She almost coughed again when she realized it was the cider instead. This was the man Paul had wanted her to contact? He had not actually told her what Samuel Taylor might look like. She decided to proceed cautiously. It could be a trick. When Paul arrived, and it was indeed proved to be the very same Samuel Taylor, surely they would all understand her initial reticence?

"My lady," Captain Taylor continued, "word of your kidnapping has reached us, although we were of the understanding it took place closer to Manhattan Island, so you can see we are a bit dubious as to your identity. Plus, and I mean absolutely no disrespect, you seem a bit young to be the wife of General Strathmore."

"And you seem a bit young for all these rebels to be calling you 'Captain'," she said boldly.

"Touché, my lady, touché." A smile played upon his lips. "Your accent, at least, would lend credence to your claim of nobility." He studied her, his gaze flickering from her head to her feet. "Although the lack of a wedding band is suspect—"

Perspicacious pettifogger. She had left the damned thing on the table next to the bed.

"—yet your dress is of exquisite fabric and workmanship."

Her husband's damned officers had dismissed her finery too quickly. But this young captain stared at the quilted petticoat peeking out at the opening of her cloak with such an intensity it felt like he was boring right through to her stocking-covered legs. She shifted in her seat.

His gaze returned to her face, his eyes sparkling with apprehension of something. Perhaps it was that her dress almost matched the blue-gray of his irises.

She flushed. Why on earth had that just crossed her mind? She hid behind her cup of cider.

"How is it that you came to be wandering in the woods, Lady Strathmore?" the captain asked with a touch of gentleness. "How did you elude your captors?"

"I ran away." Clara was surprised by the abruptness in her voice.

"Your husband has not attempted to find you? Our intelligence has told us that your husband would do anything to get you back."

"The general did come for me," she blurted before she could stop herself. She drew in a deep breath and found she was a little dizzy. Maybe more than just a little.

There was an uncomfortable silence as the tent started spinning.

"And...?" The captain raised his brows.

"That's when I ran away."

"Hmmm." His lips thinned, which was most likely an exertion on his part since they were rather luscious. "So, why were you kidnapped? Who kidnapped you?"

"My husband owed money to a man. It was he who kidnapped me."

"Ah!" He looked expectantly at her.

She returned his gaze but found it difficult to focus as the tent was still off-kilter. She concentrated on a delicate curl poised by his ear.

He blinked.

He really had lovely eyes.

"Lady Strathmore, please, go on," he encouraged with a wave of his hand.

"Then my husband's troops went after the man. I ran away at that point."

"And General Strathmore's men did not try to follow you? We understand that his men are rather loyal, to the point of brutality."

"They *did* look for me." This captain fellow was asking far too many questions.

He closed his eyes and rubbed his fingers on his temples. "Did they find you?"

"Yes," she said sullenly, remembering what had happened only that morning. Clara looked away as emotion welled inside her. "They did not realize who I was."

He leaned in. "Why would they not realize who you were when they were looking for you?"

"They thought I was a … one of the local women. They … they abused me," she said quietly. "Then I escaped."

The captain stared at her, stunned. He blinked his lovely eyes in wonder. A moment later his countenance softened. "Who was the man your husband owed money to?" The gentleness had returned.

"I cannot tell you," she murmured.

"You cannot tell because you don't know him, or you will not tell?"

Clara remained silent. She didn't have complete confidence in her ability to lie at the moment.

The captain drew in a deep breath. His luscious lips thinned again. "Your husband's soldiers, the ones who found you, where are they now? Could they have followed you? Might they know you are here?"

"No," she said succinctly.

"Lady Strathmore, are you certain? Please, how do you know?"

"Because they are dead."

He started, his expression akin to amazement with perhaps a touch of admiration. "Thank you, Lady Strathmore." He motioned to his subordinate. "Come. The lady has had an eventful day, lieutenant. Let us leave her in peace for a moment."

As they left, Clara spied the chamber pot under the captain's bed. She really had to pee.

There was very little peace to be had at the camp, for which Clara was almost grateful. She needed distraction from the anxiety that had begun to build. The captain's questioning had brought to the fore all the awfulness that had transpired that morning.

A steady stream of cadets entered the tent throughout the afternoon to mumble over maps laid out on the captain's cot, shooting her surprised glances as they wandered in and suspicious ones as they marched out. Outside, soldiers ran about shouting orders peppered with profanities. As evening descended, one regaled a sniggering colleague with an obscenity-laced story, his excited tenor easily filtering through the canvas wall. Such things were precisely why her husband forbade her to ever go near the barracks by their farmhouse. Clara paced the length of the tent, observing it all with amusement and apprehension.

Night fell quickly, bringing with it new activity. Soldiers called out sentry duties, or—quite unbelievably—protested said orders. If such flagrant disregard for authority was typical in the colonies, how did the Americans expect to win their war?

Captain Taylor came in carrying a lantern and flashed her a tired smile. "Good evening, my lady. I hope you have not been too bored in your captivity?" He set the lantern on the table.

"Oh, no, captain. There was plenty to keep me entertained."

He grunted, and went to a narrow side table with a pitcher and basin. He grabbed the pitcher, then hesitated. "I apologize for my discourtesy, Lady Strathmore. Would you like to wash up?"

The dirt and sweat had crusted on her face. She was also in desperate need of a hairbrush, but that was possibly going a bit too far. "Yes, thank you, captain. I would like that."

He called for another basin to be brought to his tent. He poured water in one and, when the other arrived, filled that up as well. Then Clara watched in utter shock as he stripped off his tunic and shirt and plunged his hands into the water. He proceeded to splash his face and upper body, wash with a well-used cake of brown soap, then splash some more.

"This is for you," he said pointing to the other basin, his face and hair dripping wet. He grabbed a dingy towel and vigorously dried himself.

She could not take her eyes off him. Lamplight played off the contours of his muscled arms, his chiseled chest, his rippled abdomen, shadows made all the more prominent by the highlights of dampened skin. A trail of dark hair teased her as it disappeared into the waistband of his breeches. His body was perfection, like that of an ancient sculpture her brother once allowed her to see at a museum.

Confusion and anxiety dizzied her brain. A very attractive man was half-dressed before her, wanting her to join him in a rather intimate activity. She hadn't really recovered from the heady experience of the cider. Was this how they planned to assault her? Get her drunk, then make her take off half her clothes under the pretense of bathing? Up until now the Americans had kept a respectful distance and she was beginning to trust them, to accept they were the ones Paul had said would offer her safe haven. Now, suddenly, she was not so sure.

She stood unmoving, staring at the captain. He put the towel down and regarded her quizzically. He spied the soap, picked it up, walked toward her, and held it out.

Clara jumped back. He was too close to her, much too close. She gaped at his nakedness in horror.

He returned her gaze, his forehead crinkling in puzzlement for only a moment before he colored from his hairline down as far as she felt comfortable looking. He sucked in his lips and calmly placed the soap on the side table, then slowly turned his back to her and shuffled into a clean linen shirt and deerskin tunic.

He said nothing as he strode out of the tent.

Sam found Pat waiting for him on the dark side of a tree trunk, out of earshot from his tent. "Christ, Pat, she's really skittish." He kicked the ground and raked his fingers though his still-damp hair.

"Of course she's skittish. She's being held prisoner."

"Yeah, I know, but, well, I mean—" Sam stopped, took a deep breath, and closed his eyes for a moment. "Look, you heard about those redcoats Andrew and Isaac found today—"

"Yeah? ... Oh, God," Pat groaned in realization, slumping against the brittle bark.

"Exactly! They assaulted her in some way, she didn't specify how, possibly raped her. And then she somehow turned the tables and castrated them. God only knows what she did to her initial captor, the man her husband owed money to."

"I'll keep my ears open for any more reports of missing cocks, sir."

Sam chuckled. Pat knew how to lighten his mood all too well. He looked out at the busy camp beyond. They were quite alone and tucked away from view.

He sighed. "It's too bad she's the enemy. We could use a woman like her."

"Beautiful?" Pat goaded.

"Cheeky bastard." Sam smacked him on the hip, letting his palm linger before sliding to cup a firm butt cheek. "No. A woman living by her wits in these troubled times, a woman willing to do whatever she needs to survive." He squeezed.

Pat shucked him off. "You court danger, my captain."

Sam slapped his hands against the trunk on either side of Pat's head and leaned in. "I'm frustrated, lieutenant."

"As are all of your men. You must embrace continence, and set the example." Pat's breath fanned hot against his lips.

"Damn this war." Sam pulled back. He could really use a frig. "What are the sleeping arrangements?"

"Concerning Lady Strathmore? I wanted to ask you the same question."

Sam groaned. "You're right. She's my responsibility." He ran his fingers though his hair then drew them across his neck and along his jaw. His rather stubbly jaw. He smoothed his hand down the front of his buckskin tunic.

Bollocks.

He looked nothing like the officer he was supposed to be. Some of the privates looked more professional. No wonder Lady Strathmore had been slightly impertinent. She probably thought the discipline as lax as the captain's state of dress. "She has to be watched, Pat. I want sentries posted on each side of my tent."

"Then she is to sleep with you?" Pat's tone dripped with insinuation.

"Not 'sleep with' me, you fool!" Sam hissed.

Patrick pursed his lips, trying very hard not to smile.

"Jesus, this is going to look bad, isn't it?"

"Not with sentries on all sides of your tent, it's not."

"Good. Then that's what we'll do. I'll need an extra cot."

"That would be prudent."

Sam glared at him.

"Sir," Pat added, the edges of his mouth trembling upward. He called for one of the night watch sentries and requested he commandeer a cot from the medical tent.

"I should check on her," Sam mused as they waited.

"As you wish, captain." A tremor of mirth edged Pat's voice.

"You find this far too amusing, lieutenant."

A grin finally cracked across his face. "Sam," he laughed, "you have an amazingly beautiful young woman—still in her lusty adolescence, mind you—in your tent at this very moment, and you are about to go to sleep. You, Samuel Taylor, who can out-perform any and all of Paul Bridgers's whores, are planning to simply go to sleep. Alone." Pat pressed forward until his nose tickled Sam's cheek. "Of course I find this amusing. As much as you find it frustrating, my friend."

"Perhaps if I were certain she was the maid and not the lady…"

Pat chuckled at his attempt at levity.

Sam sighed. "Look, we don't know what she's been through, but something happened. Like I said, she's skittish."

Pat's fingers reached for his in the dark. "You're a good man, Sam. You know I'm only teasing you."

Sam squeezed Pat's hand. "I know," he said softly.

A woman's yelp pierced the night.

"I see the cot has arrived. Duty calls, lieutenant." Sam hastened to his tent.

Inside, Lady Strathmore sat fretfully at his desk staring wide-eyed at the two ensigns who carried the cot.

Sam pointed to the side opposite his own bed. "Please put it there."

Lady Strathmore waited until the subalterns had departed before she spoke. "I won't go to bed with you!"

Oh, Christ. He shoved his fingers through his hair and gripped the strands as he drew in a breath. "Look, Lady Strathmore, you are to sleep over there." He pointed to her side of the tent. "And I am to sleep over here. I have posted sentinels on all four sides and at the door should you get any ideas about escaping, or should I get any ideas about ravishing you. As I am positively exhausted, I plan to go to sleep. I suggest you do the same. We leave tomorrow very early in the morning for Fort Revolution."

And with that, Sam stripped off his spatterdashes and shoes, blew out the candle in the lantern, and plopped down on his cot.

Alone.

CHAPTER ELEVEN

Fort Revolution was an entire day's ride away, although it seemed longer as Captain Taylor's mood was rather unpleasant and he took it out on everyone, angrily snapping orders to timorous soldiers. For Clara, it was a long ride spent on the hard wooden seat of a supply cart. According to Captain Taylor, however, she was lucky he didn't make her walk alongside the baggage carts like the other women.

They reached their destination in the black hours before dawn. The torches of the train of soldiers revealed the impressive earthwork ramparts and ditches surrounding the angled curtain walls and towers of the stone fortress. Clara breathed a sigh of relief at the sight which promised the end to bouncing on the unpadded cart bench. From her neck to her knees, her bones creaked and muscles complained.

Once inside the fort, she was led to a cot in what she thought she heard was the women's dormitory. She did not bother to inquire about her new surroundings. Once she stretched out on the cot her eyes closed in sheer exhaustion.

She awoke to the sound of dozens of women chattering and laughing. She uncurled herself and sat up to survey the scene. She was in a large room filled with cots, their heads against the lime-covered stone walls. Shabby curtains hung between each so as to separate them into not-too-private sleeping spaces. Her own curtains, she noted dryly, were pulled aside, no doubt so the other women could keep their eyes on her.

"She's up."

One of the women approached. "You look a mess, love. Would you be wanting a bath?"

Clara wasn't sure how to respond to that. She would love a bath, but weren't they in a fort? Was this woman making fun of her? She looked kindly enough, and matronly with graying hair and a plump body.

"Too tired to answer, I see. I think you do, love. Captain says I'm supposed to treat you well. Like a real lady. You'll be first in the tub with fresh water. Now take off your things while we get it all ready."

Clara slowly shed her clothes, making sure to tuck the knife belt in a deep pocket of her cloak, keeping an eye on the group of women giggling and gossiping unabashedly in various states of undress. One of them scampered up to her wearing nothing but a sheer shift shamelessly clinging to her lithe body. She took Clara's hand and led her to the bathing area.

"I hear you're a lady. Like a duchess or something. Are you a duchess?" She went behind Clara to unlace her stays.

"My husband is a viscount," said Clara. "That makes me a viscountess."

The girls oohed and aahed over this bit of information, and tittered over Clara's accent. She made sure she herself handled her heavy stays, laying them on a chair along with her garters and stockings.

"Do you have another shift with you, love?" asked the matronly woman.

"No," Clara responded as politely as she could. Obviously the women had no idea she was being held against her will. Most likely the captain had purposely led them to believe she was a traveler with baggage.

"Well, then, do you want to bathe as God made you?"

Clara looked at the tub, steam rising from the water into the cold morning air. There were screens all the way around, and plenty of women standing by to protect her from the prying eyes of men, of which she hadn't seen any yet. She untied her shift and let it fall from her body, then placed it on the chair with her stays. She tested the water with her hand, then stepped in and sank down. She closed her eyes to feel herself float buoyantly and the warm water lap at her breasts. It was like being in heaven.

"You be quick now, my lady," said the matron, handing her a cake of brown soap and a brush.

Luxuriating over with, Clara proceeded to scrub herself, then dipped her head back to wash her hair.

"You're a dirty one, aren't you?" laughed the matron. "Been out traveling without stopping at a proper inn, I hear." She motioned to one of the girls. "You're next, Susie," she said as several of the women helped Clara out and covered her with a towel.

"I get to bathe in a real viscountess's bath," said Susie gleefully, as if nobility would seep through her skin. Clearly very pregnant, Susie held onto her friends as she stepped into the tub. A sharp pang wrenched Clara's heart as she watched the young woman enjoying herself in the water.

"What's the matter, my lady?" asked a pretty raven-haired young woman handing Clara her shift. Her voice was gentle, genuinely concerned.

"I lost a child not too long ago," Clara said wistfully, putting on her stays. "I mean, before it could grow in my womb."

"I'm sorry. Susie's sister Constance lost one earlier this year, as well."

Constance? Clara dismissed the thought. Surely there were any number of women named Constance.

A blond girl couldn't help breaking in. "They say it was Lieutenant Hamilton's baby she lost, too," she whispered.

"Abby, don't go spreading rumors!" chided the raven-haired girl. She began to comb out Clara's hair. "My name's Martha. You've got some tangles here—what's your name, anyway? Should we call you Lady Something?" She continued working on Clara's mass of curls.

Clara smiled. The girls all seemed so nice, so friendly, so much her own age. "Well, if you want to, you can call me 'Lady Strathmore.' That's my title. But you can also just call me 'Clara.'"

Martha braided Clara's hair, then twisted it into a bun and secured it to the top of her head with pins. "I just keep my hair down these days, anyway, so you can have my pins. My fellow likes it that way. Do you have a cap, Lady Clara?"

"No. I think I lost it," she lied. She couldn't very well say she had forgotten to grab it as she was fleeing a burning brothel, could she?

"I'm sure I have an extra. What about a dress? You had a very fine one what you came in with. That all you got?"

"I'm afraid so."

"Susie," Martha called out. "You still got your old short gown you were wearing before you got big?"

Susie laughed. "Yes. Why? You want to tease me about my big fat belly?"

"No! Lady Clara here will need a work frock. She can't very well wear a silk gown when she's a-sweeping, now, can she?"

Clara wanted to correct Martha that it was most assuredly not "Lady Clara," just simply Clara or Lady Strathmore, but thought better of it. Susie came up to her, holding a towel to her nude body, and handed her a very plain blue-and-white striped bodice and petticoat.

"I hope it fits," she said cheerfully.

It fit Clara as well as one might expect an unflattering servant's garment to fit. The outfit hid every womanly curve. She gave a little turn for Martha.

"Why, you look just like a regular patriot's woman," Martha squeaked.

That brought up a very good point. "Martha, who are all these women? Isn't this a fort with soldiers?"

Martha laughed and took Clara's arm in hers. "I suppose it must seem a bit strange. You don't follow your husband out on the battlefield, do you?"

Clara shook her head.

Martha led her to what looked like a large workroom with a hearth and cupboards on one end and, on the other, a cozy circle of chairs arranged on a rug. Along the walls were spinning wheels and looms.

"I thought not. Well, we're all the wives and daughters and sisters of the soldiers. Some of the women are camp followers, if you get my meaning." She wrinkled her nose at that. "And some of us are servants who've taken up with some of the men. That's me. I was a maid in a colonel's house along with Mrs. Scott," Martha pointed to the matronly woman, "and they asked if I wanted to be here. So I said yes." She leaned in. "That's how I met my fellow Jacob." She giggled softly.

"So this is a patriot fort?"

"We're what's called a fortified supply station," Martha explained. "We supply other forts and regiments."

The matron entered the workroom. "And we have quite a bit of work to be done around here ourselves, girls," she said with a clap. She turned to Clara. "I don't think we were properly introduced, my lady, I'm—"

"Mrs. Scott," interrupted a masculine voice.

Clara spun around. Before her stood a very handsome man with brown hair and blue-gray eyes smiling down at her. She flushed at his attentions.

"Why, Captain Taylor!" exclaimed Mrs. Scott. "You're looking a damned sight better than you did last night. Enough to wish I were a girl thirty years younger."

"I wouldn't be able to handle your spunk, ma'am. You'd tire me in no time at all," the captain teased gallantly.

Now it was Mrs. Scott's turn to blush. Clara stared unbelievingly at the captain. Overnight he had been transformed from a wild-haired, dirty, practically bearded soldier into a well-groomed, clean-shaven officer in uniform. His dark brown jacket faced with scarlet topped off a finely tailored waistcoat and breeches of undyed linen. Under his hat, his hair was neatly combed and bound in a queue, although one or two recalcitrant curls played against his smooth cheeks.

"My lady," he bowed to Clara in greeting.

Clara bit her lip, then nodded in return. "Captain Taylor."

The young women from bath-time scurried about the large workroom, tittering and giggling as they went about their tasks. Periodically they glanced at their handsome captain and blushed.

"Mrs. Scott," Captain Taylor began. "Lady Strathmore is our guest until we can reconnect her with her husband.

However, I'm certain she would be willing to help our efforts here with whatever skills she can offer?"

"Yes, of course," Clara responded.

"Well, what is it you know how to do?" Mrs. Scott asked. "You know how to cook, love?"

"Yes, a little—"

"Nothing with knives, Mrs. Scott."

Both women regarded the captain curiously.

"For her own safety," he added with a smile that was less polite and more alluring.

"No knives, then. Can you work in our garden—"

The captain winced.

"—spin, weave, or sew?"

"I know how to sew, quilt, and embroider. And I can knit and mend stockings." Clara flushed at the last. One did not say such things in front of a gentleman. After only one morning, the American girls' immodesty was already rubbing off on her.

"Then it's settled," Mrs. Scott announced. "You will join our sewing circle." She pointed to the ring of chairs.

"Lady Clara," Martha called out. "Sit by me." She patted the seat next to her.

"Of course, Martha," Captain Taylor said. "But first I need to abscond with your lady to discuss some business." He held out his arm.

The instant Clara threaded her arm in his, a familiar but utterly unexpected warmth fluttered up her spine. The captain led her out of the women's workroom and into the vast courtyard of the fort. It was her first glimpse of her new surroundings in the light of day. Thick, partially whitewashed masonry walls rose two stories high enclosing the inner yard with its several small buildings, barracks from the looks of them. The stone walls themselves immured two levels of rooms, including the women's dormitory and workroom she had just left on the ground floor. A wooden gallery with staircases on each of the four sides of the fort clung to the masonry parapets giving access to the upper floor and its rooms. A girl with a broom disappeared behind one of the wooden doors along the second floor. Officers' quarters, most likely, which, at that moment, needed cleaning. Above, a roof of jutting logs only partially covered the opening to the sky, giving a view of the tops of two of the four crude but massive lookout towers. In the yard itself, Clara spied cannon and howitzers at the ready, while young men rushed about moving boxes and barrels labeled as containing foodstuffs, but which probably contained gunpowder and weapons. It *was* war.

As they walked into the courtyard, the captain leaned over. "'Clara'?" he said inquisitively in her ear.

His soft, deep voice so close to her sent a pleasant tingle to flush her skin and prickle the peaks of her breasts. The reaction alarmed her. She had only ever experienced such a feeling with Paul. "That is my Christian name, Captain Taylor," she responded curtly, letting him know he was most certainly not allowed to call her that.

"It is a very pretty name." He smiled a devastatingly handsome smile. "It suits you."

Clara flushed again, surely a shameful shade of crimson. "What is the business you wished to discuss, captain?" She tried desperately to maintain a tone of propriety.

He released her arm and faced her. "I would appreciate your participation in a little fiction about your situation here. I've told Mrs. Scott and some of the girls that you were traveling, your carriage broke down, and, after unsuccessfully trying to fix it, your driver fled but never returned, leaving you alone in the woods. Then we came along and found you, and you'll be our guest until we can contact your husband and make arrangements. Of course, your husband's name and reputation precede you, so they know to whom you are married."

Clara studied him. "You still don't believe I'm who I say I am."

He exhaled with a touch of exasperation. "To be honest, no, I don't. I think you are far too young to be the wife of General Strathmore—"

"But—"

"And don't say I'm too young to be a captain," he said with annoyance. "I'm twenty-six years old and I've been fighting redcoats since they massacred our men in Boston. I've earned my cockade." He pointed to a yellow bow-shaped ribbon sewn to his hat.

Clara looked up at him. "So why is my own age an issue?" she asked defiantly.

"We received reports of two missing women, one of whom has red hair." His gaze flitted around her uncovered hair. "Your color is more of a golden, honey-brown."

The heat rose in her cheeks again. It was too poetic a description from practically a stranger. "That is my maid, Annabella," she said succinctly.

"And how do I know it is not you who is the lady's maid?" he challenged, his eyebrows raised provokingly. "Never you mind. I have a very knowledgeable source near the area where we found you, and I am certain he will be able to confirm your story."

Paul. "Then this source of yours will be coming here to identify me?"

"Possibly. He also has men who work for him who might come in his stead. You see, if you really are Lady Clara Strathmore, then you are worth a lot to us in terms of recovering some of our own men who are being held prisoner by the British Army. We intend to barter your life for theirs."

Clara's heart raced. So possibly Paul, or maybe Ethan or Redmond, was coming to identify her. Then what? Would she really be able to leave with Paul? Or would the captain force her to return to her husband? Was Paul involved in this somehow and never told her? All she knew was that she could not possibly stay in the fort. She had to find Paul and get a straight answer.

"I understand, captain," she said softly. "I think I should return to the women and their sewing."

The captain led her back to the workroom and bowed graciously before taking his leave.

"He likes you, my lady," whispered Martha once the sewing tasks had been explained to Clara.

"Whatever do you mean?" Clara asked ingenuously.

"Well, I've never seen him look at a woman the way he looks at you. He looked like he was courting you."

Clara flushed yet again. "The captain is just being polite."

Martha shrugged. "I suppose. There's not a woman in this fort who wouldn't want him to act so politely around her, if you get my meaning. He keeps his distance. Not like any of the other men."

Clara kept her head down concentrating on her stitches. "Maybe he has a sweetheart back home?"

"Not as I've heard. Anyway, if he likes you, you should make the most of it. He's so very handsome."

"Yes, I suppose he is," Clara found herself saying.

"Is your husband very handsome?"

Clara sighed. "Yes, he is, rather." General Strathmore was incredibly handsome. Unfortunately, he was an utterly horrible man. She could not, would not return to him, and she could not let the captain use her as something to barter. She had to leave, had to try to find Paul. And she had to do it that night.

* * * * *

Lying awake on her cot in the women's sleeping quarters, Clara found out what Martha had meant when she said the other men of the fort did not keep their distance. Several times during the night, men came into the dormitory quietly and then entered the small curtained spaces of their chosen girls. All around her were the muffled sounds of couples whispering, moving, then finally fornicating. One or two made no secret of their climaxes, crying out as if they were alone and not mounting their amatory attacks in a room full of others.

Disgust shuddered through her. She must have been dead asleep the night before, but she was wide awake now and able to evaluate the situation. There was no reason she could not just leave the room. Surely if some of the men were coming to the women's dorm, some of the women would be going to the men's? She thought she had overheard that some of the officers even had their own rooms. Wouldn't their women prefer to be with their men in private rather than in a communal bedroom?

As quietly as she could, Clara slipped into her own clothes, then tiptoed down the central pathway between the cots, opened the door, and walked out into the night air.

Clamorous pounding on his bedroom door jolted Sam out of bed. He groaned. It was the middle of the blasted night.

"Captain! Wake up!"

It was Patrick, which meant it was serious. Sam threw on his shirt and breeches and unbolted his door.

"What's wrong, Pat—lieutenant?" he said steadying his sleepy body against the jamb. His eyes flew open the second he saw Lady Clara Strathmore standing before him, with Patrick and one of the night watchmen, Elias Bowman, on either side of her.

"She tried to escape, captain," said Pat. "Corporal Bowman here caught her and brought her to me. She was wearing this."

Pat held out a leather belt with a sheath, a sharp knife securely tucked inside.

"Christ," Sam muttered. He turned to her. "What the hell were you thinking?"

"That I don't want to be a part of your prisoner exchange scheme."

Sam studied her. She was hiding something. Why didn't she want to return to her husband? Pride? Utter disdain for imprisonment? Did she prefer wandering about in the woods to a patriot fort with a bed and food?

He turned to Pat. "What do you suggest we do, lieutenant?"

"She needs to be watched at all times, sir. I suggest you keep her here at night under guard."

"And where do you suggest I go at night?"

"You'll also sleep here. As it was in your tent the other night. Sir."

Sam wanted to throttle him, but he had to rein himself in given their present company. Earlier that day, he had confided in Pat—as his best friend, certainly not as his captain—that he had found the lady quite appealing after she had taken a bath.

"Right." Sam ran his fingers through his hair as Pat led Lady Strathmore into his quarters. "Go get a cot and blanket from the hospital, corporal," he instructed, then watched as Elias left to execute his orders.

As Patrick lit a candle stub, Lady Strathmore surveyed the small room, her expression of obstinacy melting into admiration as she took in the simple yet comfortable furnishings. Sam prided himself in his refuge from the business of war: his books, his desk, his well-worn wingback, his washstand with chipped but fine porcelain basin and pitcher, his walnut blanket chest from home.

Lady Strathmore's gaze landed on his bed, a very comfortable featherbed certainly big enough to accommodate more than one person, an idea Sam entertained for a split second.

"Where am I to sleep?" she asked with a plaintive tone.

Sam was absolutely not going to give up his bed. "In there." He pointed to a minuscule antechamber along the wall perpendicular to the entrance. Between the annex and the entry door was his bed. "If you're planning on escaping again, you'll have to slip past my bed, then slip past the guard at my bolted door."

She looked at the little room. "May I at least draw the curtain?" she asked, indicating the tattered drape that hung limply in the doorway.

"Yes." He could at least pretend she was in another room.

She turned to the bookcase. "May I read your books?"

"Yes," Sam grumbled. "But only in here. Probably not much of interest to you, anyway. Some are in Latin."

"I can read Latin," she protested.

That roused him.

"What do you have?"

Despite his annoyance at the whole situation, he had to admit having a highly educated woman in his midst would be diverting. "Caesar's campaigns and such. Please feel free to read what you like."

Corporal Bowman returned with a cot and blanket and he and Pat went about setting them up in the antechamber. Sam and Lady Strathmore glanced at each other uncomfortably until she looked away. Suddenly, her hand went to her mouth to cover a grin.

"What now?" he said. He followed her eyes to his crotch. Sam had pulled on his breeches hastily and only the waistband was buttoned. The buttons up the front were undone and a piece of his shirt poked through.

Determined to not lose this battle, he held her gaze as he boldly pushed his shirt in under the fall and fastened one button. "If we are to live together, my lady, you will need to get quite used to such indelicacies."

Her blush was enchanting.

"What was that?" asked Pat as he joined them from the annex, then shook his head with a smirk at the scene of the roommates glaring at each other. "All finished, my lady. The room is rather small, but you'll merely be sleeping there, I suppose."

The cot did indeed take up most of the space. The center of it was lined up with the curtained doorway. Elias had a difficult time extracting himself from the little room before returning to his post.

"Thank you, lieutenant," she said. "I suppose I'll just go to sleep now."

"Lieutenant, I would like to see you outside for a moment," Sam snarled under his breath.

"Certainly, captain."

Once outside, Sam dismissed Elias for a piss break before he rounded on Pat. "What the hell do you think you're doing?" he growled quietly. "You know I get in a foul mood if I can't … well, you know, in the morning. I suppose I can just stop what I'm doing during the middle of the day and go frig myself?" He raked his fingers through his hair, grabbed the roots and pulled. "Christ! You are so frustrating sometimes!" His hands continued to hold his head as if to keep it from exploding.

"Look, Sam, she might escape if she remains in the women's dormitory. That should be first and foremost on your mind. She may very well be a spy. Have you considered that? As for the other, you'll find time during the day. Or maybe you could do it once she's asleep."

"I make noise."

"Yes," Pat chuckled. "I know."

Sam couldn't stay mad at him for too long. "You are responsible, First Lieutenant Patrick Hamilton, if anything goes wrong with the workings of this fort because of my bad mood." He stood as close as he could and not cause suspicion. Their mouths were an inch apart.

Patrick licked his lips. "Yes, captain. Now go to bed. I'll wait outside until Corporal Bowman returns."

Sam went inside, closed and bolted the door, then leaned his back against it, mulling over his changed living circumstances. He would now have to wear clothing to bed— his shirt or drawers or something. And where the hell was the lady going to pee? She'd have to get her own damn chamber pot. He glanced over at the annex doorway, then froze at the scene before his eyes. Lady Strathmore had taken a candle stub into the little room with her. The light cast her shadow against the curtain, practically sheer from age and wear. Her hands loosened the laces of her stays behind her back, then she lifted the boned garment off her body and twisted around to place it on the floor. The flame of the candle flickered before she came back into focus against the curtain, this time only wearing her shift, the outline of her very feminine body clearly defined. She arched her back ever so slightly as she raised her arms above her head to toy with her hair, shaking it loose until it tumbled down her back. Sam's body grew warm in response to his now rampant cock. He had to look away, he had to, but he couldn't.

Until she blew out the light.

All through the night, Lady Strathmore tormented him in his dreams, until he woke with a start, wanting so much to frig himself, aching to spend. He couldn't, of course, not with her right there. She would hear, wouldn't she? He resigned himself to being frustrated tomorrow. Pat would get an earful at the very least.

CHAPTER TWELVE

The women said nothing to Clara the next morning. Yet they must have known something was amiss once they saw her changing out of her silk dress, then discovered she did not spend the night in their dorm and a sentinel had been stationed outside Captain Taylor's door. If anyone asked, she would admit that there *was* a war going on and she *was* the wife of the enemy, and that perhaps the captain had received intelligence that necessitated the guarding of the fort's guest.

Clara picked up her mending, inspecting it with a curious look as she joined the sewing circle. The breeches and shirts were not just torn from soldiering, they were threadbare.

"It's difficult to keep our men in uniform, Lady Clara," explained Martha.

"In fact, we really don't have uniforms at all," interjected Abby. "Which I suppose is good as we can make whatever it is the men need in whatever color we happen to have."

Clara was a little perplexed, so the women explained. The occupation of New York by the British necessitated the development of cottage industries as imports could rarely get through, if at all. Weaving homespun cloth of wool and hemp not only helped keep the New York regiments in shirts and tents, it helped the women who lived at the fort to earn their keep.

"Only officers' wives are allowed to be on the official army ration," said Martha. "Those of us what have soldiers can share in their victuals. It's especially hard if there's a baby on the way." She nodded at Susie, who was busily spinning hemp. Martha leaned in. "Many of us lost our homes and even our loved ones when the redcoats invaded New York," she said in a low voice. "This fort is our home now, so we do what we can to help out and the army gives us room and board."

Clara felt a queasiness in the pit of her stomach. She hadn't given much thought to the colonists who had been displaced because of the war. She now sat amongst them, listening to them chatter away about what role they played in their fight for independence. By "helping out," it seemed, Martha really meant practically running the fort. Not only did the women mend and make clothing and tents, they worked in the hospital, gardened and cooked, tended the pigs, cows, and chickens, cleaned the common areas and officers' quarters, and did the laundry.

"Our own Mrs. Scott maintains discipline among the girls," said Martha, once again speaking quietly. "She doesn't allow drunkenness, and no whoring, although the girls can be sweet on a soldier."

"You do so much," Clara said with awe. "What is it that the men do?" It was a bold question in the heart of a rebel garrison, but Clara was genuinely curious.

Martha laughed softly. "Well, I don't suppose I should tell you all as you just might tell your husband. We gather and distribute supplies for the militia and the regular army."

"And the men go out on scouting missions," Abby added. "They survey the terrain and build bridges." She suddenly flushed crimson. "That's what Andrew told me."

"Abby!" exclaimed Martha with a smile. "Andrew Ross? He's a nice one, he is."

Abby leaned in. "But he says some of the men want field action. They want to fight. They think they're not doing enough for the war. Some of 'em are even bored." She sat back in her chair. "If you ask me, what we do is awfully important. And I don't want my Andrew getting shot full of holes. And if any of 'em is bored he can help me do the washing!"

Susie got up from her spinning with a sigh and padded over to the mending area, her hand on her belly. She looked over Clara's shoulder. "You certainly know what you are doing, Lady Clara," she said sweetly. She stood there for a moment, admiring Clara's work, before she asked, "How long have you been in the colonies?"

Clara looked up, and offered a smile. "About a year, I suppose."

"Do you like it here?" asked Abby with heartfelt enthusiasm. "I mean, is it as nice here as it is in England?"

"Well, the two places are so very different." It was the most gracious thing to say.

"Do you think women have more rights in England?" Martha blurted.

Clara was taken aback by the question. "I really don't know." It was something she had never considered.

"Women have no rights anywhere," Mrs. Scott boomed, walking in from the kitchen, wiping her hands on her apron. "We feed and clothe our men, give them babies, and they take us for granted. Like the African slaves, except they don't keep us in chains. Don't none of you think they're fighting this revolution for *your* freedom." She nodded at Clara. "When it's all over, we and our European sisters can start our own revolt."

"But the rich have more rights, don't they?" asked Abby. She turned to Clara. "Isn't it better for titled women in England?"

"So, if we were all rich we would have rights?" retorted Martha. "I don't think that's true, Abby. We're still women."

The conversation gave Clara pause. She had never felt she lacked rights at home—until, of course, she got married. Her marriage was forced upon her. "I will admit that I don't want for anything. I have good food, fine dresses, even jewelry. But I did not make my own choice for marriage," she confessed. "I simply could not have. My father and brother made the choice for me."

There was a brief moment of silence, before Mrs. Scott asked, "And do you love the man, dear?"

No one had ever asked her that question before. Love was irrelevant for her class. What she felt for Paul was definitely love. There was not a shred of the sentiment in her relationship with the general. "We have nothing in common, really," she said evasively. "He's so much older than I."

Mrs. Scott stood with her hands on her hips. "Like I said, we have more work to be done once this war is over. And you girls have mending to do to keep our patriot men out of rags."

"Ooh, look at those elegant stitches!" Abby exclaimed, examining Clara's work.

The other girls looked over. "Your sewing is much too fancy for this lot," said a young blond woman mending a tear in a soldier's breeches. The women laughed.

"Maybe you can mend the captain's clothes, then," said Martha. She caught Clara's eye and winked.

Clara flushed. "I can certainly teach you—" A sudden pain gripped her lower right. She doubled over with a groan.

Martha was instantly at her side. "Lady Clara, what's wrong?"

"There's a pain in my side … in my belly."

"Is it your courses?"

Clara blinked back tears. It seemed a little soon. Paul had told her to not expect her body to return to normal for a while. "Perhaps. I don't know."

"The medicines and herbs are kept in the hospital," explained Martha. "Come, let me take you there."

The hospital, across the courtyard from the women's rooms, was another large dormitory with curtains separating the beds. Only a few of the beds were occupied by soldiers. Martha left Clara in the capable hands of Jenny, the nurse—really a midwife—on duty, who put Clara in a cot, gave her an herbal tea for her pains, a towel for the bleeding in case she should start, then closed the curtains around her.

Clara lay on the cot contemplating the women's conversation and wishing very much she were in the little annex room upstairs reading one of Captain Taylor's books in solitude. The commotion of a couple of newly arrived wounded militia men gave her the chance. Slipping out of the hospital was as easy as slipping out of the women's dorm. She silently made her way up the wooden staircase conveniently situated right outside, then slunk down along the covered corridor to the captain's door. She quietly and slowly lifted the latch and went in.

She breathed a sigh of relief at finding the room empty. She hadn't thought until that very moment what she would say if the captain had been present and working. He had been gruff with her that morning, so much so she had had to leave as soon as she was dressed to wash her face in the women's dorm.

She went to the bookcase and searched along the spines. She was not in the mood for Caesar so she picked one she had never heard of. *Memoirs of a Woman of Pleasure* was a slim, leather-bound volume. She opened to the title page, where she beheld an inscription in a masculine hand:

> *Sam, I sold my soul to the Devil for this one. Enjoy! And I'll see you in Hell. —Paul*

Paul? Paul Bridgers? Thoroughly intrigued, she took the thin book to her cot in her little room and began to read.

The *Memoir* was written by a girl a little younger than herself, but with a far more vigorous and enterprising spirit. Clara had never read such a story! Fanny Hill's adventures were of such voluptuousness Clara had to glance around to ensure she was actually alone. Her body heated as Fanny was seduced by a woman, her ire raised when Fanny's virginity was offered to a man far too old for her, her sex tingled and swelled as Fanny awakened to the pleasures a man could bestow upon a woman.

Clara shifted on the cot trying to relieve the wet tightness between her legs, only managing to arouse herself further. She pulled her cloak around her shoulders and leaned against the cold stone wall, her legs splayed open and crossed. When Fanny opened the parlor door to see a beautiful, sleeping youth, an idea sparked in Clara's mind that she could touch herself as she read, a thought dismissed quickly. The pleasures of the mind were far more respectable than the sins of the flesh. Better to be caught reading an immoral story than to be caught assuaging one's lust. Whatever would the captain think if he happened upon her in such a state? Clara smiled. Perhaps he would—

The door to the captain's quarters crashed open.

She jumped, flattening herself against the wall, her heart pounding so loudly she was sure whoever had just entered could hear it. She peeked through a tear in the annex curtain.

Captain Taylor and Lieutenant Hamilton entered the bedroom with a clandestine air. The lieutenant bolted the door as the captain stripped off his jacket and threw it on the bed, clearly cross and irritable, muttering about that "blasted woman," as the lieutenant countered with "Sam, Sam," and soothed him with calming words. Clara could not quite hear what they were saying but she was certain she was the topic of conversation.

Suddenly, the captain pushed the lieutenant against the wall and took him in a violent kiss. Clara froze. *Two men kissing?* She had never heard of such a thing. The men tore at each other hungrily, stripping off clothes, biting, clawing, licking each other like animals in heat, until, finally, they stood completely naked, and simply pressed themselves together in a tangle of arms, their mouths and tongues still teasing tenderly.

She stared, mesmerized by the perfectly matched bodies of the two officers, lean, sculpted muscles entwining into one knot of masculine flesh. The captain held the lieutenant's head in his hands as he covered his cheeks with kisses, murmuring something to make the lieutenant smile and nod, then pulled away and walked to his desk. He was more magnificent in the full light of day. The hair that had taunted her as it disappeared down his breeches now continued its trail to a wreath of curls framing his impressive endowments. His cock, longer but not quite as thick as Paul's, jutted out fully aroused, bouncing slightly as he moved across the room, his heavy balls swinging enticingly underneath. He went to the desk lamp, removed the top and burner, and dipped his fingers into the oil in the font. His hand dripping with the viscous liquid, he grabbed his prick and stroked, covering himself until he was slick and glistening.

"Now your turn, Pat," he said, his voice dripping with seductive desire.

Clara had to stifle a libidinous sigh.

The lieutenant, still waiting by the door, quickly glanced at the drawn bolt, then strolled over to the desk with a wide grin. His body was now on display, sleek and potent, his erection, matching the captain's in length and girth, springing proudly from a mass of brown hair. Once at the captain's side, the two men kissed luxuriatingly as the captain reached around with his oily hand to the lieutenant's buttocks, his movements eliciting a low hum of appreciation from the lieutenant.

Clara squeezed her thighs together hoping for relief, instead provoking herself with a slick massage.

As the lieutenant rolled his hips against the captain's hand, the captain murmured against his lips; "…the bed…" was all she could hear. His expression slackened with lust, the lieutenant dutifully went to the foot of the bed and bent over, holding onto the low footboard, his butt taut and round above powerful thighs. The captain followed and arched over him, licking and kissing his back, gently pressing his hips against the lieutenant's firm bottom, urging his legs apart with his knees.

And then the captain aimed his prick at the lieutenant's arsehole and pushed in slowly.

Clara clapped her hands to her mouth to suppress a gasp. Paul Bridgers had taught her a great many things about life and love. The fact that two men could join in sexual union was not one of them. Yet, she and Paul had done precisely the same thing, and the coupling of the devastatingly handsome officers seemed like the most natural act in the world.

The captain's fingers danced lightly on the lieutenant's back for a moment before he held on to his shoulders and pushed his cock farther. The lieutenant lifted his head, exhaling a groan, then twisted back to gaze at his lover. The captain grabbed a fistful of the lieutenant's brown hair and pulled his head back for a devastatingly deep kiss. Lust spiked in Clara's core. As the captain swallowed the lieutenant's tongue, she opened her mouth and thrust out her own.

The anguish of pleasurable pain wracked the lieutenant's face as the captain pushed in deeper, then pulled out slowly. The captain snaked his hand around to take his friend's cock in his fist, sliding up and down the hard shaft. The lieutenant let out a long, growling moan.

Clara's body screamed for relief. She could not possibly touch herself without making noise. Or could she? Her left hand found the ties of her petticoats and loosened them enough so her right hand could maneuver under the waistbands and slowly scrunch up her shift. Her fingers finally found her excited clit throbbing for attention. She smoothed the sticky wetness over the nub, tightening her lips against the urge to sigh, stroking slowly, then matching the rhythm of the captain's hand on his lover's cock, uniting her lust with theirs.

Captain Taylor drove aggressively into the lieutenant, pumping his prick with equal violence, pulling and lengthening the shaft toward the floor. Sweat sheened his back, his muscles flexed and tensed as he raced to completion, hissing curses, rumbling affirmations. Clara frantically rubbed her tender clit, wishing, wanting, imagining it was her the captain plundered, as she climbed to an elusive crest only to slip and tumble back down.

She needed one of the officers to climax first.

It was the lieutenant who could no longer hold out. He clenched his jaw, straining against a cry, as the captain milked him unrelentingly, sending jets of pearlescent fluid onto the wooden boards. Clara came next, her body finding its peak and holding on for the most glorious second before taking her over the edge, her eyes ripping themselves from the scene only momentarily as her head fell back in relief.

Desperately quieting her panting breaths, she watched the captain. He savagely seized the lieutenant's hips to steady himself as he slammed against his arse, his pendent balls crashing into the lieutenant's spent sac. The lieutenant gripped the footboard, his knuckles white, his face a mass of creases, his body staggering against the savage rhythm. At his final thrust, the captain closed his eyes tightly and gritted his teeth, choking back a rapturous cry. For a minute more, he continued to press his groin into the lieutenant as his body jerked in sputtering spasms, until his head fell back and he exhaled a groaning sigh. He spread his palms on the lieutenant's butt cheeks, smoothing the skin, then bent over his back and wrapped his arms around him.

"Thank you, Pat. Thank you, my friend," he said with silky satisfaction.

The silence of afterglow was deafening. Or perhaps it was the blood rushing and pulsing through her head. Clara stiffened, her hand still down her skirt. She dared not move.

The captain's prick slipped out, his emission dripping to the floor to mingle with the creamy pool. He kissed the lieutenant, gave him a little smack on the butt, then both officers dressed calmly and left.

Clara exhaled.

CHAPTER THIRTEEN

The captain seemed in a good mood for the next couple of days, despite the fact that the expected supplies were now long overdue. From gossip in the sewing circle, Clara discovered Captain Taylor was working diligently and efficiently, sending out spies and scouts to comb the area for information if not the actual hoped-for provisions.

By the end of the following day, Clara's courses had indeed started and she once again had to avail herself of the herbal concoctions at the hospital. While Jenny mixed a remedy, conversation wandered from her work as a nurse to her home and family. Clara was pleased to learn Jenny had relatives in Gloucestershire, connections, she secretly hoped, that could help her return to England.

"I've never been myself, of course. I was born here," Jenny said with a measure of pride. She turned her gentle blue eyes to

Clara. "Did you know Captain Taylor has family from there too? I think near Cirencester—"

Urgent shouts and yelling at the entrance to the fort stopped her from continuing. The commotion got closer, until several soldiers appeared at the hospital door carrying wounded men on medical litters. Battle injuries were not unheard of this far away from the fighting field, but they were rare enough to be worrisome to the fort's residents, who were quickly gathering.

"Get Captain Taylor!" Jenny called to one of the women. She quickly and capably took control, giving orders to all present, referring to the wounded soldiers as "Johnny"—"Put Johnny over there … You—go to that Johnny … Get Johnny Red a blanket."

Mimicking what Jenny and the other women were doing, Clara grabbed towels and a basin, then offered soothing words to the injured as she cleaned their wounds. She knelt at the side of one young man with sandy blond hair, his strong, robust form defeated by a bullet to his side. His clothes were soaked through, a brilliant red.

Clara grasped his hand. "The nurse will be here soon, soldier."

His face was screwed shut in agony, his breathing weak, but the sound of her voice enlivened him. His eyes flew open. A familiar shade of blue-green.

"Redmond!" she exclaimed. "My God, I never thought I would see you again." She smoothed her palm over his cheek, trying desperately to control the torrent of emotions. If Redmond was here, Paul was nearby. He had to be. "You're fighting for the patriots now?"

He attempted a grin. "You said 'patriot'."

"And you should not be speaking." She examined the shredded and bloody skin at his side and knew he would not survive long. She wiped his brow with a cool towel.

"My lady, I see you have learned a new skill," came the captain's voice behind her.

She gave him a weak smile clouded by anguished tears.

"You know this man," he said solemnly, and knelt beside her.

"Yes, captain. This is Redmond Moncrief. He was my husband's groom until circumstances made him leave our service." It was the most diplomatic way to put it. "He is betrothed to my lady's maid, Annabella. The one with the red hair."

The captain looked Redmond squarely in the eye. "Then you know Lady Clara Strathmore?"

"Yes ... sir," he sputtered.

The captain placed a hand on Clara's shoulder, his touch gentle despite his intention. "And this is she?" His tone was formal and direct.

Redmond flicked a curious glance at Clara. "It is ... indeed."

"Thank you, soldier. And thank you for your bravery in fighting for our cause." The captain squeezed her shoulder as he rose. "Excuse me. I must check on the others, my lady."

Clara's eyes burned now with tears of anger. So he got what he wanted from a dying man. She dabbed at Redmond's brow with a wet cloth, smoothing back his hair. He was quite handsome. No wonder Annabella was so attracted to him. She offered a weak smile, but Redmond surely understood his fate.

He pawed feebly at her arm. "Lady ... I saw him ... Bridgers ..."

She had to suppress a squeal. "You saw Paul? Is he alive? Where is he?" She was beside herself with frustration and joy.

Redmond was fading away quickly. "He's fighting ..."

"Oh, God." Her heart clenched. It was her worst nightmare.

"He … loves you."

Tears blinded her as her head spun. Was Paul to meet a fate like this? She couldn't bear to see his body battered and beaten.

"Lady … tell Annabella … you must tell her I love her."

Clara watched in horror as the blue-green eyes lost their vitality and went dark.

Lady Strathmore's mourning cry shattered the quiet hum of the hospital. It was intolerable. Bad for morale.

Sam quickly went to her side and took her arm, lifting her to standing.

"My lady, you should not be here. You are not prepared for such a scene. Please, let me take you upstairs." He signaled to Pat to take over his duties on the hospital floor.

She was still sobbing uncontrollably by the time they reached his quarters. Sam sat her down in the wingback and knelt beside her.

"My lady, have you not witnessed the aftermath of battle before?" She was the wife of a general, after all.

She shook her head. "No," she said, barely audible, her lips trembling.

He took both her hands in his. "It is quite normal to experience such grief when we lose friends. It is the most difficult part of war. You must feel free to talk about your feelings with those around you when this happens."

She sniffled and inhaled deeply. "Captain, I need you to do a favor for me. For Redmond. Please."

"Yes, yes. What is it?"

"Take a note to his betrothed, Annabella, my maid in Chesterton. She must know. It will kill her, but she must know."

"Yes, of course." Sam studied the woman before him. The depth of her emotions for a servant exposed the vulnerability lying beneath her usual imperious demeanor. He pressed her delicate hands between his, hoping his warmth would calm her juddering sobs. It seemed to work. She offered him a fragile smile.

Even in her despair she was beautiful. She stirred up a desire, a craving in him that had lain dormant, or possibly had never existed. Every night, he awaited her appearance at his door, only to be driven mad by her proximity as she slept in the annex.

He hated that he would have to provide his messenger to Chesterton with two notes: one for Annabella about the loss of her betrothed and one for General Strathmore requesting an exchange of supplies and prisoners of war for the return of his wife.

CHAPTER FOURTEEN

General Strathmore sat back in satisfaction, spreading his legs just an inch more, tilting his hips. He had trained the girl well, although her vigorously bobbing head at his crotch indicated she was perhaps a little too exuberant. But she would learn to go more slowly, learn to savor taking all of him down her throat, instead of making distracting choking sounds. She was still rather young. There would be at least a year's worth of training before she would be truly ready for him. Her willingness to please, without even a threat on his part, indicated she would do quite well.

She had been so scared, so submissive the first time. He had made sure that her maidenhead was intact, of course, as part of what he called an official health examination. He required promises from her and her parents that she would remain a virgin as long as she worked in his household, until he gave his permission otherwise. Little did any of them realize that it would be his prick breaching the barrier to her innocence.

He laid his hands on her head as a signal to slow her pace. "Yes, my dear, that's right. Yes." He groaned and relaxed against the back of the wooden office chair.

There was a loud and bothersome rap at the door.

"What is it?" he barked, pushing the girl's head back down onto his lap.

"General Strathmore, sir? There is a very important dispatch from the Americans at Fort Revolution."

Damn. Hawkins. If a dispatch fell into the hands of Lieutenant Hawkins then it was most definitely important.

"Come."

Hawkins entered the office and saluted, then turned a most disagreeable shade of crimson. He quickly closed the door behind him.

"Well, Hawkins, what is so damned urgent?"

Mild disgust flitted across the lieutenant's face before he looked away.

"Lady Clara Strathmore, sir, has been found. She is being held by the Americans at Fort Revolution. They are demanding an exchange of prisoners and supplies for her return."

"Oh, bloody hell," the general muttered. He wrenched the girl off and she tumbled backwards onto the floor. "Leave me," he growled, buttoning his breeches.

The disheveled girl curtsied and scurried away.

He stood, frustration fueling the urgent need in his crotch. He paced behind his desk, hoping movement would distract his unruly cock. "Damned bloody colonials think they can play games with me!"

"I'm sure you anticipated this, sir. It is a rather conventional move."

Hawkins was right. Of course. The bugger was always right. "Do they mention the child?"

The lieutenant drew the missive from his pocket and skimmed the contents. "No, sir. They merely say your wife is healthy and unharmed."

"Give me that." The general grabbed the note from the lieutenant's hands. "I suppose I have to respond in an official capacity this time. I can't bloody well go and attack them, can I?"

Ever the intelligent fellow, Hawkins held his tongue.

"This chit is more trouble than she's worth. I should have fucked her raw until I stopped up her belly and left her back home in bloody Gloucestershire." Strathmore inhaled deeply. "Go. Let me think about this. It's official military business and I have to act accordingly."

Sebastian was quite happy to oblige his superior by leaving the office as quickly as he could. As he walked toward the front door, the general called for the poor maidservant. It was despicable.

His stomach rumbled, reminding him he hadn't yet had breakfast. He walked to the barracks at a steady pace, not really wanting to get on with the business of war. It had arrived too early this morning, and autumn in the colonies, with its piles of brilliant leaves and brisk, enlivening air, deserved to be savored.

When he arrived at his officer's quarters his own lovely housemaid was pacing and fretting in the entryway.

"Lieutenant!" She jumped when he walked in.

"Miss Rogers." Sebastian nodded and removed his hat. "May I have my breakfast in the dining room?"

"Yes, yes, of course," she said nervously.

Whatever it was, Sebastian was not ready to deal with it until he had something to eat, preferably eggs and bacon. Maybe some of that oat mush with maple sugar the cook made, too.

He knew Annabella was outside the dining room door waiting for him to finish. He ate what he needed and called for her to come in.

"Miss Rogers, you have some news, perhaps?" he said, sipping coffee.

"I'm so sorry, sir. A man delivered a note today. It's for me, I know. He said it was and I can read my own name. I opened it but I cannot read it. It's in my Lady Clara's hand. I know it, sir. I know her writing even though I cannot read it. And I know her signature. She taught it to me."

Lady Strathmore. Christ. The last thing he wanted was to be caught up in some blasted intrigue. "Let me see the note. I can read it to you," he said politely.

Annabella curtsied one too many times. "Thank you, sir. Thank you." She pulled the letter from her pocket and handed it to him.

It was indeed in a woman's hand, written hurriedly. He quickly glanced over the contents, realizing he would have to relay the message truthfully and word for word.

My dear Annabella,

It has been quite some time since we have seen each other, I know. I have had my own adventures and am now in an American fort several miles north of Chesterton. While at the fort we tended wounded soldiers. Your own Redmond was amongst them. He had been fighting valiantly for a cause he feels is worthy. We spoke briefly. Annabella, sweet girl, he loves you dearly, he told me with his own lips. He died telling me this. Please know that he thought only of you until the very end.

Your humble servant,

Lady Clara Strathmore

Annabella stood stock still, eyes wide, mouth open, reddening from lack of air. She was in shock. Instantly he went to her.

"Miss Rogers." He placed his hands on her shoulders. "Annabella." He squeezed, and gently shook her.

Annabella gasped and gulped for breath, then fell to her knees. Her sobs were unstoppable. Sebastian tried to get her to stand to no avail. He picked her up in both arms, then, negotiating his way through the kitchen, carried her to the lean-to just behind, and laid her down on her bed. He knelt down beside her.

Up until the moment he read the note, Sebastian had only had suspicions about Annabella and Strathmore's former groom. Now he realized the connection was deep, something he himself longed for but had never experienced. Yet, seeing the girl in such abject pain made him reconsider his own desire for companionship and love, until she sat up, grabbed his jacket, and sobbed into his chest, clutching him to her body as if he were about to float away. He found it so easy to wrap his arms around her, pull her close, whisper tender sympathies in her ear. It felt good to be touching her like this. Too good. He nestled his nose in her fiery red hair, then pressed his lips to kiss the silky tresses.

This was definitely an agreeable way to spend an autumn morning in America.

CHAPTER FIFTEEN

Clara loved to watch Sam in the middle of the night. Almost like clockwork, he turned off the lamp, clambered into bed, then waited a few minutes before sliding off the mattress to stand in the corner by the door where it was darkest. The first time, his not-so-practiced movements roused her to the curious scene of him with one hand pressed flat against the wall, the other in front of him, his head down, his hips tucked. Moments later, the rapid slap of skin on wet skin accompanied by ragged breathing made plain what he was doing. The next night she pretended to be asleep and waited. He did it again. To her delight, he did it every night, and, also to her delight, she found she could do it too. Wrapped up as he was in his own pleasure, the captain never suspected she was taking her own.

During the tedious workday, despite the genial conversation and intriguing gossip of the women, her thoughts meandered to the captain, especially to thoughts about her and the captain alone behind a bolted door. She would wait by his bedside at night, and as he slid off she would grab hold of his thighs, kneel before him, and suck his magnificent cock. Or she would straddle him as he lay asleep, waking him with a glorious fuck...

But then her thoughts would drift to Paul and she would quickly sober, struggling to tamp down fears for his safety.

Would he be jealous? Would a brothel owner mind so much if she had an indulgent dalliance with a handsome, intelligent American officer?

Would she even have the temerity to initiate such a dalliance? What if the captain were horribly insulted? It would make their already uncomfortable situation far more intolerable. Every night they simply mumbled their good evenings, then coexisted in uneasy silence, she trying to read on her cot, he doing something at his desk.

That evening, after Clara was finished sharing supper with the women, Corporal Bowman appeared to escort her to the captain's quarters as he did every night. When they arrived, Lieutenant Hamilton was there, talking with the captain, his affable presence dissipating the awkwardness that usually hung thick in the air. The next night, the lieutenant was again in the captain's chambers when she was deposited at the door. He was a welcome fixture in their nights thereafter.

The two officers usually chatted about literature and history rather than actual military strategy or garrison concerns. Clara remained in the annex, pretending not to listen, and not being very good about it. She couldn't help herself, she had to interject comments, especially the night when the men discussed whether Pope's translation of the *Iliad* was accurate. Of course it was! And while she didn't know the original Greek, she was sure the work captured—for the English mind at least—the sense of the original. After that, she was invited to pass the evening alongside the two Americans, she continuing the ever-needed sewing and mending, while the lieutenant smoked a pipe and the captain paced, gestured, and otherwise could not keep still.

A few times, Clara looked up from her handwork only to catch the captain staring straight at her and smiling, attentions that warmed her to the very core, flushing her face and dampening her palms. At such times, she had to concentrate very hard on not letting her needle slip, not increasing the size of her stitches...

Not standing up to wrap her arms around his neck, murmuring his name, and drawing him down to kiss her.

"You know, Sam, you've been in far too good a mood every single day for the last, I don't know how long, but not long after that woman began sleeping with you—"

"Pat, she is most definitely not sleeping with me," Sam scowled.

It had become a habit for Pat to join him in his chambers before Lady Strathmore arrived in the evening. They often talked about military matters, or sometimes male concerns. Usually the topics strayed to Lady Strathmore, as she was both a military matter and a male concern. Tonight's topic was decidedly on the male side.

Pat returned an annoying smirk as he crossed his leg over his knee and settled further into the wingback. "Whatever you want to call it, but she's doing something, isn't she?"

"What?" Sam shoved back the desk chair and stood up. "You think I got her sucking my cock at night? Christ, I wish! I certainly do. But no, my friend, it is far more innocuous than that."

Pat smirked some more.

Sam paced before him. "Look, I know when she is asleep and she sleeps rather heavily."

"You know?"

"Yes."

"How?" Pat raised a skeptical brow.

"I hear her breathing deeply, like one does when one is asleep. She goes to sleep and I get up and go to the corner of the room—"

"You get up?"

"I can't very well do it on the bed, now, can I? She'd hear the bed frame squeaking or banging against the wall."

"Right." Pat shook his head in disbelief. "Go on."

"So I get up and do it in the corner. It's far too dark for her to know what's going on even if she did wake up and try to look."

"Hmmm." There was that smirk again, this time with a dubious squint. "And, my friend, how do you know she is not waking up and watching?"

"Because, when she's fast asleep she makes a little noise. Sort of like, well, a purring kitten."

"A kitten!" Pat tilted his head to the ceiling and threw up his hands. "For Christ's sake! A kitten?"

"Don't worry, she is completely unaware of what's going on." Sam grinned. "I do it every night."

"Well, thank the heavens you found a way to frig yourself, captain," pronounced Pat. "You are extremely difficult to work with if you do not. You know that, don't you?"

"I am quite aware of my own needs, thank you, lieutenant," Sam snapped.

Pat reached into his pocket for his pipe and tobacco. "You do realize she's probably doing the very same thing while you're going at it. That's most likely what that kitten sound is."

Sam's jaw dropped. "You think she...?" He trailed off, imagining it. His body responded far too quickly.

Pat flicked his gaze to Sam's crotch. "I have no idea." He took his first puff. "But I rather like the thought, don't you? She's quite lovely. I would love to see that beautiful face of hers abandoned to ecstasy."

Apparently Sam wasn't the only one who considered the viscountess in improper predicaments. "You think I should bed her, don't you?"

"I think every soldier in this garrison would like to bed her. You, my dear captain, have the opportunity." Pat sucked on his pipe.

Sam chuckled. "I do, don't I?" Now it was his turn to smirk. "However, lieutenant, I am supposed to be the example of ascetic continence for my men."

"And," Pat added, "the safety of this fort would be threatened if General Strathmore ever found out that his beautiful wife had been violated by rebel scum."

There was a knock on the door.

"Come, corporal," called Sam as he circled back around to his desk.

Corporal Bowman entered with Lady Strathmore, saluted, and left to take his post outside the door.

"You two look guilty," she said as she took a chair near the lamp and gathered her sewing on her lap. She looked back and forth between them. "Cat got your tongue tonight, gentlemen?"

Sam and Pat exchanged glances before Pat began to laugh uncontrollably, dragging Sam with him in his mirth. Lady Strathmore merely thinned her lips and went back to her handwork.

"Don't give us that look, Lady Strathmore," said Sam wiping tears from his eyes. "You know the women do the same. I see you all whispering and giggling so the men don't hear."

"Well, we are just women, after all. It's not like we need to command respect and obedience from our subordinates. As women we understand our place is at the bottom," she said provokingly. "We have no subordinates."

"Uh, oh." Pat grinned.

"Certainly a viscountess would never find herself at the bottom," countered Sam, now pacing along the foot of the bed. "You'll always have servants beneath you."

"Yes, captain, that is true. But, and I only say this as a guest in your land, when your revolution is finally won, and your republican government installed, will women be included in your councils and congresses? I think not."

"Damned free-thinking Mrs. Scott!" grumbled Sam.

"You'll even free the African decades before you free women because there are men amongst the race."

Sam stopped and turned to her. "You, madam, are infuriating."

"I know." Her smile was wonderfully beguiling.

But Sam couldn't be defeated by a pretty face. "How does your husband deal with this insubordination? I cannot imagine he, of all men, would allow such an undisciplined tongue in his house."

"He doesn't have to. With him I am complacent and conciliatory," she said, subdued. "I would never contradict or challenge him."

"I cannot believe that," countered Sam. "Or rather, I cannot believe you do that willingly."

"No, but he is my lord and master, so I must act accordingly." There was a bitter bite to her words. "And he treats all his subordinates the same." She glanced up at him. "We all, captain, must hold our tongues in his house."

Sam gazed at her. If her husband didn't enjoy her barbs and wit, the man was a damned fool. It was a shame. To pass an evening with a beautiful woman as she performed simple domestic tasks and boldly challenged his views would be the height of marital bliss. That, and waking up wrapped around her nude body, her honey-brown locks draped loosely against the pillows of their bed, breathing in the fragrance of her arousal as his needy cock nudged between her thighs...

Pat cleared his throat, bringing Sam back to the present. He adjusted the fullness in his crotch as discreetly as possible.

But Lady Strathmore had stood up and was coming toward him, her mending in her hand. Sam panicked momentarily and looked over at Pat, who shrugged his shoulders.

She unfurled the dark brown jacket she had been fixing and held it out for Sam to take. "Here you go, captain. Is the repair to your satisfaction?"

Nonplussed, Sam took the jacket from her. "What? Oh, right, the tear. Why, yes. In fact, I almost quite forgot I had torn it." He ran his fingers along the scarlet facing, then held the jacket out for Pat to see. "You really can't tell, now, can you?"

She took the newly mended coat from him and placed it on the bed, then began to unbutton the dingy green woolen jacket he was wearing, her fingers calmly working as his head whirled in astonishment at her touch. "I think the morale of your troops will be uplifted when they see their captain in his dress uniform." She tugged the green jacket off him. "That is what this is, right?" she asked as she guided his arms into the sleeves of the brown jacket.

"Yes, yes." Sam was less concerned about the morale of his soldiers at the moment and more about the now-visible sign of desire in his breeches.

"It's a little worn," she sighed, fussing over him. "The women tell me that you are lucky to have a uniform at all, much less a dress uniform." She stood back. "You look quite handsome, captain."

Sam flushed and hoped to heaven she would not glance lower than his waist.

"If it weren't for this damnable civil war I would like to see you dressed in some frippery." She tilted her head. "You've a fine figure." She waved her hands about his person as if draping him in fine materials. "Yes. Mustard-brown velveteen with golden silk lining. Some lace perhaps."

He could put up with mustard and gold, not so much the lace.

"And a wig, of course."

He hated wearing a wig. The very thought dissipated his ardor, until he met the twinkle in her eyes and saw she was teasing.

"Civil war, my lady?" baited Pat. "Are we then rebellious Caesar to your Pompey? I rather thought we were being treated more like the Gauls."

"Yes, but the Gauls were utter barbarians, were they not, lieutenant?" she shot back. "You lot may be savages, but at least you know your Latin."

Sam laughed. She was perfect.

"Forgive me, my lady, I forget myself sometimes," Pat said snidely. "What with the quashing of my freedoms and such." He blew out a steady stream of gray smoke as his lips twitched into a wry smile.

She took up the gauntlet. "Well, I suppose your General Washington must consider himself as Vercingetorix, then, uniting the thirteen disparate colonies against us."

"No, my lady," countered Sam. "That would be our Congress, our people's own representatives, who united us. General Washington takes orders from Congress." He raised an eyebrow at Pat. "Nor should we think of our great commander as a tyrannical Caesar."

Lady Strathmore removed Sam's newly mended officer's jacket, considering it as she hung it on a peg. "I've been wondering, how is it that someone as young as yourself leads this group of men, Captain Taylor?"

"I distinguished myself in service under General Washington—"

"And he's highly educated. Classics at Harvard. He won't tell you that part," grinned Pat.

"Harvard! That's impressive," Lady Strathmore said as if she truly meant it. She picked up a shirt and resumed her mending.

"A veritable hotbed of sedition," Pat sneered. His lips formed an O as he blew smoke rings.

"And Patrick won't tell you he is just as educated," Sam smirked. "William and Mary. He's an honorary member of that treasonous secret society Phi Beta Kappa—"

"It's a debating club, Sam," Pat said with annoyance.

"Debate in the king's colonies, my friend, is treason," Sam retorted.

Pat chuckled. "And you, Lady Strathmore, how is it you are so well-read?"

"I was allowed to be tutored with my brother," she said. "Except for Greek. I had to learn how to sing and play instruments so I would be more attractive to suitors."

"I'd rather you had learned Greek," Sam muttered as he buttoned up his old jacket.

"Well, I am hardly worthy of being amidst such scholars," she said, this time with a cutting edge. "I really should be back downstairs with the women."

"So you can escape again?" countered Sam. "Clearly, it's far too easy to break out of the dormitory at night."

"You don't know the half of it," she said, suppressing a grin.

Pat laughed heartily. "No, he does not! My lady, you are quite correct in that regard. Our abstemious captain does not avail himself of the pleasures of the women's dormitory." He winked at Sam.

"Presumably you do, lieutenant?" Lady Strathmore raised a brow in his direction.

"It is not beneath me." Pat continued blowing smoke rings.

"Really? Who?" She bit her lip and leaned forward.

"He won't tell you, my lady. Patrick has an honorable streak."

"Well, then," she said as she threaded a needle, "I will just have to keep my eye on you at the dance tomorrow night, lieutenant, and see which of the colonial beauties captures your attention."

What? Sam stared at her. "Dance? There's to be a dance tomorrow night?"

"The womenfolk have arranged a small affair, yes," she said smoothly.

"Need I remind you, Lady Strathmore, we are in the middle of a war?"

"We've already discussed that, captain. Did we finally decide it was a colonial war?" She cocked her head demurely.

"I do not find this amusing." Sam gripped the edge of his desk. "We don't have time for such nonsense."

She rested her sewing in her lap, and looked him directly in the eye. "Captain Taylor, with all due respect, sir, after seeing the wounded soldiers the other night, your men are restless. They are tired of drills and scouting, of counting and distributing supplies. The chatter amongst them is that they are impatient for a chance to fight for what they believe in. The women thought it would be a good idea for the men of the fort to relax with the wounded soldiers, get them talking, remind your company that what they are doing is valued and needed. The women feel this might prevent some desertions, so it's in the best interest of everyone. You wouldn't want good men deserting you, even if it is to fight the war, and the women don't want their menfolk to leave." She lowered her gaze to her sewing.

Sam slumped in his chair. Lady Strathmore was right, of course. He had noticed a greater level of frustration at the fort. Discipline in the ranks was getting more difficult to maintain. Maybe a little dancing and merriment wouldn't be so bad. He might even make a speech commending his men for their good service.

She looked up at him once again. "And it would be well-received, I'm sure, if you said a few words of praise to your men, captain."

A chill crept up his spine. She had read his thoughts. Like a wife might do. "Yes, yes. Thank you. That is an excellent idea."

A twinge of regret chased after the chill. General Strathmore most definitely did not deserve this woman. And Sam was sending her right back into his clutches.

Sam's chest swelled with pride as he watched the fort's residents gather in the yard for their first ever social event. Lady Strathmore had been correct in her assessment of the positive effect it would have. He gave a brief speech, then, under the viscountess's direction, the women made introductions among the wounded soldiers and the garrison men, and all the men began to talk, to exchange stories, to explain duties. The logistics of war and each man's place became clear to all involved. And once the women felt some amount of success had been achieved, they gathered the musicians together and encouraged them to play. The first dances were spontaneous reels, somewhat disorganized, but enjoyable to watch.

From the fringes of the assembly, Sam exhaled a sigh. He would have to deal with a few transfer requests to join the fighting army and even deserters to the militias, but that was to be expected when eager young men came in contact with battle veterans. He glanced around the crowd. The women looked especially fine that night, with scrubbed faces and combed hair. One woman in particular caught his eye.

Pat sidled up alongside. "She's enchanting in her aristocratic finery, don't you think, captain?" he said in a hushed voice.

Lady Strathmore seemed to be thoroughly enjoying herself with her new friends and watching the couples swing and skip. She was dressed in the blue-gray silk gown she had been wearing the day they found her. It was tailored to fit her perfectly, accentuating the swell of her breasts, the neckline revealing just a touch of cleavage. The outer skirt was covered with embroidered vines in a green to match her eyes. Simply enthralling.

"Don't be cruel, Pat," Sam murmured. "You know I can only admire from afar."

"Ah. Of course. Unless you dance with her."

Sam flashed him a perturbed look. "I leave that task up to you, lieutenant."

"As you wish." Pat smiled and was off to join the fray.

Pat took his position as dancing master over the confusion of twirling bodies, organizing couples, calling out steps, and enticing wallflowers. It was a task Patrick enjoyed immensely, and Sam could not help laughing out loud at the sight.

"I think your men would enjoy seeing you lead the dance, Captain Taylor."

Sam hadn't noticed Lady Strathmore's presence at his side, then had to wrestle against a pang of bashfulness as he considered his response. He was acutely aware that they were at a social event, an event where men and women conversed and danced, flirted and courted. "I don't dance, Lady Strathmore," he said, turning back to face the assembly.

"No? Not at all?" She seemed genuinely disappointed. "Even your General Washington dances, captain. Or so I hear."

He flushed. "It's just that I haven't done so in many years." Her closeness was distracting, but he did his best to keep his focus on the merriment in the fort's yard. "And yourself? I noticed you have not yet joined in."

"It's a bit different from what I'm used to, I'm afraid. However, I think I have figured out that this is quite like what we do back home called 'Sir Roger de Coverley'." She stepped a little in front of him as if to get his attention. "I was hoping that you would join me as top couple."

Sam grinned. "Is this the latest English custom? Women ask men to dance?"

She blushed delightfully. "The women resolved to encourage all able-bodied men to participate in the evening's activities." Her voice was firm, but not without a tremor of shyness. "We decided that as I am a married woman and, as you always remind me, merely a passing guest, it would not be improper for me to ask you." She looked him in the eye. "It was either me or Mrs. Scott, captain. I'm not asking you to perform a gavotte, sir. I'm just requesting you join your men in a little fun."

Now it was Sam's turn to blush. She was right. Her marital status along with her social rank made her the proper partner demanded by etiquette. He offered his arm. "As you wish. I will do my duty, my lady. One dance."

And when she wrapped her arm around his, his thoughts turned perfectly improper.

Clara could barely suppress a squeal of glee at her triumph as the captain led her to the now organized sets of dancers. It had been over a year since she had danced, and never in such an uncivilized way. The boisterous familiarity of the Americans was so refreshingly unlike balls back home. She grasped ungloved hands, was turned about most indecorously, and yet had never had so much fun in her life. The captain danced two sets with her, his elegant turns in utter contrast with the almost savage swings performed by the fort's soldiers. They led the first dance and let Lieutenant Hamilton and his pretty blond partner lead the second. The lieutenant was a terrible flirt with the garrison's women folk, but the captain kept a polite distance. After he felt he had done his duty, he gracefully stepped back to the fringes of the party. Clara followed him a moment later.

He angled toward her. "I do thank you for coaxing me, madam."

"A bit of fun is great for morale." She smiled up at him. "I do think seeing you enjoy yourself humanizes you amongst your troops. It helps create loyalty."

He merely nodded as he rocked on his heels, his hands behind his back, grinning at the scene before them.

A social affair was a good time to bring up thoughts that weighed heavily on her mind. "Captain, the nurse Jenny says you have family back in England, in a village called Cirencester. Is this true?"

"Why, yes," he said in astonishment. "My grandmother and grandfather live there."

"Have you ever been?" Clara tried to hide her excitement. The captain having a connection with the place might afford her the opportunity to travel back home.

He chuckled. "No, my lady. I am American, born and bred. I have not been outside my homeland." He regarded her curiously. "How is it that you know of this place? I understand it is rather small."

"Yes, yes it is, quite. My family home is just outside the village, in the countryside."

"Strathmore?" He stood in thought for a moment. "I don't recall my grandmother ever mentioning the name, and as she is from a lesser aristocratic family, she's rather obsessed with the doings of the nobility."

Clara cleared her throat. "No, not Strathmore. My husband's family is from elsewhere in Gloucestershire. My family. Hastings."

His forehead crinkled in astonishment. "Hastings? *You* are Lady Clara Hastings?"

She smiled as expectation spiked her heart. "Well, I was, before I married. But most likely you have heard of my great aunt, my grandfather's sister. She never married so she shares my name." Clara turned a little away from the activity in the yard, hoping to draw the captain's attention with her. "If you have never been out of the colonies, how do you know of my great aunt?"

He offered his arm and motioned with the other that they should take a turn around the yard. She nodded and slipped her hand around his elbow, her fingers tingling at the point of contact, shooting a little thrill through her. She glanced to the side in hopes he would not see the flush on her cheeks.

"My grandfather was sent to America as a colonial administrator," he began as they strolled. "During his service my father was born, in fact he was born here in New York. At the end of my grandfather's tour of duty the family returned to England. My grandmother much prefers it there. But my father always held some romantic sentiment for the place where he was born. He emigrated here as a young man and married a girl from an old established family."

"Your mother is American, then?" The noises of merriment and music dimmed as their tête-à-tête grew increasingly intimate.

"Yes, and like me a native of New York. My grandparents spent a few summers here after I was born. My grandmother loved to tell me stories of England, and felt compelled to send me letters keeping me up to date with the goings on of the fashionable families near Cirencester." He leaned in. "Including yours, it appears." He chuckled. "I suppose she felt I would return, but she doesn't fully realize that, for me, there's nothing to return to. I belong here."

"Ah," Clara said softly. The sting of defeat for her plan to return home was overcome by a strong curiosity toward the captain's story. Their aimless sauntering had led them to the darkened passage under the second floor gallery, reminding Clara of the last time she had wandered away from the crowd at a dance. But being alone with Jeremy Strathmore in a dark garden was far different from being alone with Samuel Taylor. The captain lacked the seductive artifice of the general and, for that very reason, her burgeoning desire was genuinely felt and not a contrived reaction.

She released her hold on his arm and leaned back against a supporting post. "How is it that you can fight against the British when you still have familial connections?" she asked, absently biting her lip, gazing up at him for an answer.

He turned to her in the darkness, cutting off her view of the crowd, standing just a little too close for propriety's sake, the warmth of his body penetrating the tight space, wrapping around her, reeling her in. His breathing quickened imperceptibly, but noticeably, no longer the captain in control of a garrison, but a man struggling with control of his desires.

No, there was no artifice. It was all very real.

Sam could not take his eyes off her. She was posed provocatively, her chest thrust forward ever so slightly as her hands grasped the post behind her. The light of now-distant torches and lamps illuminated her face—still glowing from dancing—and her hair—coyly disheveled. His arm still tingled where she had touched it, the heat of her body radiated into his, coiling in his crotch.

"I suppose we're back to the civil war-colonial war debate, eh?"

She laughed softly.

"It's a fair question, Lady Strathmore. I was born and raised in Brooklyn, on the western edge of Long Island here in New York. My father is a lawyer for the colonial administration. He wanted the same path for me, so he sent me to Harvard College for my education, thinking it the only alternative to his own Oxford."

The unabashed giggling and tussling of soldiers and their women echoed around them. Sam placed a hand on the post above Lady Strathmore's head to carve their own private space. She did not flinch at the hint of intimacy, yet his own heart skipped a beat at the closeness.

"He set me up as a law clerk with a colleague in Boston," he continued. "So, I was in Boston when British soldiers massacred five innocent men, and there when we dumped crates of tea into the harbor. The taverns were filled with talk of separation and rebellion. Pamphlets and treatises arguing independence and freedom littered the streets. My friends and I were convinced of our cause so we joined the militia in Boston."

"With Lieutenant Hamilton?" She subtly adjusted her position, moving closer.

"No, no. I met Patrick later." He drew in a breath, gathering his thoughts, calming his pulse. "Eventually the militia became our Continental Army. I served under General Washington and we were sent to defend New York. When the British attacked Long Island last year the rebellion was suddenly real, not just some fantastical ideal. Unfortunately, my father has found it necessary to remain loyal to the king and, as a rebel, I was unable to return to my family. I'd have been arrested. During the fighting, we heard the Hessians had burned farms to the ground and slaughtered anyone in their way." He stared out into the shadows. "Our retreat in the middle of the night was so close to where my parents live, but I simply could not desert to see how they fared. I felt angry and frustrated. That's when I realized I needed to defend my home to the death, and I enlisted with the New York regiment."

Lady Strathmore's quiet gasp brought him back to the present. "That's where I met Pat," he said.

"And your family? Do you know anything?" Her voice held a tremor of despair.

"As my father is connected officially with the British government, they were spared. They only suffered property damage. Some of our patriot friends, however, were killed."

"Captain," she began, her voice quivering with emotion, "I know it means nothing, but I apologize for the vicious actions of my countrymen. And, although it is little comfort, please know that my husband was not involved in the matter. We arrived some time later."

Sam looked down at her. "I do know that, my lady."

She blinked up at him, the pale light reflected off the tears forming at the corners of her eyes. The sounds of lovers in the dark grew stronger, emboldening him. He lowered his head. She remained as she was, her décolletage rising and falling infinitesimally more rapidly. He could make her his if only for one moment, and, in the distracted darkness, no one would know. He brushed aside a tear as it coursed down her cheek, his thumb lingering on her face as his fingers cupped the back of her head. She relaxed against his palm in acquiescence, and licked her lips in invitation. He moved toward her until his lips hovered above hers, her breath hot and moist as it mingled with his. She closed her eyes.

And then Sam remembered that the young, beautiful, seemingly willing woman within his grasp was the wife of the enemy. She could never be his. To think otherwise would be foolhardy. He pulled away, dropping his hand. "Please, forgive me, my lady," he murmured.

"No, don't apologize," she said softly. Her fingers threaded through his, firing every nerve in his body. She squeezed gently before letting him go.

Sam stepped back, his head still spinning from their almost-union. "I think I should have Corporal Bowman escort you upstairs, my lady." His voice was husky, unwittingly revealing his unfulfilled desires.

"As you wish," she replied.

"Unless you feel you would like to continue dancing." Sam was finding it very difficult to tear himself away.

He followed her gaze to the yard. Very little dancing was still going on. Couples had paired off into the dark recesses of the fort. It would be unseemly for Lady Strathmore to spend any more private time with him.

"No, thank you. I think I will retire for the evening, captain." She righted herself from leaning against the pole. "Please take me to Corporal Bowman, sir."

It was going to be very hard to get any sleep that night.

CHAPTER SIXTEEN

Several nights later, Clara was sure the captain regretted ever wanting to kiss her, for at that moment, red-faced and pacing before the fire in his quarters, he looked like he wanted to throttle her.

"The 'divine right of kings,' madam?" he bellowed, waving his arms in disbelief. "You have got to be joking!"

She looked up from her darning. She was repairing a hole in his stockings, a far too intimate chore which she initially balked at, but relented when the womenfolk all agreed her handwork was by far the best. "I assure you captain, I am not. Why else would our King George be monarch?"

"Yes," snickered Lieutenant Hamilton. "Rumor has it that he is certainly not qualified for the task."

Behind the captain's back, Clara winked at the lieutenant who returned a smile. Earlier that evening, they had conspired to tease the easily aroused Captain Taylor.

"And what gives your leaders their right, captain?" she goaded.

"They are elected by the people, madam."

"Except for Ben Franklin," the lieutenant quipped. "I do believe God himself gave Mr. Franklin some sort of divine right."

Clara tried to hide a laugh. "And what, pray tell, gives the American people the right to elect their leaders, sir?"

Outside someone clomped noisily up the wooden stairs, yelled to Corporal Bowman, then ran back down to the yard.

The corporal banged on the door. "Captain!"

Captain Taylor went to the door and threw it open.

Bowman stood at the threshold, his face sober and pale. "Captain, they found him, sir. They found Bridgers. He's dead, sir."

"No," Clara gasped. *It can't be Paul.*

Captain Taylor bolted out and down the stairs. The lieutenant grabbed Clara's arm. "You're coming with me," he said.

"Yes, of course." She stood up, dazed. The lieutenant had to practically drag her down the stairs.

The fort's residents milled about in the yard, some with torches, some gathered near a wooden cart that looked as if it had seen battle action. The captain questioned a bedraggled soldier, cuts and bruises still fresh from a recent skirmish.

"What happened?" Captain Taylor was gentle but firm.

Clara stopped cold in her tracks. The soldier was none other than Ethan Pitt, Paul's boy-of-all-work.

She looked frantically for Paul. Surely he would appear and all would be well. Maybe he was outside, or in the hospital, or…

"You're not going anywhere, my lady," Lieutenant Hamilton murmured in her ear. "Corporal Holmes!"

The corporal approached instantly and saluted.

"Hold on to Lady Strathmore. She appears to want to escape again."

"Yes, lieutenant."

The corporal's grip was cruel. Clara acquiesced. Surely Paul would be there at any moment and explain everything.

"After the brothel was burned—"

"The brothel was burned?" Sam was incredulous.

Pat approached and stood at his side. "What about the women? Ethan, what happened to the women?" he asked, barely masking his fears.

"They had been sent away well before then." Ethan looked at the two officers. "Mr. Bridgers never told you any of this?" he asked under his breath.

"No." Sam tried to remain calm. "I'm sure he had his reasons. Go on."

"Well, we joined up with the band that Redmond Moncrief had formed, you know, to dig at Strathmore's incursions. He had sent a handful of soldiers—"

"Up this far?" Sam snapped. "Why would he do that?"

"Sam," Ethan said in a very low voice. "I thought you knew. You have her here. don't you?"

"'Her'?"

"Lady Strathmore, Sam."

Sam cast a glance behind him. Corporal Holmes looked like he was holding on to her for dear life. "Yes, Ethan, she's here. Please go on."

"Mr. Bridgers kidnapped her so he could get the money the general owed him." Ethan spoke in hushed tones. "And because of what he did to Constance."

"Constance?" Pat yelped. "What's wrong with Constance?"

"She's fine now, Pat," Ethan assured him. "The general beat her pretty bad and she had to recover at one of the houses up the Hudson. That's where the other girls were sent, too." He looked from one officer to the other. "The truth is that the situation became somewhat personal for Mr. Bridgers." He glanced around again. "He sort of fell in love with Lady Strathmore," he said quietly. "And she returned his affection, if you understand my meaning."

Sam's chest tightened, but he remained stoic as he nodded.

Ethan continued in his clandestine manner. "And Redmond had it out for the general, too, what with his raping his girl. They acted together. I helped. They just didn't account on the general taking things into his own hands. They figured he would act like a proper English commander. We've been fighting his men for weeks now."

Confusion and despair roiled Sam's gut. He closed his eyes and drew in a deep breath, which only served to drag up an uncomfortable emotion. "Where is Bridgers's body now?"

"There." Ethan pointed to a plain wooden cart.

"Oh, God!" Lady Strathmore ripped herself away from the corporal. She ran to the cart, leaning in to examine the face, touching the body gingerly, murmuring her disbelief.

Her wail cracked the solemn silence of the small crowd gathered in the yard. One of the women went to her, embracing her in their mutual grief. More of the women began to cry.

Sam's gut twisted at the scene. *Jealousy.* He hated being jealous. He turned to Ethan. "What's the state of your militia?"

"We're only about five men now, but with the native tactics, we're able to seem like more."

Sam motioned to Pat. "Lieutenant, round up your riflemen."

"Yes, captain," he said, and took off to do as ordered.

"Pat's the best marksman we have, Ethan," Sam explained. "With his aim and the addition of a few of our men, you'll be free of the British just after dawn." Pat was trained in the use of the fast-loading Kentucky rifle and could probably take on the redcoats himself, but it was best to be cautious.

"Thank you, Sam."

"Now go get cleaned up and attend to your wounded." Sam patted Ethan on the back as the boy hurried away. He looked over at the cart containing Bridgers's body. Questions buzzed in his head as he approached the mourning women. "Lady Strathmore?" he began.

She wrenched around and reached for him, her hands sinking into the shoulders of his jacket, desperately clinging for solace.

Sam stroked her back warily, fearing for his own emotions. She pressed into him more closely, her sobbing body shaking against his. He had no choice but to hold her a little more firmly. Between sobs she repeated Paul's name like a litany.

Bridgers and Lady Strathmore? Paul Bridgers? It was incomprehensible. Lady Clara Strathmore was refined and educated. Paul might have been a handsome, friendly chap, but he was ... well, a whoremaster to put it bluntly. It was the most unlikely pairing Sam could think of. But, then again, Paul was masterful when it came to women, and Lady Strathmore, with her beauty and beguiling innocence, was quite a prize. For a brief moment, Sam imagined Bridgers and the viscountess together. Then, finding it possibly the most inappropriate thought to have while consoling the grieving girl over her lover's lifeless body, he shook away the reverie.

Ethan approached the pair. "My lady, please accept my sympathies."

"Thank you, Ethan," she said, wiping her tear-stained cheeks. She grabbed his arm in entreaty. "Ethan, the day of the fire, when Paul left me in the woods, what was the shot I heard?"

Ethan pursed his lips. "The British soldiers dragged me from the house and chained me to the hitching post. Mr. Bridgers had to shoot the chain in order for me to move." Tears rolled down his cheeks. "There was fire all around and he had to shoot though two chains because of the iron ball at the end of one of them. The shots caught the attention of the soldiers and we had to hide." He searched her face with apologetic eyes. "Please believe me that we looked for you, but it was too late."

"I understand, Ethan," she said gently.

"I have something for you, my lady, a letter from Mr. Bridgers. He said I should give it to you in case he didn't make it back to the fort." Ethan handed her a tightly folded piece of paper.

"Thank you," she said, with fresh tears. She looked at the letter and, with a tremulous hand, put it in her pocket.

"And one for you too, Sam." Ethan held out a note.

Suddenly, sorrow overwhelmed Sam. He choked back the sobs that threatened to burst forth. He was the captain, after all. He motioned for one of his soldiers to come forward. "Have him buried as quickly as possible," he said, trying to steady the shaking in his voice. "You might have to wait until dawn." He put an arm around Lady Strathmore's shoulders. "Come. Upstairs."

Only once inside his quarters did Sam allow himself to cry. He would never have known Paul if it hadn't been for the war—their backgrounds, their social circles, everything about them was too dissimilar. Yet Paul had become not just a trusted ally, but like family, sometimes a nagging father, more often an advice-giving older brother. Most of all, Paul had been a confidant and a good friend.

It seemed it was the same for Lady Strathmore.

She lay on his bed and sobbed into the pillow. Sam stared at her wretched form as he sank into his desk chair, then opened his note from Paul and stared at the words by the light of a flickering candle. It was written on the back of a page from one of Paul's ledger books. Those he kept in the kitchen building, to ward off suspicion from his various enterprises. The brick and stone structure must have burned last.

In his letter, Paul briefly explained the kidnapping and that he had given instructions for "Clara" to go to Sam. He had only recently heard she had arrived at the fort safely.

> *I know you'll see her person as a military opportunity, but Sam, you must reconsider. She is perfect for you. I'm sure you know that by now. After I realized she and I could never be together, I knew she could be—she would be— happy with you.*

Jealousy faded into envy. Paul had been a lucky man.

Sam returned his attention to the woman lying on his bed. She had exhausted herself and was sleeping, albeit somewhat fitfully. Paul was right. She was perfect for him. Except for the fact that she was already married to a loathsome monster. A monster Sam had just sent a dispatch to requesting negotiations for her return. His fingers pressed and massaged his temples. *What the hell have I done?*

He went to the bed and folded her in his quilt. He then took off his shoes, hung up his jacket, grabbed the woolen blanket and pillow from her cot, and laid down on the other side of the bed next to her, staring at the ceiling and wondering what he was going to do next.

CHAPTER SEVENTEEN

Clara did not know how long she had been sleeping, but it was the most comfortable night she had spent in a long time. She stretched against the feather mattress. The familiar feather mattress...

She sat bolt upright and saw the captain sitting at his desk, disheveled from slumber, holding what looked like a page from a ledger book. Then she remembered. It hadn't been a dream. Her beloved Paul, her Mr. Bridgers, was dead.

"Did I sleep here all night?" she asked, not really sure what else to say.

"Yes," was his glum answer.

To her left she saw her own pillow and woolen blanket in a crumpled heap on the mattress. Startled by the implication, she looked at the captain.

"Lady Strathmore," he said gently, "why did you not tell me of your connection to Paul Bridgers?"

His tone was not angry. No, instead he seemed sad. Very sad. Sorrow for the loss of Paul, or for the revelation of her relationship with him? Clara flushed at the thought. Why would Captain Taylor care about her and Paul?

"For very much the same reasons you never believed I was Lady Strathmore even when I insisted. There was really no reason for either of us to trust the other. This is war and anything and everything can happen."

He stood and paced behind his desk. "He told you to come here, to find me. You should have explained all that to me."

"And you would have believed my story?" She swallowed a sob. "Captain, I am the wife of an enemy officer, and you did not believe *that* until a patriot soldier you did not even know confirmed my identity. And why would you ever believe that I, a viscountess, would have a relationship with a brothel owner?"

"Touché, my lady," he snapped. "You win. You are correct. I did not trust you, and I apologize now." He raked his fingers through his hair, inhaling deeply, exhaling deliberately. He looked at her across the room, holding her gaze with his own. "I am so sorry, my lady," he said with genuine feeling. "Please, believe me."

"I accept your apology, captain." Tears welled in her eyes. "And I am sorry, too."

He stood motionless for a moment, studying her. "How long has your affair with Bridgers been going on?" he asked tentatively. "I mean, he only mentioned you once to me, that he met you in the village of Chesterton sometimes. And that your husband did not deserve you."

Clara smiled. It was somehow satisfying to know Paul had mentioned her in conversation with his friends. "I found Paul rather appealing since the first time I met him. He was always so pleasant to me and Annabella, my maid. We saw him in the village one day, and Annabella told him I was with child."

The captain gaped at her, his eyes wide.

"When Annabella and I were sent away for my confinement, Paul and Redmond—and Ethan too," she reminded herself, "kidnapped us and took us to his property. We were kept apart, and Annabella was never told what it was all about. My husband owed Paul a considerable sum. That, and," she drew in a fortifying breath, "his abhorrent treatment of Constance just pushed Paul over the edge. He knew my husband did not care a fig for me, but he did care about his unborn child. So Paul's plan only came together when he discovered my condition."

She tossed aside the quilt and sat on the edge of the bed.

"While I was with Paul, I lost the child. He took such good care of me. And then we—" She gulped air before letting loose a deluge of emotion. Her hands flew to her face, to hide the pain that twisted there. "Oh, Sam!" She slumped against the mattress.

Immediately he went to her, sat beside her, held her against him. "Shh, Clara." He rocked her in his arms as he pressed his lips against her hair.

His warmth, his nearness calmed her. It was easy to slip her arms around his waist. She sniffled against his chest. "It was only then we started our affair. My husband's troops set fire to the brothel while we slept in the kitchen outbuilding." She looked up at him. "I presume you know the property?" she teased.

He chuckled, the deep sonorous tone reverberating through her. "Yes, my lady, I know the property."

"We were able to escape, except that the soldiers had done that awful thing to Ethan, and Paul felt compelled to go to him. He left me in the woods, told me to count to three hundred, and, if he wasn't back by then, to come here, to find you." She nuzzled into him. "Sam, I was so frightened."

He smoothed a hand slowly down her back. "Clara," he began haltingly, "I saw the bodies of the two British officers you killed."

She pulled back, terror-stricken. "Sam, no. Don't use that against me, don't. You cannot tell General Strathmore. He'll have me hanged."

"Shh, shh," he soothed, stroking her hair. "I would never." He stared at her, his eyes asking questions left silent on his tongue.

"They did not succeed in their molestation of my person, captain." The memory broke the dam of fresh tears.

He clasped her close. "Thank God." His hands spread against her back, warm and comforting. "I had feared the worst. Don't worry. No one will ever know. This is war, anything could have happened."

Clara drew in a long, deep breath. "Sam, my husband does not know I lost the baby, and I don't know what he will do to me when he finds out."

"Hmm. We'll figure something out." He lifted her chin with one finger until their lips hovered apart by a hair's breadth. "We'll get some breakfast first, then we can discuss strategy with Pat." He remained tantalizingly close for a moment, before releasing her.

"Right," she smiled. "I must look a fright. Let me wash up."

The cold water felt good on Clara's eyes and cheeks, still burning with the salt of her tears. She didn't want to cry anymore. She would have to dredge up the necessary detachment with which every proper English lady was instilled since childhood. She loved Paul, but she would have to put the grief behind her. She was still alive, and Paul would have wanted her to live her life. As she washed her face, she even felt grateful for the crude brown soap and, when she dried herself, for the worn linen towel. Suddenly, she wanted her whole body to be immersed in water, to cleanse herself of all pain and sorrow, and she wondered when bath day would come around again.

"If you are quite finished with the basin, my lady, I would like my turn."

Sam's voice was like a soft, warm blanket after being out in the rain on a cold afternoon. *Sam*. It was so wonderful to think of him as Sam. She looked up at him, smiled, and stepped aside.

He dunked his face in the water, then came up for air, one wet hand searching for the cake of soap he usually kept on the corner of the table.

"Are you looking for this, captain?"

Sam grabbed a towel from the shelf below and wiped his eyes. She stood before him waving the piece of soap.

"Yes, my lady."

He reached for it and she pulled it away and behind her back.

"You, my lady, are toying with the wrong man." He flung the towel over his shoulder.

He moved to snatch it around her right, and, as she stepped farther to her left, he lunged around her left. She stood trapped between his arms, his embrace no longer comforting, but imbued with seduction. Clara looked up into his eyes, the blue-gray clouded by desire. Her heart raced, his breath mingled with hers in the tight space between them.

It was wrong to want him. Paul was not even in his grave and here she was in the arms of another man. A man, who, from the hunger in his eyes, wanted her as much as she wanted him. She gripped the soap behind her back.

She wanted him to take her so she wouldn't have to make the choice.

"By God, you are beautiful." Sam dipped his face and brushed her lips with his own. She didn't pull back, and he kissed her softly.

The soap slipped from her grasp and dropped to the floor with a dull thud.

His mouth ravaged hers, his tongue exploring, tangling, his hands spanning her back, supporting her as she arched into him, wanting, needing him to be closer, to feel his strength leading her along the path they both knew was right. She wrapped her arms around his neck and wove her fingers in his loose brown locks, pulling, holding, binding him to her. Carnal cravings ripped through her, arousing senses that had lain dormant the last few weeks. She lost herself in his embrace, wallowing in her body's sensual response, nipples hardening against her cambric shift, a tingling heat spreading through her belly.

Sam broke from her lips and trailed kisses to her cheeks and down her neck. "Clara, I want you." His breath was hot and damp on her skin. "I want you now."

"Yes, Sam, oh, yes, please."

His trembling fingers struggled with the bow of her short gown. The garment unfastened, he pushed it off her shoulders, off her arms, letting it fall to the floor. He bent over to kiss the pale flesh of her bosom peeking out over her stays, reaching behind her to loosen the garment.

A loud and insistent rap on the door stopped him cold. Clara froze in his arms, meeting his panic-filled gaze. Together they turned to the door.

The bolt had not been thrown.

* * * * *

The knocking continued in earnest. "Captain!"

It was Pat. Sam moved first, picking up Clara's top and handing it to her. "Get dressed. Quickly," he hissed.

Clara turned her back to the door. He gave her a mere few seconds before grabbing his towel and responding.

"Yes, lieutenant. Come in." He pretended to be drying his face as Pat opened the door. "Sounds urgent. What is it?"

Luckily, Pat did not seem to notice anything was amiss. Instead he glanced worriedly at Clara as he closed the door behind him. "We received a dispatch from General Strathmore, sir. He'll agree to our terms." He once again cast an apprehensive look in Clara's direction. "He wants to know if the baby is unharmed," he said.

"Oh, God." Clara fell to her knees.

Sam went to her, helped her up, then sat her down on the bed, taking his place beside her. "Pat," he said steadily, "Lady Strathmore lost her child several weeks ago." He took her hand in his.

Clara shook with emotion, her face twisted with all the sorrow and anxiety that wrenched in Sam's gut. The air lay thick with her impending sobs, but they did not come. She pulled her hand from his and wiped her eyes. "I should go," she said quietly, standing. "You have something important to discuss."

"As you wish," was all Sam could think of to say. He watched her leave his room, still poised sullenly on the edge of his bed.

Pat sat down beside him. "She told you everything, didn't she?"

"Yes."

"You're going to tell me, right?"

"Yes."

"What do we do now?"

Sam took a deep breath, regret shuddering his lungs. "I've done a horrible thing, Pat, and we're going to think this through."

Clara stopped briefly at the top of the stairs. She did not want to go to the women's workroom just yet. She was far too flustered to be able to sit with her friends, to endure their questions of how she knew Paul. She needed time to calm down. Near the foot of the stairs was an alcove used by the women for storage of brooms, mops, rakes, and the like. Usually only the bottom half of its Dutch door was kept closed, making it perfect to hide behind if one squatted down, something, as a lady, she should really eschew. But she desperately needed a moment of privacy. She went inside and sat in the darkest corner, resting her back against the cool limestone wall.

Something sharp poked up into her petticoat. The letter. Ethan had given her Paul's letter and she had not yet read it. With shaking hands, she pulled out the folded piece of paper, a page from one of Paul's ledger books. Her lungs weighed heavy with impending sobs, her face hurt from the strain of sorrow as she slowly unfolded the page.

Her wedding ring fell from the folds.

"*My love,*" Paul began, "*if you are reading this letter, you will know of my fate, although I fear I am most likely dead.*"

She screwed her eyes as her heart clenched in despair. She drew in a bolstering breath and read on.

He loved her, he wrote, and knew that she loved him. He was grateful for their short time together, but realized their love was not meant to be.

We are far too different, Clara, and while a man and a woman may enrich each other's life with such differences, eventually one can only sustain a relationship based on commonalties...

As far as the circumstance regarding your return to your husband, if it must come to pass, then believe me when I say that you can trust only one man in General Strathmore's camp, Lieutenant Sebastian Hawkins. He is truly honest and incorruptible from what I can tell of my dealings with him, and he may be willing to safeguard you from the general's wrath, which may mean transporting you home...

I know you are ensconced at Fort Revolution. I hope that those in charge of the fort will see your importance not in terms of revolutionary tactics. There is one man in particular, Captain Samuel Taylor, whom I consider my rightful heir in the throne of your heart. I am fairly certain Sam will fall madly in love with you the moment he sets eyes upon you, but I am quite biased in my views. However, if the two of you do not find yourselves attached in that regard, he will be a good ally for your endeavor to return home. He knows the law, he knows politics, he has connections, and you have the currency.

With all the love in my heart,
Paul

Clara rocked on her feet, silently freeing the tears of mourning and relief that had dammed in her eyes. Paul had just given her permission to offer her heart, her soul, her body to Captain Samuel Taylor.

CHAPTER EIGHTEEN

"We've decided to wait a few days before responding to the general's dispatch," Sam explained later that night when Clara had joined him and the lieutenant in his room. "That suggests to the British we consider ourselves to have the upper hand, and it gives time for our scouts to make sure General Strathmore does not have rogue soldiers near the fort."

The lieutenant turned to her, his demeanor particularly dour, not his usual jocular self. "Do you trust him, my lady?"

"Absolutely not." She couldn't go back to her husband, she just couldn't. She looked down at her sewing while gathering her courage. "Captain," she finally said. "If money were not a barrier, would there be any way for me to return home to England?"

Something akin to distress flitted across Sam's face. "You mean could you purchase your way back home?"

"Yes."

He sank back in his chair, stretched his legs out, and folded his hands on top of his head. "We don't have any English officers in our debt. The best we could do would be to get you on an American or possibly a French ship. They would only take you to France or Spain. I don't know how you would get to England from there. You'd be on your own." His gaze bore into her with an uncomfortable intensity. "But, of course, there is the issue of the money."

Clara flushed and glanced over at the lieutenant, then decided that modesty was irrelevant at that moment. "Before I left for my confinement, I sewed some of my jewelry into my stays in the event I was widowed and would have to purchase passage home. They are still there."

Sam's forehead furrowed in thought. "Are these jewels family heirlooms or items your husband presented to you as gifts?"

"Both."

He leaned forward and placed his chin in a palm, drumming his fingers on his cheek. "Legally, there is no difference. As a married woman you can own virtually nothing. The difference is that the Strathmore jewels could be traced while he is here on American soil. We would have to find someone who would be willing to purchase the other items."

It sounded long, drawn out, and not a certainty. "What about a divorce?" she asked.

Sam looked at her incredulously. "You want to try to obtain a divorce between two English subjects under the laws of New York colony in the middle of a revolution?"

Clara saw his point. "Quite right. I suppose that would be out of the question."

The lieutenant yawned and stretched out of the wingback. "I'm going to bed. Let's sleep on this and discuss it in the morning." He bowed and slunk out of the room.

The lieutenant's absence was palpable. She and Sam were alone for the first time since they had kissed that morning.

"He doesn't know," he said.

She turned to him and saw the longing in his eyes, her own heart a tangle of desire and fear. "Sam," she said as she rose, placing her handwork on her chair, "I should just go to bed."

"No," he said quietly.

Clara hesitated, hoping he would read her quiescence as an invitation, wanting him to simply take her. He went to her, took her hands in his, and bent down to kiss her. She closed her eyes, giving herself up to the sensual delectation of his mouth, his kiss so soft, so gentle, not at all like the furious passion that morning.

He left to bolt the door, then returned to her side. He pulled her into his arms, and rested his forehead against hers. "Come to bed with me."

"Yes, Sam."

Her words shot straight to his groin.

Yet she did not move, perhaps uncertain, the depths of her naiveté in matters carnal apparent. It was simply charming.

"I want to see you, all of you," he said. The nervousness of that morning was replaced by urgent need. He swiftly undid her bodice and slid it off, untied her two petticoats and pushed them to the floor, grabbed her cap and tossed it on the pile of clothes. His cock strained against his breeches at the sight of the shadow of her quim beneath her thin shift.

He lifted her at the waist amidst her surprised giggles, sat her on the edge of the bed and knelt before her. One by one he slipped off her shoes and unbuckled her garters, then drew his fingers down the backs of her pale thighs to pull down her stockings, eliciting the most appealing sigh when he tickled behind her knees.

He stood back to admire her, then disrobed with quick impatience, while she smiled and stared. When he finally stood before her, naked and erect, she gasped and blushed.

He climbed onto the bed and knelt behind her, smoothing his hands along her stomach, rounding over her breasts. "So, these are the infamous stays with the jewels," he said as he worked the laces. He lifted the undergarment from her body, surprised by the weight. "You have been wearing this heavy thing all this time?"

"Yes," she said meekly, positioning herself so he could remove her shift.

And then she was utterly nude, too. Oh, what a lovely sight to behold!

He wrapped his arms around her perfect form, pressing his chest against her back, his face at her neck, breathing her in. He cupped her breasts, each a perfect handful, and teased the delicate pink peaks with his thumbs. She arched against him, leaning her head onto his shoulder. His mouth took hers in a tantalizing upside-down exploration.

"Lie back," he said, urging her to the pillow. "I want to taste you."

He lay beside her, caressing the soft white flesh of her arms and belly as he took a nipple in his mouth. Clara's moan was music to his ears. She wove her fingers through his hair, holding his head steady as he sucked. His fingers drew circles around her other nipple, already puckered and hard.

"You're cold," he said.

"It's cold in here, Sam."

He grabbed the quilt and threw it over them, then slid down her body warming her with his breath until he finally nestled his face between her legs. In the tented darkness he could only hear her wetness as he parted her slowly. He drew his tongue through her slick slit to play with her aroused nub before delving into her depths, her hungry orifice nipping at his invasion. He moved his attentions back to her clit, teasing and sucking, as she rocked her hips and moaned in encouragement.

But it wasn't really a moan. Sam quieted his frenzy to concentrate on the sound she was making, a sound like low guttural breathing. A sound like a purring kitten.

He scrambled up to her face and opened a corner of their tent to let in the dim candlelight. "That sound. It's not you sleeping, it's you in ecstasy."

Clara looked perplexed. "What sound, Sam?"

He mimicked her deep breathing as best he could.

She giggled.

"You've been watching me all this time, haven't you?" He wasn't sure if he should be mortified or aroused.

"Yes," she said grinning uncontrollably. "And taking my own pleasure during your performance, captain." She pecked his lips.

Sam groaned and rolled onto his back. "Damn. Pat was right. He said you were probably doing precisely that."

"Of course, the virtuous captain could not fathom such a possibility," she giggled as she climbed on top of him, straddling his hips, rubbing her wetness against his cock. He closed his eyes to indulge in her touch as she massaged his chest, threading her fingers through the hair. "Just as I had no idea two men could make love."

Sam jumped up, throwing her off him. "Christ, Clara! You saw us?"

She righted herself onto her knees. "Sam," she said softly, "it was beautiful."

This simply could not be. "You can never tell anyone. Ever."

She gaped, nonplussed. "I would never reveal your secret. Please, Sam, believe me. I have my own, remember."

Indeed, she had murdered two British officers. Both crimes were capital offenses. Sam studied her, then drew her lips to his to seal their mutual pact of silence.

She smiled as they parted. "You know what I've been fantasizing about since I've been watching you?" she said seductively.

"Having me and Pat inside you at once?" he tantalized.

"What?" Clara's eyes widened in disbelief. "Is that even possible?"

He kissed her open astonished mouth. "Yes, my love."

Her astonishment turned into delight. "Well, I suppose I was thinking of a far more simple pleasure." She slid down his body slowly, nibbling the skin of his chest, his stomach, his hips, until she reached the head of his cock. She pretended to bite that too, tormenting him only briefly with her teeth before taking him into her mouth. Inch by inch, she gently wet the skin of his shaft with her tongue, then surrounded his glans with her hot, moist lips. She took her time, lingering lusciously on the sensitive skin under his prepuce.

Whatever she wanted to call what it was she was doing, it most certainly was not a simple pleasure. Sam had to cover his face with the pillow to silence his blasphemies and groans of satisfaction. She was taking him—all of him—all the way inside her mouth to the back of her throat. After what seemed like an impossibly long time, she pulled him out and massaged the tip with her magical mouth and tongue, while her hands continued to pump his shaft. And then she proceeded to draw his length inside her once again. It was nothing like what Pat did to him, perhaps a little more like one of Paul's girls, and yet it was something so exquisitely more. Sam reached for her, grabbing fistfuls of her hair and holding on to that one shred of reality as his senses were transported to an unworldly plane of pure ecstasy.

He had not frigged himself that day, and he couldn't hold back. He tried to suspend the sensation but she was too good, too damn good. With a muffled cry he thrust up into her, cradling the back of her head, exploding inside her, groaning as her throat clenched him and she swallowed every drop of his ejaculate.

Sam was spent, but desire still coiled inside. He wanted to thank her, to please her, his reason protesting his body's exhaustion. He would have to wait until morning to make love to Clara in the way he had wanted to ever since he saw her undressing by candlelight. He pulled her back up alongside him and kissed her, tasting himself on her tongue, sensing her excitement at what he might to do to her.

He wanted to take her on the same ride of absolute joy, wanted to watch her face as she reached her peak. He rolled her onto her back, glided his hand along her skin, past her belly, tangling in her curls before stroking her sex, swollen and unsatisfied. She caught her breath as he drew her wetness to the sensitive nub, pressing and massaging the slippery flesh. He touched his lips to her mouth, murmured an admonition to silence her building moans. He held his thumb on her clit and slid two fingers inside her yearning passage, the smooth, slick walls throbbing and pulsing at the intrusion. She clenched tightly around him, surprisingly strong. Now it was his turn to gasp in stunned amazement, to know how wonderful it would be when it was his cock inside her, pulling and pushing as her hot wet flesh gripped and released.

She thrust her hips against his hand, her face twisted in agonizing rapture, looking as if she were going to scream. He wished he could let her, wanted so much to hear how he was giving her pleasure. He cursed the war, the fort, their forced secrecy, and propriety. He covered her mouth with his own as she took him with her to the heights, then came down again sated and breathless.

Sam rolled over, his body heavy with sleep, his cock having ideas of its own. He reached for Clara, finding instead her pillow, still warm. He clutched that to his chest and reached some more. His dreams distracted him with too many noises, banging, running, metal clanking against metal. All he wanted was Clara's lovely body knowing how it would fit his own perfectly. He stretched further across the mattress.

"Captain?"

It was a man's voice. It must be part of the blasted dream. He ignored it. *Clara.* He needed Clara.

"Sam?" the voice repeated.

He shot straight up in bed. "Patrick! What the devil is going on?"

"It's morning, sir," Pat dutifully answered, his lips twisted in an unsuccessful attempt to not grin as he took in Sam's naked, excited state. "You've overslept."

"Where's Clara?" Sam looked frantically around the room.

"You mean Lady Strathmore?" Pat glanced at the alcove curtain obscuring equally frantic activity behind it. "It appears that she is dressing in the annex." He raised an eyebrow at the faint impression of a body which had not very long ago lain on the bed next to Sam. "Should she be somewhere else?" he inquired. "Sir?"

Sam looked down at himself then up at his friend, catching Pat's meaning. "No, no, of course not," he grumbled and ran his hands through his hair. "What needs to be done today, lieutenant?" He got off the bed to search for his drawers amid the garments strewn on the floor.

Pat took a seat at the desk. "We have to go over the list of needed supplies, you know, the ones we were expecting from Bridgers—"

Clara appeared in the doorway of her little room, wide-eyed and frozen. She caught Sam's eye then continued downward, perusing his semi-aroused, naked physique, all the while biting her lower lip.

"Good morning, Lady Strathmore," said Pat with far too much amusement.

Clara whipped her head toward him. "Good morning, lieutenant," she nodded, startled and blushing. "I must be off," she mumbled and fled the room.

As soon as the latch clicked shut, Pat slapped the desktop. "Hell and damnation, you slept with her!" he grinned.

Sam pulled his head through his shirt. "Well I suppose we finally did get some sleep."

"Sam, as your best friend and first officer, I am obliged to remind you that she is a married woman—"

"I am very much aware of that."

"Married to our sworn enemy—"

"He does not deserve her."

"—and as our captive—"

"'Guest'."

"—her well-being is in our trust—"

"For God's sake, man, she fellates like a whore!"

Pat's jaw dropped.

Sam combed his fingers through his hair. "Damned Bridgers must have taught her," he muttered as he put on his waistcoat. "She's good, Pat. Christ, she's good. I need her."

"Sam, this is simply not a situation we—you—can sustain. We've got politics to consider." Pat moved around the desk to pace in front of him. "And are the two of you going to be able to keep this covered up?" he growled quietly. "Martha already gossips about how you're in love with Lady Strathmore."

"'Clara'."

"That's what I'm talking about! One slip like that and Strathmore's spies—and don't tell me there aren't any—will have it out for you. Let me get you a whore. I can find Prudence—"

"No," Sam snapped. He stood in rigid frustration next to his friend knowing full well that Pat was right.

Pat touched his hair, smoothing the unkempt locks. "Sam, I could ... you could use me."

Sam stilled his hand and brought it to his lips for a brief kiss. "No Pat. We have to be even more careful. Truth is I would rather be caught in bed with the general's wife than with you. I might get shot by the general, but I would most definitely hang if I were found with you. We both would."

Sam gazed at him, their fingers entwined, the desire for more of Pat's touch so palpable, so dangerous. Instinctively, he moved closer until their lips brushed lightly, inexorably sparking a need to explore his mouth. For a brief moment, Sam reveled in the forbidden kiss, a kiss that, despite the damnable law, felt as right as a woman's.

"You need a shave," Pat complained when they parted.

Sam rubbed his cheeks. "Yes, I do." He filled the basin with more water. "Look, give me some time. With Bridgers dead there's no need for her to escape, so there's no reason to keep her in my room, but no else one will know that. No one will be expecting her to return to the women's dormitory. Yet."

Pat sat back down at the desk and crossed his arms. He gave Sam a dubious look.

"Please, Pat. Indulge me."

CHAPTER NINETEEN

Sebastian pulled Annabella's supple nude body closer to him, wanting so much to protect her from anything and everything. She was the most sweet-natured girl he had ever met. She did not deserve the sorrow the fates had laid at her feet with the death of her beloved Redmond and her treatment in the Strathmore household. He, Sebastian Hawkins, would be sure no man would ever harm her again.

And yet, he couldn't help thinking that his exhortations at protection had been far too persuasive. She had spread her legs far too willingly, and he had been far too willing to be between them. She was beautiful, she was beguiling, but she was barely seventeen. At ten years her elder, he should have known better than to seduce such an innocent. Still, something inside him insisted it was she who seduced him. Now he could not foresee a future other than being in Annabella's arms in these extraordinary and exciting American colonies.

But there were his obligations to General Strathmore. The more Sebastian spent time with the man, the more he hated him. He was intimately involved with the general's negotiations for the return of his wife, a wife for whom the general admittedly cared not a whit except that she was carrying his heir. Strathmore contemplated all manner of deceptive promises, only to be shot down by Sebastian's own reminders that the Americans' intelligence was quite possibly as good as theirs, and that the rebels would see right through any tricks and conspiracies.

Sebastian caressed Annabella's spine languidly, tracing the peaks and valleys of each vertebrae, until he reached the soft pillowy flesh of her buttocks. His erection roused slowly while he explored his lover, until it sprang insistently from the thatch of curls at his groin and nudged against her thighs. He wanted her, he found he always wanted her, he could not stop wanting her. She, however, was still sleeping. He refused to wake her for his own pleasure. He was happy to wait. Now that she was his, he was happy to wait forever.

Forever. His mind wandered to their future together. The possibilities seemed endless in these wild colonies, or "states," rather. These Americans had decided they were living in free and independent states, places where any man could do as he pleased as long as he did not infringe upon the rights of his fellow man. Position at birth did not matter, only will and determination. So different from England, where Sebastian, as the third son of a fairly wealthy member of the gentry, had so few options before him, and really only one, as his father purchased his army commission without even consulting him. Of all the Hawkins sons, only he had the requisite management skills and farming blood in him. He knew his dissolute eldest brother would simply go through the income as it came in, then have to start selling off parcels in order to support his libertine lifestyle.

But here in these American states he, Sebastian, could purchase his own bit of land, could grow what he wanted to grow. Apples. He wanted to grow apples for cider, he knew that at least. He still wasn't sure what the soil could support.

Annabella sighed in her sleep and rolled onto her back. Sebastian shifted for her, his hand now gently caressing her belly. She said she was pregnant with Redmond's child, that although it wasn't showing and she hadn't been sick like her lady had been sick, she just knew. In this new life he would share with her, Sebastian was content to raise Redmond's son— a truly American son—and hoped they would then raise a healthy, happy brood of their own. One delightful consequence of this premonition of pregnancy was that she never insisted on precautions when they had intimate relations.

She stretched against him, yawning.

"Are you finally awake, my love?" he asked tenderly.

Annabella reached down to grab his erect prick. "I suppose you have been waiting patiently."

"Ah, not so patiently. I confess I am at bursting."

She giggled. He loved it when she giggled, laughed, enjoyed herself. He wanted to never see her cry again. She clawed playfully at his body indicating she wanted him on top this morning and he heartily obliged. The moment he entered her warm, inviting flesh he realized how close to bursting he really was. Her sleepy satisfied moans made him comprehend how much he wanted to find a life for the two of them ... a life of freedom ... with no limitations ... a life that was of their own making and not according to the dictates of a society no longer viable in this modern age.

Oh God, what if the British won? Then we would have nothing...

Annabella writhed beneath him as he plowed into her. *No, never.* They were not going to take this away from him. The British could not win. He would not let them win. The Americans must be victorious in their revolution.

With his resolution, Sebastian fervently spent his seed deep into the womb of his beautiful, fertile, free-born American compatriot.

Chatter in the sewing circle was that Constance Gibbs was coming to Fort Revolution during the final days of her sister Susie's pregnancy. She had been convalescing at Mrs. Blanchard's Home for Women—a useful euphemism for a whorehouse—farther up the Hudson, but was finally recovered enough to travel. Clara was tormented by thoughts of how best to handle the situation. What does one possibly say to the woman who was beaten almost to death by one's husband? The woman for whom one had committed murder?

Constance, however, turned out to be a very sweet girl, polite and endearing. Clara was immediately set at ease in her presence. Somehow it also helped that Constance, with her creamy skin, full smile, and bounteous body, resembled Annabella, albeit blond and a little taller. The two were able to talk privately for a few minutes in a corner of the workroom after all the other women had said their hellos.

"Miss Gibbs—"

"I know who you are, my lady. Please, call me Connie." Her blue eyes shone with sincerity.

It felt strange to be on such intimate terms so soon, but the Americans had very different ways. "Thank you," she nodded. "Connie, please understand that I know my husband to be emotionally cruel, yet I had no idea he could be so physically cruel. If I could have stopped what he did to you, I would have. With all my heart I would have."

"I understand, I do. My lady—"

"Please, 'Clara'."

Constance smiled warmly and took Clara's hands in hers. "Clara, how is the baby?"

Clara's stomach turned. Constance knew she had been pregnant. Of course, her husband need not bed his own wife if she were already pregnant. He must have informed his whore of this fact. "I lost the child." Clara looked at Constance pleadingly. "Please, my husband does not know this. He must not ever know."

"And I hope to never see your husband again, Clara."

"Yes, of course. I wish I could say the same." She had but a few moments with Constance before she needed to attend her sister Susie. Something else had been weighing on her mind. "Connie, did you ever sleep with Paul Bridgers?" she blurted.

Constance regarded Clara with a little bit of curiosity, and took a moment to gather her thoughts. "Yes, Clara. All the girls did. He insisted on knowing what each of us was like and, sometimes, corrected us." She closed the space between them. "However, he never loved any of us, and we, each of us, knew it. With us, it was business. But with you, I am certain, it was different. If he woke up next to you in the morning, then it must have been love."

"Thank you, Constance." It was what Clara had wanted to hear. What she needed to hear.

She returned to her place at the sewing circle, and Constance started for the hospital to join her sister. She stopped when she saw Lieutenant Hamilton at the door.

"Connie," he gasped, his face twisted in worry and relief.

He ran to her and she to him. They met in an energetic embrace, he swinging her around for a moment, before suddenly putting her down, a horrified expression on his face.

"Oh, God. I shouldn't be doing such things to you, not in your condition."

"Pat, love. I'm quite recovered now." She cupped his cheek with her palm. "You can touch me, love. I *want* you to hold me."

The lieutenant pulled her to him.

"I only ever want it to be *you* who holds me, Pat," she said, her voice shaking with emotion.

The lieutenant dipped his head and kissed her passionately. Constance responded in kind, clinging to him tightly.

Clara and the other women in the workroom simply sat and gawked at the reunion, then watched as the couple, oblivious to the world around them, walked out and up the stairs toward the lieutenant's bedroom.

Pat stared unbelieving at the scars on Constance's back. "My God, Connie, how did you live?"

"I kept thinking about you, about coming home to you, Patrick."

They were in his bed in his officer's dorm. Pat had bolted the door, letting his roommates know he was not to be disturbed for this long-awaited reunion. For the first time in months, they had made love. And for the first time, it was truly as woman and man, not whore and patron. She had cried when he offered his heart and professed his undying devotion. He would never, ever not be there for her.

Afterward, she was at first unwilling to let him examine the disfigurement of General Strathmore's attack, but finally turned her back to him giving him a full view of the scars left by the general's abuse. The whip had lashed around her torso, leaving marks not just on her back, but around her waist toward her abdomen, on the sides of her breasts. Patrick traced the silvered lines with the tips of his fingers, wishing so much they could simply be erased. Anguish and hatred boiled inside him, and yet, thrilled to be with his true love, he gave in to relief and joy instead.

He kissed her lusciously, then settled her under the covers in the crook of his arm.

"Connie," he said with a touch of trepidation. "Sam and I had just left. We could have saved you."

She sighed heavily. "Patrick, I've done it before. There was no reason for you to think something horrid would happen this time."

"Why didn't you scream? Bridgers would have stopped them." Pat snuggled against her a little more closely.

"I did scream. Then I was gagged and Strathmore refused to follow the rules when I stomped. He just kept beating me."

"Did he say or do anything to indicate why he was acting so violently?"

"Only once, at least I think. He mentioned his wife and her pregnancy." She looked up at him. "But why would a man be angry about having children?"

Pat snorted. "A reminder of his own mortality. He probably considers a son to be a usurper."

She inhaled deeply, then exhaled with a shudder. "At one point I fainted." She pressed against him, her eyes screwed shut, squeezing out tears that dampened her lashes. "You know I can withstand quite a bit, but this was more than that. This was too real. My mind usually can control the pain, but I couldn't this time. I was terrified. I truly felt trapped, like a scared rabbit being attacked by a pack of wild dogs. I had no chance."

Pat tried to smother the sorrow and anger welling within. He had to be strong. Had to protect her. But when her arm wrapped around his waist more firmly, the emotions burst forth. He tried to muffle the sobs, but could not stop his body's shaking.

Constance pulled back. "Pat!" She reached up to trace the trail of tears down his cheeks, then nuzzled her own tear-stained face against his chest. "Patrick Hamilton, why haven't you asked me to marry you yet?"

His heart swelled as anguish bled out. "Connie? Would you?"

"I don't want the other life anymore."

"You'd have to live here, in the fort."

"My sister lives in the fort with her cadet. I already have family here."

"And if I have to move, you have to follow me. I'll never leave you alone again."

"You have to promise to make this war end soon. I want a normal life with cooking, cleaning, and making babies."

Pat laughed at what she thought was a normal life. It had never been as such for either of them.

He cupped her face and brought it up to his. "Constance Gibbs, will you be my wife?"

"Yes, Patrick Hamilton, I will."

She was smiling the biggest smile he had ever seen on her lovely face. For a moment he just wanted to look at how happy she was. But she protested, wanting her first kiss as an engaged woman. As he kissed and wrapped his arms around her, a torrent of emotions rose inside of him. This sweet, kind, beautiful woman, his woman, had been subjected to the most vile abuse. It would never happen again.

General Strathmore would never harm anyone again.

CHAPTER TWENTY

When Corporal Bowman deposited Clara at the captain's door that night, the first thing she noticed was the absence of Lieutenant Hamilton.

"Pat's with Constance," Sam explained, pacing behind his desk.

"Yes, of course." Clara quickly shuffled to one of the straight-back chairs, setting her sewing basket and shirts to be mended on the floor.

"Take the wingback." Sam smiled weakly and indicated the stuffed chair.

"Thank you." She moved her sewing while Sam moved the lamp for her benefit. She picked up a shirt.

Sam sat. He gathered up some documents and tucked them away in a drawer.

It was just too painfully obvious that the lieutenant had been the impetus of conversation for their evening colloquia.

But what was she supposed to say to Sam? Ask him how his day had been after she had fled from his room, and his arms, that morning? That she had thought of nothing all day but his touch, the memory of their intimacy still smoldering in her core?

Perhaps a bit of gossip from the women's workroom. "Susie Gibbs will be having her baby any day now." Well, it was something to say, anyway.

"Yes, Jenny is excited to be overseeing a birth rather than the dead and wounded." Sam ran the knuckles of one hand over the other in rhythm to some unheard melody.

Their vacuous words simply prolonged the agony of unspoken desire. Clara had to say something.

But it was Sam who finally conceded. "How did you sleep on the featherbed last night, my lady?" he asked with a quirked brow. "Much better than the camping cot, don't you think?"

She hid a smile. "I will admit it was a far better experience than my attempts at comfort in that pathetic solitary bedstead, captain."

He got up from behind his desk and walked toward her, unbuttoning his jacket and waistcoat. "I would like you to share my bed tonight, Clara, if you so wish." He shed his outer garments.

Clara's breath hitched in her throat. It was far too early to actually go to sleep.

He offered his hand and she stood before him, biting her lip to suppress a smile of desire and happiness. For a moment they stood staring at each other, their fingers lightly touching. Clara flushed, then raised herself on tiptoes and brushed his lips delicately with her own.

Instantly, his mouth devoured hers, his hands tearing at every button, untying every string, until, finally, they held each other, panting, clad only in shirt and shift. Before she knew what was happening, he had lifted her in his arms and carried her to the bed, unceremoniously depositing her on the mattress amidst her giggles. He straddled her lustfully, his shirt tenting out from his body indicating precisely how he felt about her at that moment. She peeked under the hem playfully before he tore off the garment, revealing his spectacular masculine form in all its glory, his erection bobbing tantalizingly before her.

She propped herself onto her elbows and flicked her tongue along the eager purplish head, lapping up the drop of excitement that pooled at the tip. Sam pushed her onto the bed, holding her down at her shoulders.

"Not tonight, love. Tonight, I want you in the proper way, as a man should be with a woman." He tugged off her shift then pulled away and simply stared. "My God, you are so ... so ... *perfect.*" His gaze wandered over her admiringly.

She grabbed hold of his hips and lightly drew her thumbs over the ridges of muscle leading to his groin, licking her lips in anticipation. "So are you." She smiled up at him.

He urged her back down to the mattress, then cupped her breasts with both hands, pinching the peaks between his fingers, inciting desire below. He bent over and took a nipple in his mouth, his teasing tongue liquefying her core, swelling her sex. He trailed kisses down her belly, stopping at the hairline of her mons, moving lower at an excruciating pace, his hot breath hovering over her yearning clit, taunting her with the promise of pleasure.

"Please, Sam. Please."

She exhaled a juddering breath as he drew his tongue slowly through her wetness. But it wasn't enough. She needed more. She tilted her hips, encouraging him.

He chuckled. And then he sucked her clit mercilessly.

It was exactly what she needed.

She thrashed against him as he gripped her hips, digging his nails into her bottom, holding her steady as he took her to the heights, then clamping his hand over her mouth when her moans began to rise with her climax. She jerked against him in glorious culmination as he drank her release, continuing his ravishment even as she was beyond satiated.

And when he was finished, he settled his body on top of hers, nudging aside her legs to nestle between them, laying his cock in her spent wetness.

"Have you had enough, my lady?"

"No, captain. I fear you have not quite finished the act."

Sam chuckled and pecked her neck and shoulders. "Insatiable wench." He rocked his hips to slide his cock through her swollen sex, until the head found its aim. Yet he did not enter her fully, instead continued to tease her, poised over her on straightened arms, his unbound hair falling in loose waves to frame his face.

She reached up and touched his cheek, rough and masculine. She wanted him, his body in hers, but something so much more than that. "Sam," she said softly. "I want you to stay inside me." She met his eyes. "I want you to spend inside me."

His playfulness dissolved. "Clara, you know what you are asking? I cannot do that, love."

"Please, Sam."

"Sweet, there might be ... consequences."

She swallowed the lump of emotion in her throat. "My husband does not know I've lost my child. And now you're returning me to him, childless, barren." Tears stung her eyes. "When we married our agreement was that I could not go home until I bore him two sons. Two, Sam. Now I don't even have one in my womb."

His brow furrowed. "Is that why you want to make love to me?"

Shocked at his implication she grabbed his arms. "Oh, God, no. Sam, no. I didn't mean it in that way." She tried to calm the torrent of regret and mortification that welled within. "Sam, love, believe me, if I were to stay with you, I would insist you ... be cautious, but as you are sending me away, I must ask this one favor."

Sam rolled onto his back, his legs still tangled in hers. "Clara, I'm not sending you away," he said bleakly.

She drew in a long, steadying breath. "Then what is it you are doing?"

He stared up at the ceiling. "I don't know," he sighed. "I guess, if I had known about you and Bridgers I never would have sent the missive to the British. I would have waited for him. But, I cannot go back on my word now."

She lifted herself on an elbow. "Why not? Why not simply say you are ignoring your previous bargain? This is war, isn't it?"

Sam inhaled deeply, tremulously. "Because when I sent the letter to General Strathmore, I also sent one to my superior, Colonel Axford of the Continental Army, informing him of the situation." He touched her face, wiping her tears, his own trickling down his cheeks. "I have to honor the bargain. Bridgers did not provide us with some expected supplies, so unfortunately you are the only way to get them. The army is desperate."

A bargaining chip. Like what she had been for her father's ambitions.

Sam disentangled his legs and folded her in his arms. "I've been attracted to you since the day we met. In fact, I had hoped you were not Lady Strathmore. Had you been the maid I would have bedded you a long time ago. Pat, too, most likely." He chuckled grimly. "Now I regret I did not trust you, or, at least, claim to trust you. You would have told me about Bridgers and we would have waited." He kissed her hair and spread his hand on her belly. "You have every right to ask for my complicity in your scheme. But, you do realize that even if you were to become pregnant tonight, your baby would not come for another nine months. That's nine months in addition to the how many months you are supposed to be pregnant at the moment? Wouldn't your husband be suspicious that the child was so long in your womb?"

Clara sniffled and laughed bitterly. "Once I'm returned to him he'll simply send me away again. He'll have no interest in when the child is born, just whether he has a son or not." She flattened her palm against Sam's chest, threading her fingers through the soft hair. "I would love to have your child, Captain Taylor." Her teary eyes found his and she smiled.

He grinned and pushed her onto her back, easing his way between her legs once more. "And I, my lady, would love the opportunity to give you one."

He bit her neck and she arched her back in response, pressing her breasts against his sculpted chest. His fingernails grazed down her sides, her hips, tickling her. She jerked a shivering retreat from his touch. He held fast to her waist.

"Where do you think you are going, my lady?" His breath was hot on her neck. "Trying to escape again? Perhaps you need to be restrained."

The shivers shot straight to her sex. Somehow he knew it was what she wanted.

He massaged her clit and bent over to lick and nibble her too-sensitive nipples, her natural instinct to writhe kept well in check by the weight of his body. She submitted to the all-encompassing ecstasy, letting him take control, letting him take her to the brink. He smiled at her purring moans, a devious smile, a thrilling smile that took her to the absolute edge. She gulped air to bolster her climax…

And then he took his hand away.

"You want to spend, my lady, do you not?" he said, casually sucking her nipples.

"Yes," she breathed helplessly.

"'Yes'?" His tone was velvety smooth.

She was aching to come, even more so with his sensual teasing. "Yes, please. Sir."

He slammed into her. She shattered around him with a sharp cry muffled quickly by his dew-slicked hand. He was hot inside her, hard as iron, and she clenched so tightly he slipped out, only to plunge in more deeply, more resolutely with every thrust, holding her gaze as she stared up at him, open-mouthed, delirious.

"Touch yourself," he commanded.

A thrill coursed through her even before her fingers stretched to rub her aching clit. One touch shocked her into oblivion, and she flinched her hand away.

Sam grabbed her fingers and pressed them to her mons. "I did not tell you to stop," he rasped.

"No, sir." His forcefulness was exciting, the perfect accompaniment to her ministrations, taking her to a glorious climax.

She exhaled a sigh.

"Again," he commanded, his face somber, his eyes solidly black.

She was determined to take him with her this time. She massaged the slick folds just below her clitoris, keeping herself on edge, all the while teasing him with relentless squeezes.

"You're not coming," he admonished.

She squeezed him tighter. "Neither are you."

"We'll just see about that, you little minx." Sam swatted her hand away, replacing it with his thumb. As he pressed down, he plowed into her. Clara gave in to him, choking back her cry of release. She relaxed under him in suffused exhaustion as he came hot and deep inside her.

Sam collapsed, panting, then rolled to her side and hugged her close. As sleep crept over him, he murmured something that sounded like, "I love you." She wasn't sure as she was quickly lost in the depths of her own dreams, snug and safe in his arms.

Sam had been nervous before his meeting with Colonel Axford, and not even the memory of Clara under him the last few nights could dispel the anxiety. She was partly to blame, of course. With every slip of his cock inside her, he lost a little piece of his heart. Returning her was going to be sheer hell.

But when he met his superior officer at the gate and showed him to his war room, Sam felt immediately at ease. Jocular and fatherly, the colonel was strict but never harsh and, as they walked through the bustling yard, was complimentary of Sam's management of the fort.

"General Strathmore has agreed to our terms, sir," Sam said, offering his superior a seat at the meeting table in the center of the war room.

"Good work, Captain Taylor." The colonel did not sit. Instead, he unfolded a large map he had brought with him and spread it out over the table. "However, there is some activity just south of here, in this area, that is of concern to me." Colonel Axford leaned over the map. "Here," he said circling his finger over a spot that was just north of Paul Bridgers's property. "We understand that there was a fire on this property here, and some skirmishes between the British and local militia men."

"Yes, colonel, sir. The man Bridgers, who owned the property, was one of our local sutlers."

"Never heard of him, captain."

"Yes, well, he, uh, remained neutral," Sam said warily.

"Ha!" bellowed Axford. "You mean he worked both sides for his own profit. That's fine, son. You won't get any argument from me. Just as long as you didn't trade any secrets," he said, flashing a smile and winking. "Where is he now?"

"He's dead, sir. He was killed in one of the skirmishes you mentioned. Fighting for our side, sir."

"Too bad, too bad." The colonel perused the map again. "What I wanted to show you was—"

There was a tentative knock on the door.

"Yes?" Sam called out.

"First Lieutenant Hamilton, sir."

"Come in, lieutenant," Sam called. "Colonel Axford is here."

Pat entered, then beamed when he saw the red-faced jovial officer at the table.

"Patrick, my boy. Come here, and let me look at you." Colonel Axford held his arms wide.

"Colonel, sir." Pat grinned shyly as he approached the officer. The colonel embraced him in a big bear hug, slapping his back with good humor. "Have you seen Major General Hamilton recently, sir?"

"Yes, son," Axford said gently. "Your father is well." Pat's father and the colonel had served in the Seven Years' War together and were good friends.

Patrick seemed a little edgy. "Would you be able to deliver a letter to him?"

"A letter? Of course, my boy." The colonel regarded Patrick quizzically. "What's this about, son?"

Patrick looked down at the buckles of his shoes and shifted side to side. He drew in a deep breath. "I want his permission to marry." He looked up at the colonel. "Sir."

That was clearly not what the older man was expecting. "Marry?" he roared, his face turning a slightly deeper shade of crimson. "Who is she?"

Patrick blushed like an admonished school boy. "A girl at the fort, sir."

"I see." The colonel paced briefly before turning to face Pat. "You didn't get her with child, son, did you?"

Pat flushed briefly once more and flashed a glance at Sam. "No, sir," he said sheepishly.

Colonel Axford shook his head. "You boys are too quick to move ahead in life. It's this damn war." He placed a fatherly hand on Pat's shoulder. "How old are you, son?"

"Twenty-three, sir."

"You think you're in love with her, don't you?"

"Yes, sir," Pat said emphatically. "I've known her since the beginning of this year. We've grown close."

Sam watched the struggle of emotion on Pat's face. What Pat couldn't tell the colonel was that he wanted to make sure Constance was protected, something he was determined to not fail at again.

Colonel Axford turned to Sam. "You know the girl?"

"Yes, sir," Sam dutifully responded. "She's kind, pretty, and completely devoted to Lieutenant Hamilton."

The superior officer grinned broadly. "Ah, well, I was young once, too," he said, putting an arm around Pat's shoulders for a brief hug. "I'll take the letter to Josiah, son. He's down in New Jersey mustering his troops. We're more encouraged now with the victory at Saratoga and the Hessian retreat from Ticonderoga."

"Retreat?" Pat looked questioningly at Sam, who shrugged his shoulders.

"Ah, I see word travels rather inconsistently in this war," mused the colonel. "The Hessians destroyed Fort Ticonderoga two weeks ago and retreated into Canada. We've beat them back for now."

Sam exchanged a triumphant look with Pat.

"But, my boys, this thing with Strathmore worries me. We can't have the British encroaching from the south. Let me show you."

"Blast!" Pat muttered. "Sir, my apologies," he said to Sam. "We received a note from Strathmore's camp with a request to reconnoiter the exchange location. The note is from a Lieutenant Sebastian Hawkins." Pat looked at the colonel and Sam. "Have you heard of him?"

They shook their heads.

"He wants to meet alone," Pat added.

The colonel cleared his throat. "Well, Strathmore's got plenty of troops spread out all over the place," he said pointing to spots on the map. "So this fellow Hawkins probably feels he's pretty well protected." He looked at Sam. "You'll be sending my boy Patrick for the job? He's the best."

"Yes, sir," Sam responded with a grin.

"Well, Pat, you take some men with you. Have them follow you, out of sight. I don't trust Strathmore."

"Agreed, sir," said Pat. "I'll take my leave to work on the supply list. Captain Taylor and I can discuss specifics later." The lieutenant bowed to his superiors.

Sam stared at the door after Pat left. Everything was moving too damned fast. It would be a bloodless battle for Clara, but the wound in his heart hurt like a jab from a bayonet.

* * * * *

Pat headed over to the kitchen to review the supply list with Mrs. Scott. It gave him an excuse to poke his head into the women's workroom and say hello to Constance on the way. His brain buzzing with far too many worries and thoughts— marrying Constance, meeting this fellow Hawkins, checking supplies—he did not notice Lady Strathmore skulking behind him when he greeted Mrs. Scott.

"I am under strict orders to not let you work in the kitchen, my lady," Mrs. Scott warned when she saw her standing in the doorway.

"I was hoping to speak with Lieutenant Hamilton, if I may," she said timidly.

Pat had been avoiding Lady Strathmore since his reunion with Constance, but he could not continue to do so in front of others. "We'll continue in a moment," he said to Mrs. Scott. He steered the viscountess by the elbow out into the yard. "What is it, my lady?" he said, barely suppressing his irritation.

She looked at him perplexed. "Patrick, why are you so cross with me?"

Because your damned husband nearly killed my girl. "Is that what you needed to ask?"

"No," she stammered. "I wanted to know about the man with Sam."

Pat once again grabbed her arm and guided her along the covered walk toward the captain's war room. He glanced around furtively before pushing her into the broom closet along the passage and closing both halves of the double door behind him.

"Hey—" Her palms slapped against the limestone wall as she fell forward.

Pat covered her mouth with his hand, forcing her to stumble backwards against him in the dark. "Lady Strathmore, I would appreciate it if you would refer to the captain and myself by our military titles when we are in public."

She nodded and he released his hold on her mouth. "Yes, lieutenant," she murmured obediently.

He encircled her waist with one arm and her shoulders with the other and pulled her close, restraining her. "Strathmore's got his troops all over the bloody place," he growled. "What say you, my lady? Is all this for you?"

She tensed. "No, no, it couldn't be. He's planning something," she whispered hoarsely.

"Planning what? Planning to attack us? Was your kidnapping merely a ruse to get you into Fort Revolution? I think you're working for your husband."

She twisted around in his arms. "No!" she hissed in his face.

In a flash, Pat had her up against the back wall of the small closet, his hips weighing into hers, his hand crushing hers against the cold stone above her head. "Then, pray enlighten me, my lady. What is it you think your husband is planning?"

Her panting breaths were hot on his lips. "Where are his troops? Is there a river or stream, something to bathe or swim in nearby?"

Arousal sparked in his groin. "I believe so." Her body grew warm under his. It took every ounce of control to not rock against her.

"And a house, a bawdy house. Is there one nearby?"

"Only Bridgers's and it was burned down." He breathed her in. She smelled like Sam, his soap, his sweat. His cock throbbed.

"All the buildings, lieutenant? Some of the buildings are of brick and stone and built to purposely withstand fire. I know Paul used those for his clients, as well."

Pat swallowed hard, unable to erase the image of Constance being brutally flogged in the blacksmith's shop. "Go on."

She squirmed, then emitted a quiet groan of despair when he merely pushed into her harder. "Before a battle General Strathmore gives his men time for relaxation. He believes it helps them fight better. They spend a few days resting and training. He may have also procured prostitutes, or even pressed some village girls into such service."

"And how do you know this?"

"Dinner conversations when other officers joined us. The general would never speak to me directly about military strategy."

She once again shifted under him, unwittingly rubbing against his erection. He pressed into her harshly to assuage his needy cock, the heat and scent of her body goading him to explore.

He drew his hand along her waist to her hip. "What about a Lieutenant Sebastian Hawkins? Do you know him?"

"Yes. Not well." A breathy tremor infused her voice. "He's General Strathmore's aide-de-camp."

"Do you trust him?" Pat released Clara's arms and hips from under his weight to allow both his hands to follow the curves and contours of her body.

"Paul wrote me a note saying I could trust Hawkins." She sighed imperceptibly.

He brushed his lips against her neck as he untied her top. "Do you still have the note?"

"Yes." She stretched, giving him more access. "It's the only thing of Paul's I have left."

She did not resist his touch. Instead, she moved as if inviting more intimacy.

He slid his hands under her top to cup her breasts through the stiff stays, and ran his thumbs over her bared cleavage, his mouth a hair's breadth from hers. "Sam's in love with you."

She leaned in a little. "And I with him." Her lips touched his.

Pat hovered for only a second before he took her in a violent kiss, his tongue plunging viciously, demanding the satisfaction his mind and body craved. He scrunched up her skirts and shift, tickled the bare skin of her thighs, and slid a finger through her silky slit. "You're wet," he breathed against her neck, thrusting two fingers inside her.

"Yes," she whispered, moving her hips in rhythm with his probing touch.

Pat unbuttoned the fall of his breeches with his free hand. "You're ready for me. You want me."

"Yes, please."

Clara found his stiff cock in the dark and guided it to her entrance as he bent his knees and lifted her leg for better access. She was wondrously warm and tight and climaxed instantly around him, stifling a sigh against his shoulder. She grabbed his buttocks and pulled him to her, encouraging his thrusts.

She was as skilled as a whore and as passionate as a randy maid. Her unceasing orgasms clenched him, gripping forcefully as if not wanting him to leave her body at all.

"Christ! You're so damned tight," he groaned. He couldn't hold on much longer. He tried to pull out as far as possible to make longer strokes, only succeeding with two complete thrusts. As he drew back for the third, his prick popped out, jetting his emission over the inside of her petticoat. For several minutes, they held each other, panting.

And then reality descended. "Christ, what have I done?" He relaxed his hold on her.

"Please, Patrick, don't send me back," she pleaded. "You saw what he did to Constance. I can't go back to such a monster. I want to stay here with you and Sam."

"Clara, that's impossible." Pat pulled away to button his fly. "You know that."

"I will do anything, please. If I can help with strategy, I will." She reached for his hand. "You want me to be with you, don't you?"

"You belong with Sam." He was thankful she could not see the shame on his face for betraying his best friend.

"Please say you will try to make that so."

He touched her face, her cheeks wet from crying. "Yes, Clara, I will see what I can do." He felt around in his jacket for a handkerchief. "Now please, wipe your tears. I'll take you to meet Colonel Axford. He'll be interested in your information. Only, don't mention anything about, uh, you know."

"Coition with you and the captain?" she offered.

He knew she was smiling. "I see why Sam loves you." He opened the door cautiously, looked both ways and, seeing no one about, gave her butt a gentle swat. "Let's go."

The captain's war room was two doors down along the same passageway as the broom closet. As if she would escape, Patrick held Clara's arm at the elbow while he walked her there and knocked on the door.

"Yes?" came Sam's voice from the other side.

"Lieutenant Hamilton, sir."

"Come."

The color drained from Sam's face the second she walked into the room. He gave Pat a chiding look, then shuffled about for a moment, clearly getting his thoughts in order.

"Lieutenant Hamilton, I see you have brought the fort's guest with you. Is there any particular reason?" he said acerbically.

"Yes, captain," Pat nodded. "Colonel Axford, this is Lady Clara Strathmore. I have just had a discussion with her about a few points of interest. I think she should tell you herself."

Clara stared at the portly, bewigged, middle-aged man, dressed in a fine blue uniform, whom Pat had just addressed. He looked rather jolly and pleasant, with kind eyes. He probably was not much older than her husband, or her father. Maybe the colonel would listen to her, take pity on her, and not send her back to the general.

"This beautiful young creature is the wife in question?" Colonel Axford grinned broadly. "I now see why General Strathmore has complied with our demands so readily." He approached her and bowed slightly. Instinctively, Clara held out her hand and he politely kissed it. "He is a very lucky man."

She wanted to scream that she hated him, did not want to go back to him. She wanted to throw herself on the ground at the mercy of this American colonel. She glanced up at Sam and saw the apprehension in his eyes.

"And why would you want to help us, my lady?" the colonel said with a touch of distrust.

"Honestly, sir, I do not love my husband and do not wish to go back to him. These young men have been very kind to me. If at all possible I would like to stay here in the fort."

"Nonsense," Colonel Axford said unequivocally. "You are worth at least twenty American prisoners and two cart loads of needed supplies, plus the horses and wagons the supplies come in on."

Clara had to suppress a gasp. She had no idea she had been valued at so high a price.

"You will go back to your husband and you will raise that child of yours." The colonel's tone was vaguely paternal. "Now, young lady, what is it that you wish to tell us?"

Her heart sank, yet she clung to a shred of hope. "Lieutenant Hamilton asked why General Strathmore has his troops nearby. I believe he is planning to attack. I suspect he is planning to engage in battle during the prisoner exchange rather than make an assault upon the fort."

"Ah, I see. Then why are they not amassed at one site?"

"My husband likes to give his men rest and relaxation before they fight, as well as review military exercises. From my discussion with Lieutenant Hamilton, it sounds like the British are located at points that contain swimming and bathing spots, a brothel, and fields for exercises?"

Colonel Axford studied the map. He looked up at Sam. "A brothel?"

"The house that burned down here," Sam explained, pointing to the map, "was a brothel, but there are other buildings on the property that could be used as such."

"Very good, very good," mused the colonel. "Is that all?" he asked Clara.

Patrick leaned in to her. "Hawkins," he said quietly.

"No, sir. I understand you need to know about Lieutenant Sebastian Hawkins? He is a very trustworthy man. Even Paul Bridgers always thought so."

"Bridgers?" Colonel Axford queried with curiosity.

Sam cleared his throat and she discreetly glanced in his direction. He gave her a warning look and mouthed the word "supply."

"Mr. Bridgers worked with my husband to acquire goods beyond what the military supplied. Or rather, Mr. Bridgers worked with Lieutenant Hawkins. I used to see Mr. Bridgers in town and would chat. He commented once to me that the

lieutenant was an honorable man, honest and incorruptible."
Clara flushed slightly at her little white lie. She looked at Sam,
who appeared somewhat pleased with the tale.

"And you can describe this Hawkins fellow to Lieutenant
Hamilton, enough so he will know he is dealing with the right
man?"

"Yes sir," she said. "In fact, Lieutenant Hawkins looks a bit
like Captain Taylor."

"Thank you, Lady Strathmore. I do appreciate your
willingness to disclose your knowledge openly," Colonel Axford
said with a genuine air. "Now, lieutenant, if you will please
escort the young lady out, the captain and myself have a few
items to discuss."

Pat placed his hand at the small of her back, warming the
chill that prickled her flesh. The shred of hope had flashed and
burned.

CHAPTER TWENTY-ONE

Patrick directed his small squad of soldiers to hang back among the trees while he rode forward. He stopped on a knoll to look down on the meadow where in a few days Lady Clara Strathmore was to be exchanged for goods and men. In the clearing, a British soldier stood next to a horse, his musket topped with a scrap of white fabric indicating the present truce. The redcoat kicked the ground with his foot, turned his gun upside down to scratch the frozen earth with the blade of his bayonet, then knelt and picked up a handful of the cold dirt, weighing and sifting it in his palm. The man looked up and around, his breath hanging momentarily in a cloud, nodding his head as if some thought were agreeable to him.

Pat rode down the hill and pulled his horse to a slow walk as he reached the British soldier.

"Hullo there," he called out.

The man looked up and took hold of his horse's reins. "Hello. First Lieutenant Patrick Hamilton, I presume?"

His voice held a twinge of excitement beneath the British accent. Pat decided to meet the man on his terms, so he dismounted and walked to the center of the clearing. "Yes," he said once he stood before the redcoat. "And you are Lieutenant Sebastian Hawkins?"

"Correct."

They shook hands.

"Right," Patrick began. "I've a list here of the agreed-upon supplies which we should go over." He reached into his jacket pocket and pulled out a folded piece of paper.

"Yes, of course." Hawkins pulled out a similar document as he inhaled the chilly air. "Beautiful country you're defending, lieutenant. Rich soil. A man could farm quite profitably here. Create a good life for himself."

Patrick did not feel the romance of tilling the land, but he did understand that it was a powerful draw. "You're a farmer then, lieutenant? When you're not at war, I mean."

"I come from a long line of farmers. The Hawkinses are a landowning family, yes." Hawkins looked up at him. "And you?"

"I'm from a military family myself."

"Ah. Then you understand this business of war better than I."

"Frankly, I think no one understands war. We just do it. Like you said, we're defending what we feel is rightfully ours."

"Yes," said Hawkins, almost with a sigh.

Pat began listing the desired supplies. "…candles, salt, gunpowder—"

"No," interrupted Hawkins. "We'll not supply gunpowder, lieutenant. However, in its stead we are willing to supply saltpeter and brimstone. You'll have to make your own gunpowder," he said with a wink. "You understand, I'm sure."

"Yes, of course," Patrick responded with a little amusement.

They began to review the specifics of the exchange. While they were in the thick of it, Hawkins abruptly changed the subject.

"Lieutenant Hamilton, you are aware that you are being watched, are you not?"

"As are you, Lieutenant Hawkins," Pat chuckled.

"Well done. I am going to tell you something but I respectfully request you not react in too broad a manner. Understood?"

Patrick was intrigued. "Yes."

"I have promised someone—someone who cares very much for her ladyship—that I would see this exchange through, that I would see Lady Strathmore safely ensconced at the house near Chesterton." Hawkins pretended to glance at the list and look up as if they were still in the midst of negotiations. "After that, I will become a deserter from the British army. I would like to seek asylum at your Fort Revolution, for myself, my common-law wife, and her unborn child."

Pat covered his surprise by perusing his own list. "Is your wife American? I mean, besides yourself, can we expect any trouble from the British?"

"She is American, in fact she is the former personal maid to Lady Strathmore. Her name is Annabella. The child she carries is not mine, but that of her betrothed who died recently at your fort. His name was Redmond Moncrief. He was working with Paul Bridgers."

Pat inhaled deeply to maintain his composure. "And Lady Strathmore, she should not know of any of this, right?"

"Correct." Hawkins sighed. "I feel for her ladyship. She is an innocent who should not be with Strathmore. He is a brute and a blackguard. If there were a way for her to be free of the man, I would wholeheartedly support it. Unfortunately, she is tied to him for life." The lieutenant casually folded his list in half. "For the duration of his life, at least."

Such an astute soldier would be a valuable asset to the patriot cause. "Lady Strathmore does indeed find herself in a grievous marriage." Patrick folded his list and met the lieutenant's gaze. "Hawkins, is there anything else we need to discuss? Any surprises?"

Hawkins grinned. "No. Except that Strathmore plans to slaughter the lot of you. But, of course, you already know that and are well-prepared."

"Yes, we do know that."

"And I intend to delay the attack, for my own personal safety," admitted Hawkins. "That would be the only surprise. You might want to bear that in mind when considering your own course of action."

Patrick saluted his colleague. "Thank you, lieutenant. I will see you on the battlefield."

Colonel Axford was absolutely brimming with war stories and eager to regale Sam and the other officers. But, despite the diverting, almost theatrical, way in which he told his tales, the man was simply no substitute for passing a quiet evening alone with Clara.

The colonel remained at the fort until Patrick had returned and reported on his meeting with Lieutenant Hawkins. Axford was pleased with, but not entirely surprised by, Hawkins's impending desertion. "Strathmore is a brutal lunatic, if you ask me," the colonel said and proceeded to relate relevant anecdotes from the Seven Years' War. Then, after discussions and plans were finished and a letter for Major General Josiah Hamilton was in his jacket pocket, Axford left to retrieve troops for backup during the exchange.

While the colonel was at the fort, Sam felt it politic to send Clara back to the women's dormitory and place Corporal Bowman on night watch duty there. Day by day, the truth of the situation had slowly crept up on him, but now bald realization fully engulfed him. Clara was no longer to be a part of his life. Worse, she was to face an uncertain future with a man she loathed. All of this because Captain Samuel Taylor, soldier and patriot, had done his duty far too efficiently. He missed her terribly, imagined her under him every night as he lay in his bed stroking himself. He wished she would disobey his orders and come to him, and to that hope he never bothered to bolt his door. But his bed remained cold and desolate. After Axford had departed, he could have had Clara back, but propriety and duty demanded that he leave her where she was. During the day he sought her out to exchange pleasantries, but there was never the opportunity to reestablish their previous intimacy as friends, confidants, and lovers.

He cursed the war, cursed himself, and cursed society's choking dictates.

Pat had warned him against getting involved with the wife of the enemy. It was stupid to have ignored him. Sam's only sustaining pleasure was that perhaps she was carrying his child. His lips curled in a smug smile when he envisioned his son raised in privilege, inheriting a title, and, ironically, living not too far from his true family.

Clara stared through the bleak darkness at the dormitory ceiling trying desperately to fall asleep. For probably the dozenth time that night, the door to the dorm opened and shut. Another soldier searching for his sweetheart. There were still a few men in the room, but everyone was rather subdued that night. Clara shifted onto her side on the small bed, putting the door at her back.

Behind her, quiet footsteps approached, then the curtain to her space opened, and someone stood at the side of her bed. A chill of anticipation crept up her spine. She turned to see. His height, his lean form, and his long unbound hair gave him away. *Sam!* The captain had risked his reputation to visit her, to make love to her. He said nothing as he quietly sloughed off his outer garments, then slid under the covers alongside her. His arm snaked around her waist and he pulled her close. His shirt bunched up at his mid-section to allow his erection to nudge between her legs.

She reached down and stroked the muscles of his thigh, her touch eliciting an unsteady breath, masculine and hot. He nuzzled his face in her hair as his hand drew her shift up. He tickled her motte, then insinuated his fingers delicately in her wetness.

"Oh, yes, you're ready for me," he said in a soft sultry whisper.

Clara stiffened. It wasn't Sam. She grabbed the hand that had just found her clitoris and tore it away.

"Connie? Love, what's the matter?" The seductive air was laden with concern.

Connie? Clara turned around and faced her midnight would-be lover. "Patrick?" she hissed.

"Clara?" His voice was devoid of its earlier charm.

"Pat, Constance isn't here. She's in the hospital with her sister. Susie's having her baby tonight."

"Oh." He moved his hand to rest on her bare hip.

His touch was startlingly titillating, making her mind a muddled mess. "Her bed is far more comfortable than mine," she babbled. "And I had no idea you would come here. I thought she went to visit you in your quarters."

"Yes, usually she does." The sultriness had returned.

He gently caressed her hip, then smoothed his hand along her thigh as far as he could reach. She made no protest and he continued his wanderings, moving along the back of her leg to her butt. He cupped a cheek and pulled her to him.

"And who were you hoping for?" he said, kissing her forehead.

"Sam."

"Of course," he said softly.

It felt good having Patrick so close, his warmth calming, his embrace exhilarating, his body so much like Sam's. She struggled to tamp down tears. A cool, gentle breeze lifted the ragged curtain at the window. The fabric twisted on itself, letting the pale moonlight cast its glow across the bed. Patrick was smiling at her.

And then the tears broke.

He kissed her cheek. "Shhh, love. Sam would like to be with you, too."

"He's bolted his door to me."

"If he's bolted it, it's for his own sanity. The situation is unbearable to him." Patrick met her eyes. "Clara, he's terribly in love with you."

"He is?"

"I've never seen him this way around a woman before. He brightens when you walk in a room. Listens when you talk. He talks about you constantly when you're not there." He closed the small span of space between their faces until their lips were almost touching. "He admires you. He desires you. He's probably frigging himself right now and thinking about you."

Clara reached up and caressed Patrick's cheek. "You're not jealous?" She trailed her fingers down his neck. "I know about the two of you," she said below a whisper.

He pecked her lips. "I know. He told me. And no, I'm not jealous. I'm glad." In one sudden move, he was on top of her and between her legs. He looked down at her, his brown hair spilling over to frame his face. "I rather like you myself." He sat up and tore off his shirt, revealing his beautifully sculpted body, the twin of Sam's. The moonlight heightened his erect nipples atop the angled planes of his pectorals. "And now your turn."

A flame of desire scorched her core as he skillfully pulled her shift up and over her head. She lay naked before him, vulnerable to his demands, hoping he would demand a great deal.

He licked his lips. "Christ! You are as he says. Beauty, innocence, and sensuality all at once."

Clara raised her hand to stroke his chest, but he stopped her. "No. Not yet," he said.

He leaned over and unwrapped the twisted curtain, sending their small space into darkness. He lay on top of her, pressing the length of his body against hers.

"God, I want you," he breathed into her ear.

The evidence of his desire nudged against her sex, rubbing the lips until they parted and he remained poised at her entrance.

"Let me make love to you, Clara." He kissed her lips, her cheeks. "Pretend I'm Sam. When I touch you, it's his touch." He trailed kisses down her neck, across her shoulders. "You're wet for him." He sucked a nipple into his mouth. "You'll open for him." His insistent erection proceeded forward. "You'll spend for him." He embedded himself fully inside her and she gasped in astonished pleasure.

"Clara, my love."

In the darkness, it was Sam's voice she heard, it was Sam's muscled back she gripped with her nails. Her lover moved to Sam's rhythm, respired the same breathy grunts, knew precisely how to thrill her with his touch, and how Sam demanded his own satisfaction. He took her to the heights of ecstasy, sustaining her there, body and soul, while he climbed toward his own release.

"Sam, come inside me," she moaned. "Like I told you before. I want you to come inside me."

He paused for only a brief moment before he pushed on, driving through her clenching encouragements, murmuring her name until the words were merely delirious groans of lust. Then and only then, lost in his imminent culmination, it was truly Patrick pleasuring her.

As if she were engaging in carnal delights with both men at once.

He slowed his pace, trying to hold on, and the urge to force him over the edge overtook her. She slumped down, tucked her hips under, and bent her leg up as far as it would go. She reached her hand around his downy cheek to search for the tight aperture nestled in the ridge of his buttocks. She slicked her fingers in her own moisture, and massaged his puckered hole until it softened for her invasion.

"I'm Sam, too," she whispered wickedly, plunging her middle finger into his tightness.

With a jerk and a stifled cry, Pat let loose his satisfied desire in hot jets inside her. For a moment he held himself aloft, his cock still spasming as she removed her finger.

He collapsed on top of her and burrowed his face in the crook of her neck. "You cruel wench." He kissed her burning flesh. "Blast it, I'll miss you," he murmured morosely. "I can barely comprehend what Sam must feel."

CHAPTER TWENTY-TWO

Sam stared at the piece of paper lying on the desk in front of him. He had read and re-read his letter from Paul seemingly for hours, not quite sure what he hoped to glean. Some new piece of wisdom, perhaps. Or something to appease his guilt. The candle had burned down to a stub. The wax-sodden wick flickered weakly, reminding him that the better spermaceti candles were dear and, for that reason, were among the items for which Clara was being traded the next day.

He sighed.

Patrick had already left his quarters. He had wanted to say his goodbyes to Constance before the meeting—and presumed battle—with Strathmore and his troops. Pat had been lousy company anyway. He was fretful and secretive about something—probably that he had slept with Clara. That wouldn't surprise him at all and, with Clara now in the women's dormitory, Sam half expected it. For some reason it didn't bother him, either. She was never really his, was she?

He rubbed his tired eyes. He had cried earlier, but now was too aggravated with himself to be sad. He bent his neck and ran his fingers through his loose hair trying to massage away the tension. It didn't work. He held his hands on either side of his head and pressed on his temples. A slight breeze and the sensation of a presence sparked him to look up.

Clara leaned against the door watching him, her face wet with tears.

"Clara." He tried to mask his enthusiasm by rising slowly. "How did you get in here? Aren't you under guard?"

"Corporal Bowman only has instructions to keep me from escaping, not to keep me from you."

"Oh." He couldn't stop staring at her. She was a vision from his fantasies.

Clara's eyes flashed at the page lying on the desk. She bit her lip. "Is that from Paul?"

Sam glanced down at the letter. "Yes. He says I should be with you. That you're perfect for me."

"He told me the same thing."

In the dim light their eyes met, their mutual longing palpable. Sam took the lead, skirting his desk to move toward her. He stopped at the foot of his bed and held out his hand. Clara lowered her eyes and came to him, grasping his fingers. He pulled her to him, enveloping her, holding her tightly as she slipped her arms around his waist.

He breathed her in. "I was a fool to not believe you."

She tilted her head back. "And what would you have done? Continue to hold me captive? He would have attacked the fort."

"Hmm. I was thinking about that. He might have sent an emissary after a month or so to see you in person." He kissed her nose. "To see how his child grew in your belly."

"Ah. And when he saw I was no longer pregnant he would have left me alone?" She shook her head. "Sam, I'm still his wife. I'm his sole vessel for a legitimate heir. He could not very well find another English lady here in the colonies."

Sam pulled her against him once more. "You're right. I'm doubly a fool." He pressed his face into her hair. "Clara, my love. I'll come for you. Wait for me. We'll win this war and I'll come for you."

"He'll make me go to Manhattan Island again, for my confinement. You can't possibly go there. It's a British stronghold."

She was right. Again. "What do you really know about Lieutenant Hawkins?"

"He's loyal to a fault. He's young and, I assume, ambitious."

He stroked down her spine languidly. "He told Patrick he would desert when this mess with Strathmore is finished. He wants to see you to safety, then he will seek asylum with us at Fort Revolution."

She pulled back, incredulity flickering in her eyes, quickly replaced by apprehension. "Might Hawkins have information that could be used against General Strathmore to relinquish his hold on me?"

"I don't know. I can only hope." It was odd how she referred to her husband by his military title. It spoke volumes about a marriage founded on nothing but political and social ambition and about an antiquated society that let such things happen.

He cupped the back of her head, threading his fingers through her hair still twisted under her cap. This woman in his arms, this utterly perfect woman, was going to be out of his life tomorrow and, despite what they were both hoping for and fantasizing about, she would most likely be out of his life forever. One side of him wanted to tear off every shred of clothing from their bodies and make passionate, rutting love to her. The other side of him wanted to simply hold her, like a precious jewel, guardedly yet jealously.

"Sam, take me to bed. Make love to me."

He wrapped his arms around her. "Clara, I want you, you know I want you. But I'm afraid. Afraid it will be our last embrace." He squeezed a little more tightly. "I don't want our final union to be melancholy."

"Sam, don't think of it as the end." She nuzzled into his chest. "Think of it as what we feel at this moment, this night in this place."

"I want it to be perfect."

"It will be you and me and that is always perfect." She gazed up at him. "Remember, we are perfect for each other."

He chuckled. Once more she was correct. He released her, took her hand, and led her to the bed. He sat on the edge of the mattress, curved his hands along her form as she stood between his thighs. She was beautiful. She was his. He was determined to make the night last as long as possible for the both of them.

He waved her away. "Undress for me. I want to watch you." He pulled off his shoes and sat cross-legged on the mattress.

Her mouth fell open as she blushed. His cock tingled at her artless modesty.

"Perhaps if you started with the tie of your bodice," he suggested with a salacious grin.

She proceeded to untie the boxy top, slipping the garment off her shoulders too quickly. With a shiver, she wrapped her arms around herself against the chill of the night air.

She would need a little incentive.

"Ah, my lady, you know how deliciously warm my bed is, how soft the coverlet. If your performance does not please me,

I will send you back downstairs to sleep in the frigid dorm with its scratchy woolen blankets."

She held his gaze, her features twisting into mischievousness, a scintillating smile curling her lips. His heart beat a little faster.

She turned her back to him, removed one arm from a sleeve, then the other, still keeping the top poised on her shoulders. She turned her head and glanced back to toss him a smile.

Damnation. He was utterly hard.

She reached her arms behind her and untied her overskirt. It dropped as far as her knees where it hovered while she untied her under-petticoat. She crushed both skirts down to the floor, thrusting out the white mounds of her shift-covered derriere in the process. Still bent over, she bunched up her shift, inching it up only enough to reveal the backs of her pale thighs and her garters fastened below her knees. She untied one garter, then the other, flinging each in their turn behind her, just missing him. As she straightened to standing, her shift and stockings dropped simultaneously, concealing and revealing her luscious ivory flesh.

His fingers trembling with excitement, he unwound his cravat.

She reached her hands behind her once again, this time to untie and loosen the laces of her stays, the top still balanced on her shoulders screening the activity. She bent her head down to carefully untie her cap and untwist her bun, then arched backwards. The bodice dropped to the floor as her tresses fell in waves down her back.

His cock ached. He unbuttoned the fall of his breeches, the fly of his drawers, and reached inside to allay his desperate need.

She curled forward to strip off each shoe and bunched stocking in its turn, then shimmied out of her stays.

She stood with her back to him, clad only in her sheer shift, the delicate fabric clinging to her curves accentuated in the shadows cast by the flickering candle. She looked over her shoulder. He grinned at her.

She loosened the tie at her neckline and, clutching the delicate garment to her body, she pulled one arm out, then the other. She held the underdress to her breast as she sauntered over to him. With a provocative twitch of her lips, she let go and the filmy fabric floated to the floor.

Sam wrapped his legs around her hips and his cravat around her shoulders and pulled her to him, taking her in a languid and lustful kiss. Her hand roved under the opened plackets of his breeches and drawers to tickle his hardness. He pulled away. "Get under the quilt before you catch cold, love."

As she scrambled under the covers he tossed the cravat on the pillows, then went to his desk, divesting himself of his jacket and waistcoat along the way. He retrieved the sputtering candle, then spied the oil lamp. He grabbed that too and placed both objects on the nightstand. She stared as he stripped fully, and giggled when he joined her in bed.

He held her, warming her in their downy cocoon, bracing against the November cold. The heat of their bodies mingled and spread through their chilled limbs. She burrowed and nuzzled in the crooks created by the tangle of arms and legs, as his hands wandered, stroked, caressed her silky, taut flesh, memorizing every sensuous curve.

He propped himself up on an elbow to better brush his fingers across her breasts, watching the rosy peaks crinkle and stiffen, their color deepening against the dove-white skin. Another memory to hold on to. He drew delicate circles around each nipple before continuing down to her belly button, then raked his fingers through the hair of her motte. Clara sighed and snuggled against his chest, offering up her lips to his kisses. His tongue in her mouth mirrored his finger tormenting the locus of pleasure below. She was more than ready for him, swollen, slick, and eager.

He moved on top of her, separating her thighs with his knees, and entered her, groaning at the rush of relief. She was warm and inviting. He worked slowly, remembering every inch of her, ensuring she remembered every inch of him. He crushed his mouth against hers as he quickened his pace, encouraging her climax, knowing her orgasms came swiftly and often. Another memory.

She clenched around him forcefully, a declaration of her initial wave of satisfaction, and the second followed soon after. He did not try to silence her, needing to hear the music of her ecstasy, no longer caring what others thought.

She sighed and he resumed his easy rhythm. "Clara, love, I would like us to share a new pleasure." Create a new memory.

Her eyes widened in anticipation.

"I would like to do to you what you saw me do to Pat," he said with soft seductiveness. "Except I want to do it in this position, the one we're in."

"Yes. Yes, please," she said excitedly.

"Put the pillows under your arse, love," he directed as he pulled out.

She propped herself up as he commanded.

He reached for the lamp on the nightstand. "It works best if we use oil, like this," he said scooping some into his palm. "It's hemp seed oil. Mrs. Scott makes it here, but I don't think she knows what I do with it," he chuckled. He smeared the entire length of his prick with the viscous liquid, massaging and caressing as she watched. He poured a little more into his palm, then circled her puckered hole, coating the outside before gently inserting an oil-slicked finger, then two, inside the tight channel. She jerked slightly.

Sam kissed her forehead. "Sweet, this may feel, well, perhaps a bit uncomfortable at first. It might even hurt."

She pressed two fingers against his lips. "But if you stroke the nub of my pleasure, it will be the most wondrous ecstasy a woman may enjoy."

His mouth fell open. "You've done this before."

She nodded.

"With Bridgers."

She nodded and bit her lower lip.

"Ah," Sam murmured. "Then, I'm sure you'll indulge me this as well." He snatched her hands and the cravat and swung the length of cloth around her wrists, wrapping them together above her head. He grabbed hold of her bent knees and pressed gently, lifting her, as he aimed his prick. He pushed in slowly, groaning at the taut but lubricated entrance, then stopped when she flinched with a little protest. The first ring of muscles.

He licked his thumb and massaged her clitoris. Her eyes widened, her mouth fell open as bliss infused her body, melting her resistance. He pushed through, the passage coaxing him, drawing him to the second ring of muscles. He pulled out slowly, building to a rhythmic thrusting, never letting go of her clit. She closed her eyes, lost in the dissolute rapture of pleasure mixed with pain. Her first orgasm swallowed him. She was so tight, her expression so alluringly wanton, he could barely hold on. He delved deeper, battering the second barrier until another orgasm loosened her muscles and he was all the way inside her. Conquered and bound, for this brief moment, she was utterly his.

She thrust her hips up, encouraging him, taking him once more to the brink. She moaned and writhed in her abandon, struggling against her bindings, squeezing him. Her cries grew louder, too loud perhaps. He placed his free hand on her mouth. Her tongue wrapped around his fingers, sucking them in. She held his eyes as she bucked up against his other hand demanding he take her over the edge. He was more than happy to. The strength of her contraction, her orgiastic roar hot on his fingers, were his undoing.

He pulled out and slammed into her cunt, driving deeply, forcefully, until he came inside her. She climaxed again, gripping his prick, milking every last drop of his seed.

He slumped over and she slung her bound arms around his back, hugging him. Their chests rose and fell in the same panting satisfied rhythm, their hearts pounded in unison.

"Clara," he murmured, kissing her cheeks. "I'll find you. Trust me. Wait for me. Whatever happens, just wait for me. We'll find a way to be together."

Tears dribbled down to wet his kisses. He held her face in his hands and looked her in the eyes.

"I love you. Be secure in that." He wiped her tears with his thumbs. "And I know you love me."

"Yes," she said with a quiet sob. "I do. I love you, Captain Samuel Taylor."

Sam kissed her mouth softly before sliding out from under her arms. He freed her wrists, then pulled her to his side. "Let's try to get some sleep, love. We have a long day ahead of us."

He wrapped his arms around her, hoping his closeness would calm her. He did not fall asleep until the shaking of her sobs had stilled.

Patrick was surprised to find Sam's door unbolted. No one had answered his usual early morning rapping and only a whim made him actually try the latch. He slipped into the bedroom cautiously, glancing around warily, before realizing Sam was still asleep.

Clara clung to him in their bed, one arm gripping his bare shoulder and, under the quilt, one leg twined around his. A pang of emotion pulsed through Pat. The two lovers belonged together, yet today was the day they were to be separated. Possibly forever.

Sam's eyes blinked open and met his. Pat only nodded.

"Clara, love," Sam said, stroking her hair lightly. "It's time."

She roused sleepily, then bolted upright when she saw Pat. "No, no," she whimpered. She fell back onto the bed and burrowed her head into Sam's chest.

He pushed her away gently and scrambled out from under her. "No long goodbyes, sweet. The men are waiting."

She took her time climbing out of the shelter of the down covers. She was clad in Sam's shirt, a defense against November's cold or a reminder of her lover. Probably both. The morning air was still bracing and enlivened her skin under the linen. Her erect nipples tented the fabric, provoking Pat's memory of her naked and under him. She met his gaze and wet her lower lip, then went to him and put her arms around his neck. Panicked, Pat glanced at Sam. The captain sat on the edge of the bed, naked, slumped over, running his fingers through his hair, brooding.

Pat wanted nothing more than to continue to hold Clara in his arms, but this was Sam's farewell. He reached up to untangle himself from her embrace.

"Enjoy her while you can, Pat," said Sam, rising from his perch.

Clara stood on her toes and kissed him. Pat flinched, startled. When she continued to press her lips to his, he gave in and kissed her back, deeply, passionately, his arms encircling her waist to pull her to him, his hands roving over her swells and curves.

"I'll miss you too, lieutenant," Clara said softly, lowering herself back onto her heels.

Sam came up behind her, huddling close. He raised the hem of the shirt to uncover her buttocks, then slid his morning arousal in the furrow of her cheeks. He pressed into her, pushing her into Pat. Pat pressed back, grasping Sam's waist, trapping her between them. The heat of their bodies rose to challenge the chilly air.

"It's too bad we have to leave now," Sam said, trailing kisses along her neck and shoulder. "I had hoped we could both enjoy you at once. Pat in front, and me behind." Sam bent his knees a little, then thrust up.

Clara gasped, her expression cast in pure ecstasy.

You bloody bugger. Pat's erection strained against his breeches, nudging Clara's belly.

Sam rocked his hips slowly, then bit the nape of her neck, jerking Clara forward. Pat held her steady and gawked while Sam continued his sensual assault, holding on to every shred of control his mind could muster.

Her eyes were closed, her breathing ragged, her body gently undulating. She was no doubt dripping wet. "I think I would like that very much," she purred.

Pat's cock ached with need.

She flicked her eyes open to meet his. "But with the little time we have, I think I would merely like to see the two of you kiss."

Pat gaped as Sam chuckled.

"What say you, lieutenant?" He leaned in. "Shall we accede to the lady's wish?"

"Damn you, Captain Taylor, damn you."

Pat laid his hands on either side of Sam's head and delved in with an open-mouth kiss, grinding his bedeviled cock against Clara. She squealed in delight, twisting between them, reaching

Pat's cheek with her lips, trailing pecks and licks along his jaw until she reached Sam's, he responding by tormenting Pat's mouth with a thrust of his tongue punctuated with a dig of his hips.

If it continued any longer they'd be late for the battle.

Pat jolted back, freeing himself from the seductive embrace, and Clara from Sam's intimate connection. He met Sam's eyes with an admonishing look. "You are cruel, captain, for tempting us." He kissed Clara's forehead, then went to the desk chair and sat down, adjusting the bulge in his crotch before he crossed his legs. From his position he would have a nice view of his lovers as they dressed. "But I must request the two of you make haste."

"Yes, of course," Clara assented, suddenly sullen.

"Madam," Sam said, glancing at his shirt that she still wore. He pulled it off her, revealing her lovely nude body.

Pat had never seen her in the light of day. With her round breasts just big enough to fit in his palms, her firm backside needing a spank or two, and her slim yet shapely form, she was truly a prize. She would be well worth winning back when the time was right.

And there was only one way to secure her return.

CHAPTER TWENTY-THREE

The chill of the mid-November morning still lingered when the Americans and British met in the appointed clearing, melted frost still sparkling on the tenacious weeds carpeting the ground. Sam reviewed his men from astride his horse. He was grateful Colonel Axford had been able to send him some backup soldiers, knowing full well the Continental Army could ill afford the temporary loss. Compared to the British regiment, his troops looked like the hastily assembled ragtag group they really were, but at least the two armies matched in numbers. In total, there were several hundred men on the field, all standing in uneasy silence.

Sam knew General Strathmore instantly, and not just by his officer's uniform. He had the bearing of an arrogant, cruel man who maltreated everyone he met, not just his own wife. As Strathmore's horse approached, Sam was taken aback by how strikingly handsome he was, although Clara had to have been seduced by something initially.

"You are Captain Taylor, I presume?" General Strathmore's voice dripped with disdain as his eyes surveyed Sam with disbelief. He raised an eyebrow in disgust.

Sam looked down briefly at his own faded uniform, only then realizing he was wearing the jacket Clara had mended for him. He hoped the pang of regret did not register on his face. "I am indeed Captain Taylor. You are General Strathmore, I presume?"

The general shook his head in incredulity. "The Americans are so desperate for rebels to join their cause that they promote mere boys to their ranks of officers," he drawled. "I wonder your men obey you at all."

"Enough so, general, that they were able to keep your wife's whereabouts a secret until I deemed it appropriate to contact the enemy. Despite your spies."

"My wife, though, is easy to subdue and keep hidden. She is rather compliant." He looked around at the American troops. "Where is the girl?"

"You mean Lady Strathmore? She's here. Where are our requested supplies and men?"

Strathmore waved to a soldier in the distance who drew back the canvas coverings of two carts to reveal several crates. Two more carts carrying a couple dozen ill-looking men drove up alongside. Sam nodded to Corporal Ross, who immediately rode to the wagons and inspected them, his prolonged, meticulous attention to the matter heightening the tension on the field. Assured of the British compliance with the terms of their agreement, the corporal waved to Sam.

"Corporal Mercer," Sam said to the soldier behind him. "Our guest, please."

Strathmore snorted.

Mercer ran back through the ranks of the Americans. From the mob of cadets Clara emerged, the American soldiers parting as she walked through their lines. She clutched her cloak around her not just against the cold. They had decided it was the best way to conceal her childless body. Patrick walked with her, his fingers gripping her elbow, steadying her. Once they reached the captain's horse, Pat left her in the capable hands of Corporal Bowman and returned to his place among the ranks.

"Lady Strathmore," Sam began, "can you identify this man as your husband?"

He had warned her about her role as only she knew for certain what her husband looked like. She had protested at first, but relented under Sam and Pat's gentle persuasion. Sam's gut wrenched watching her now, her hands trembling, her face twisted in distress, her lashes damp.

"Yes, that is my husband," she said hoarsely, barely looking at the man.

Strathmore raised a brow in amusement, then narrowed his eyes at Sam. "You're a fine looking fellow, my boy." He turned his attention to Clara. "Did you fuck my wife? That's really all she's good for."

It took every shred of self-control to not pull the villain off his horse and thrash him. Clara blanched in horror then quickly looked away.

"Hawkins!" Strathmore bellowed.

A man fitting Pat's description of the lieutenant appeared immediately. "Sir," he saluted. As Clara had said, Hawkins did look a bit like himself.

"Please escort the lady off the field. This is no place for a woman."

Lieutenant Hawkins offered Clara a weak smile along with his arm and led her through the ranks of British soldiers.

Behind the redcoats waited a conspicuously elegant coach emblazoned with a heraldic crest.

Clara did not look behind her as she walked away. With every step she took, Sam's heart broke a little more.

Sebastian had to practically drag Lady Strathmore through the ranks of British soldiers. Her steps were maddeningly unhurried, and slowed even more the closer they got to the coach. She inhaled sharply when they reached the door.

Sebastian opened the door and offered his hand. She hesitated.

"I don't blame you for not wanting to go back to him, my lady," he said below his breath, "but I really must ask you to step into the carriage."

She blushed. "Yes, of course." She took his hand and climbed inside.

He closed the door behind her. He had only a few minutes.

The carriage rocked as she settled herself, and as long as there was movement inside the driver would not dare depart. Sebastian went around and quickly entered through the other door.

Lady Strathmore looked at him, perplexed. She pulled the wool blanket up over her shoulders. "Lieutenant? Are you to accompany me?"

"Stay quiet and move along the seat," he growled, indicating the side farthest away from the door she entered.

She slid across the bench instantly. He moved to the door, then knelt down and pushed aside the curtain just enough to look out the window.

"You hate him, don't you Clara?" he asked.

He felt her tense behind him. He had never spoken in such a familiar manner to her before.

"Yes, I do," she whispered warily.

He glanced back at her, drew the curtain a little farther so she could see as well, then turned to peruse the scene outside intently. He wanted to be absolutely certain the patriots had secured their supplies and prisoners of war. The carts of men and crates were moving ploddingly off the field under the direction of a small contingent of men. A hundred or so Americans still stood at attention facing their British counterparts, the faces of the rebels exhibiting both fear and determination, the redcoats looking merely vicious and bored. As he watched and waited, Sebastian very carefully and as quietly as possible opened the carriage door just an inch. He unbuttoned his waistcoat and pulled out a flintlock pistol, then balanced it on his bent arm. He had counted the steps from General Strathmore's horse to the coach. *Fifty paces. Dueling distance.*

The carts were off the field. It was time.

General Strathmore lifted his arm above his head, the signal to engage in battle. Sebastian took aim and fired his pistol from the coach, the crack reverberating with an eerie echo.

Strathmore's head exploded. His body jerked and slid off his saddle. Lady Strathmore barely suppressed a scream.

Sebastian blinked. One bullet should not have caused the utter destruction of a man's skull. He scoured the field, catching a glimpse of the American officer he had met several days before. Lieutenant Patrick Hamilton had not been on horseback previously that he remembered, but now was dismounting a ride and surreptitiously passing an American rifle to a waiting ensign.

Sebastian grinned in morbid satisfaction.

On the field, chaos reigned. Soldiers fought while others fled. In the back of the lines, redcoats stood in confounded amazement. At the front, Captain Taylor shouted orders while British troops tried to drag him off his horse.

The time to join was now.

"Give my love to Annabella, my lady," Sebastian said hastily as he tore off his red coat and leapt from the carriage. Before closing the door he spied her terrified and confused expression. "Tell her I will come for her when I am able. It won't be too long. Keep her safe."

He closed the door and pounded on the side of the coach signaling to the driver to depart, then fled into the melee.

CHAPTER TWENTY-FOUR

New York, May 1778

From her perch on the second-story window seat, Clara looked out onto the greening and blooming yard below and pulled her wool shawl more closely around her. Spring had been much anticipated. It meant the house was not as cold as it had been during the harsh winter. Yet, with the shortages, they still had to conserve wood. She never started a fire in the upstairs bedroom anymore, and Annabella had set up a bed downstairs in the kitchen where it was warmer. Her baby had come early and Annabella feared for his health.

It had been a cold, long winter, made seemingly colder and longer as the Americans had not come for the two women. The British forces, having been strengthened under General Strathmore's command, were able to beat back the patriots until the snows came. After that, there was only the occasional skirmish. The patriots, it seemed, were holed up on their side of the battle lines.

The British had not been quite certain what to do with Clara once the general's carriage had returned to Chesterton camp without Lieutenant Hawkins. As the general's right-hand man in all matters administrative, the lieutenant would have known precisely what the general would have wanted for his widow. The remaining officers decided to simply establish her in the farmhouse she had once occupied until they could organize passage back home to England.

And for the first time since arriving on the shores of the wild colony, Clara did not want to leave.

But the redcoats quickly forgot her, as the general's second in command decided to decamp for Fort Knyphausen. First, however, they ransacked the general's stock of wines and spirits, as well as his pewter, silver, and plate. They even took General Strathmore's eager young maidservant. In the scramble of looting and troop movement, a distraught, pregnant Annabella joined her mistress at the farmhouse, having been evicted from Hawkins's former abode in the officers' barracks.

Left alone without army rations and with the storms of winter fast approaching, the women had to act quickly to ensure their survival. Although she did not lack for money—having her jewelry to pawn—Clara knew she would need local help in getting food and fuel during the winter. She asked the Cuyler family to return to their homestead. Despite the ill-treatment by General Strathmore, the farmer, his wife, and their four children displayed great generosity by giving Annabella and Clara one of the bedrooms. The general had been hated in Chesterton, but, Clara discovered, she and Annabella had been held in high regard.

When the slow thaws of spring arrived, Clara sought out gossip and rumors about what had actually happened on the field during the prisoner exchange. She learned General Strathmore had been killed by two men—not just Hawkins—that there had been an ensuing fight, that Sam had been wounded but was alive. Word was the Americans were making headway into the Chesterton area hoping to secure positions for a future assault on Manhattan.

Clara missed Sam terribly, his company, his conversation, his body, his touch. Her fantasies were filled with the when and how of their reunion. Despite the daily tasks of farm life, the boisterous play of the Cuyler children, and the good-hearted conviviality of the farmer and his wife, emptiness oppressed her. Tears accompanied her unsuccessful attempts to satisfy herself, the solitariness of masturbation only heightening her loneliness.

The emotions of pregnancy stirred Annabella's pining for her Sebastian, and night after night she cried herself to sleep. In the darkness of winter, Clara and Annabella, while sharing the warmth of the same bed, eventually discovered comfort in each other's arms. Annabella's lips were soft, her cheeks smooth, sensations so unlike being with Sam, but sensations she was willing to explore. Clara discovered new delights in pleasuring her former servant whose uninhibited nature was infectious. Another woman's pliant curves were certainly no substitute for Sam's hard muscular form. But until spring, when she could try to search for him, Annabella's soft flesh would have to do.

The jangle of horses in the front yard woke Clara from her late morning reverie. American rebels. Her heart pumped loudly as she frantically searched for Sam amongst them. The clamoring of soldiers in the entryway sent her running to the landing. She stopped upon seeing the tall, lean, handsome figure of Samuel Taylor dressed in his officer's uniform, resisting the urge to scream in delight, to fling herself into his arms. He relayed orders to his soldiers to secure the house and grounds, his masculine authority sending long-awaited sensual thrills to rile her core. He looked up and locked eyes with her, easily dismissing the soldier at his side as he approached her on the stairs.

"My lady, I must inform you that the Continental Army now controls this area and will need to make use of this farm." His tone was firm, but tempered with an underlying expectancy. "Are you alone in this house?"

"No, I—"

A rebel ran through the front door, panting and eager.

"Major Taylor, sir—"

Major Taylor? Clara tried to make sense of Sam's uniform. It was clean and new-looking. His cockade was no longer yellowish, but red. He must have been promoted. Her heart skipped a beat in pride.

"—we found the owners, the farmer Cuyler and his wife, in the field," the young soldier pointed behind the house. "They have welcomed us, as anticipated."

"Thank you, cadet. Clear the house of any soldiers and fetch my officers." Sam licked his lips as one corner curled into a sly smile. He took a step forward.

As the cadet shouted orders and men filed out into the yard, Sam simply stared at her. It took every ounce of self-control to remain where she was. She stared back, desire quickening her breath while joy dampened her lashes.

Sam could barely maintain his veneer of authority as his men filed out. When the last man had closed the door behind him, he let out a much needed exhale.

"Clara," he said, his voice shaking from restraint, "love, please accept my apology. The plan had been to follow your coach, and then everything went horribly wrong. We had to wait until after the snows to make our move. I've been—"

The wail of an infant came from down the hall.

His mouth fell open as he turned to face the sound. "Yours?" he asked softly. "Ours?" He swallowed the incredulous hope welling within.

Clara beamed as tears wet her cheeks. "No," she said. "My maid Annabella had her baby. The father was Redmond, Strathmore's groom who died at the fort after fighting alongside Paul."

"Oh. Of course." He had never met Annabella, but Sebastian had gushed over every detail of his sweetheart. The man was head-over-heels smitten.

"The child came early. Annabella stays in the kitchen by the fire for her son's sake."

The front door swung open and Sebastian and Pat charged in.

"You called for us, major?" said Pat.

Sam raised a brow and nodded in Clara's direction. She stood frozen, her hand over her mouth to barely stifle a squeal. Pat and Sebastian grinned broadly.

The infant cried out again.

"Captain Hawkins," Sam said, "Annabella and her son await you in the kitchen."

Sebastian quickly sobered. "Thank you, Sam." He rushed toward the sound of the crying child.

Sam leaned in to Pat. "As we planned, captain," he whispered.

Pat flashed a smile and saluted before he left, closing the front door behind him.

Finally they were alone. Sam hastened to Clara on the stairs, grabbing her around the waist with so much enthusiasm she squealed and gripped his shoulders for purchase. She kissed him, tenderly at first, until his mouth sought to slake the thirst of desire his body craved. She drew back, his desperate need reflected in her eyes, and clasped his hand to lead him up the stairs. Once inside her bedroom, he led the frenzy, tearing at her clothes, she following suit, touching, kissing, licking, as they both removed layer after layer. Finally nude, he pressed against her, the pounding of his heart matching hers, sighing in relief as she gripped and kneaded his muscles, memories and fantasies flashing through him with every caress of her flesh.

Clara nestled her head on his shoulder. "Sam, Sam. I've been so worried—"

"Shh. Hush, love." He pulled her cap off, then released her hair from its prison of pins. "I'm here now. We're together. There is nothing to worry about anymore." His cock grew impatient, jutting insistently against her belly.

"I heard you were wounded," she sniffled as she smoothed her palms across his shoulders.

"Only a scratch, my love." He stepped back and pointed to a scar on his left thigh. "See?" The bayonet blade had seared and shocked him with pain, but he had fought back, preventing the British from pulling him off his horse, avoiding more injuries, or even death. Yet the tussle had held him back and Clara's coach was long gone by the time he had broken free. "Thinking of you, knowing I would—must—find you again, helped me heal quickly." He kissed her forehead. "Clara," he said against her ear. "I want to make love to you." He pulled her closer to feel the heat of his prick. "Christ, I'm desperate for you!"

Her lips curled in a sultry smile as she led him to the edge of the bed. She climbed under the covers and reached her hand out for him to join her. He snuggled against her under the quilt, stroked the tender skin of her thighs and belly, cupped her breasts. She arched her back, her nipples peaked from the chilly air and arousal, willing him to suck. She gasped as he rolled the tender flesh against his tongue, then raked her fingers through his hair when he nipped gently. He turned his attention to her other breast while his fingers coursed over every once-familiar curve.

But something was different. Winter had been harsh.

He propped himself on an elbow. "Clara," he said brushing aside a stray curl from her face. "You've changed. You're—" he hesitated for a moment "—thinner, love." He kissed her cheek. "You gave your food to Annabella, for the baby, didn't you?" he asked gently.

Tears pooled in her eyes. He clutched her close, blinking back his own tears, angry with himself, with the well-stocked British who had camped so close by, with the entire damn war. He laid her against the mattress and kissed her, letting his lips and tongue touch every inch of her yearning, undulating body. He urged her thighs open and pressed his lips reverently against her clit before his tongue explored the swollen folds of her sex. She was deliciously wet, and he was more than ready.

He slid up her body until they were face to face, his legs between hers. He guided his prick to play in her wet folds and watched her expression dissolve to wanton desire. He poised himself at her entrance while he toyed with her clit.

"I have dreamed of this moment, Clara. It has been too long. I promise, we will never be separated like that again."

She traced a finger around his lips. "There have not been others with whom you could have bided your time, Major Taylor?" she said teasingly.

He smiled. "After you, I could never have another woman. However, I do confess I used the willing services of my next-in-command. But even he was far too preoccupied with his own lady love to offer condolences with any frequency."

Clara giggled until his ministrations between her legs caused her to catch her breath and exhale in a lustful moan.

"And you?" Sam asked suggestively. "A farmhand perhaps?"

She giggled again. "No, love. Never." She raised a brow. "Only Annabella."

"Truly?" His cock sparked with interest. Sebastian had described his love as voluptuous and lusty. "I regret having missed your frolicsome romp." He pushed an inch inside her. "As you haven't had a man in over six months," he murmured, nudging in a little more, "then you will enjoy what I have to offer." He filled her slowly, fully, watching her emerald eyes widen in abandon with every measure of penetration. When he was utterly sheathed in her warmth, he slowly pulled out, again marking her reaction at every inch.

And then he slammed inside her with winter's pent-up energy.

Clara let out a sharp cry and clutched him to her, digging her nails into his back, raising her hips in pleading. Her first climax engulfed him, taking him to the edge, her body continuing its release with a seemingly unending succession of orgasms. He was trapped between needing to explode and wanting to prolong her utter joy. He had to hold on for her sake.

He bent his back to take her sensitized nipples in his mouth, one after the other and back again. Clara wailed, clenching him in her sensual rhythm. She tugged him away from her chest and lifted her body to press her mouth to his, the thrusts of her tongue mimicking his forceful penetration. Dizzy with lust, they tumbled to the side, never breaking contact. Clara righted herself on top, straddling him as he continued driving into her from below. She closed her eyes and shook her head, her hair whipping the air, her absolute abandon challenging his control, her moans tearing down his otherwise sharp defenses.

She bent over him, her hair falling like curtains on either side of her face, creating a private space for their feasting mouths. Unbelievably, she still climaxed. Sam closed his eyes, relaxing, focusing on her pulsating grips...

"And I thought the two lovers downstairs in the kitchen were lost in their own world."

"Christ!" Sam jerked back, grabbing Clara at the waist to shield her from the intruder.

Patrick stood at the side of the bed, sloughing off his waistcoat, smirking. His jacket and hat lay on the ground near the door.

"Damn you, Pat!" Sam scolded as he fell against the mattress in relief.

Unwinding his cravat, Patrick chuckled and grinned wolfishly at Clara, locking eyes with her before he pulled off his shirt. She still straddled Sam, unmoving, as his cock twitched in complaint. She flashed him a sated smile before reaching to stroke Pat's chest, tracing the muscles with her fingers. Placing both hands on his shoulders, she pulled Pat to her and took him in a devastatingly sensual open-mouthed kiss. He growled his appreciation as he gave in willingly, and raised no objection when she unbuttoned his breeches.

Clara drew back to free his erection from his fly. Slowly riding Sam, she flashed him a provocative look before curling over to take Pat's cock in her mouth. Pat let out a shocked gasp, then groaned contentedly. Finally, he would understand. The lady was good, so very and amazingly good, with a remarkable tongue and lips every bit deserving of Sam's panegyric. As Clara sucked and licked, Pat's expression slackened in stunned delight.

He protested when she let him slip from her mouth. She smiled wickedly at them both, her chest rising and falling in anticipation of some imagined scenario. "I want both of you," she said. "Both of you inside me at once."

Sam's cock jumped, shooting desire through him to coil in his stones so utterly ready to burst. Pat bit his lip, thwarting the smirk of victory that tugged on his mouth. It was something they had both fantasized about, had talked about, had strategized as a diversion during the long winter nights. They knew exactly what to do.

Sam repositioned himself to the middle of the bed and spread his legs. "Come here, love. Straddle me."

Clara scrambled over and opened her thighs wide, ready to take him inside her.

"Not yet." He touched her belly to halt her descent. "Just bend forward, so your face is near mine."

Clara hunched over a little, then more so when Sam pulled her closer. Patrick knelt behind her, between Sam's legs, naked and erect, holding a small bowl in one hand. She turned around to watch Pat, then looked at Sam, perplexed.

"How—" she began.

He pressed a finger to her lips. "Shh, shh. Just do what you're told, sweet."

"Yes, Sam," she breathed.

Pat stroked the cheeks of her buttocks, pulling them apart. She dropped forward with a gasp when he found her tight hole, giving Sam a better view. Pat scooped his fingers through the bowl, the flexing muscles of his arm making plain what his fingers did to her.

Clara's mouth fell open at the sensual assault, her breaths hot and ragged on Sam's neck. She glanced over her shoulder at Pat.

"Butter," he explained, tossing the bowl onto the bed. "I almost tripped over Hawkins and Annabella in the kitchen to get it."

He continued his ministrations, lubricating and loosening Clara's tight muscles, her panting moans so deliciously beguiling. Sam pulled her mouth to his in a plundering kiss.

"I think we're ready," came Pat's voice.

Clara pulled back, curiosity clouding the cast of lewdness on her face. Sam delved his fingers between their bodies to toy with her aroused clit, drawing her natural wetness to coat the little nub, massaging steadily. Clara moaned and her eyes fell shut as she faded into lubricious oblivion.

Until Pat prodded her with his engorged prick.

She gasped as he entered her slowly, deliberately. Sam worked her harder, taking her to the inexorable peak. She came on his hand, soaking his palm, his abdomen, and Pat took the opportunity to press in fully.

Pat gripped Clara's waist as he pumped in and out, digging his fingers cruelly into her flesh as she undulated to the tempo of his thrusts. Sam grabbed his yearning prick, the rapturous expressions of his lovers as they merged in carnal union taking him to the brink of need.

"Lift up a little for me, love. I want to enter you now."

She raised her hips just enough. Sam wet his cock in her slickness, then entered her, slowly, watching every twinge of emotion flitting across her face at the double invasion. Pat waited patiently as Sam filled her, pushing in to the hilt.

"Oh, God!" she screamed, grabbing Sam's chest hair, clawing at Pat's fingers on her waist. Both men remained still as she clenched and released unceasingly, panting and growling with each climax.

She was already so exquisitely tight, but this, this was torture. Sam had to muster every ounce of control to keep himself from coming, knowing if he did, it would not be a satisfying climax. He needed to move inside her.

"Clara—"

She clenched again. "Please ... Sam ..." she rasped, her eyes tightly shut, her face red from want of air. With one final scream she slumped forward.

Sam lightly caressed her shoulders. "Sweet, are you well?"

"Oh, God," she exhaled, barely recovered, yet smiling. "Sam, love. Pat," she turned her head weakly over her shoulder, "spend in me. I want you both to spend inside me. I want you to feel what I just did."

Released from her sensual torment, Sam laughed out loud, exhilarated, meeting Pat's relieved gaze. Sam set the rhythm, and Pat followed, thrusting in as Sam pulled out, his cock sliding along the length of Pat's through warm wetness, the excruciating tightness relieved only when he was embedded fully and Pat had pulled back.

There was simply no more luscious feeling than a double fuck.

But the time for indulgence was over. The need for release had never been so strong.

"Now!"

Pat grinned at the command and followed Sam's lead, matching his movements, pumping in and out simultaneously, two men as one. Clara offered fresh encouragements, moaning and tensing, taking them to the edge. Sam hung on as Pat gripped Clara's waist, threw his head back, and with one final thrust, loosed himself deep inside, the heat of his emission penetrating her core, enticing Sam to let go.

He gazed up at Clara, his Clara. She smiled as a tear fell from her cheek. "I love you," she whispered.

It was his undoing. Sam jerked up in release, filling her with his seed amidst curses and blasphemies.

For a moment, the three lay in a spent heap, catching their respective breaths, the pounding of their hearts slowing in concert. Pat pulled out first.

"I expect our guest is here by now, waiting in the parlor downstairs," he said as he cleaned himself with a handkerchief before starting to dress.

Clara tumbled off Sam's body. "Guest?" she said, looking from man to man.

Sam pulled himself up on his knees and took both her hands in his. "Clara, love, the man downstairs is the parson from the town of Chesterton. I've had a license prepared. He's here to marry us, if you will have me."

Tears welled in her eyes. "Oh, Sam," she said with a soft sniffle.

He cupped her cheek with his palm. "Clara, will you marry me?"

Her eager eyes answered him first. "Yes, Sam, I will."

He bellowed in gleeful laughter as he took her in his arms and kissed her everywhere his lips could reach. "Thank you, thank you. You have just made me the happiest man in the world."

Clara giggled. "But, love, won't Patrick be jealous?" she teased.

Pat let out a sharp guffaw.

Sam grinned. "Patrick is already married these last few months."

Clara's eyes widened. "Constance?"

Pat blushed. "Yeah. With our baby due, I wanted to get her on the ration for officers' wives." He buttoned up his waistcoat. "Sam will do the same for you. But with all the shortages, there's no guarantee."

"Mr. and Mrs. Cuyler are fervent patriots," said Clara. "I'm sure they will allow you to use their lands to grow whatever is needed."

Patrick chuckled. "And I'm sure we can get Hawkins to liaise with the Cuylers. He's got farming in his blood." He wagged a finger at Sam and Clara still naked on the bed. "Get dressed, you two." He grabbed his hat as he opened the door. "I'll meet you downstairs in the parlor."

Clara had never dressed more quickly in her life. She even had to goad Sam into hurrying up.

"Darling, you are marrying an officer of the Continental Army. I must set the example and look presentable."

Clara simply cursed the war.

And when Sam was finished she grabbed his hand to lead him downstairs and into the parlor. She giggled when she spied the Reverend Daniels, a sharp little man with dark hair, a pointy nose, and reading glasses, who now wore patriot blue instead of his usual neutral green frock. Once the British had left Chesterton, the true sympathies of many of the villagers had been revealed in a similar manner.

He smiled and nodded his greeting. "Lady Strathmore." The smile turned into a smirk when he turned his attention to Sam who fidgeted at her side so much he was practically dancing. "Major Taylor, I presume?"

Clara giggled some more.

Sam flushed. "Yes, sir."

Pat stood silently by, trying most unsuccessfully to hide a grin.

And then it happened. As her heart thumped in her chest, the reverend opened his *Book of Common Prayer* to the "Form of

Solemnization of Matrimony," drew in a deep breath and began. "Dearly beloved, we are gathered—"

The parlor door creaked open and Sebastian Hawkins poked his head into the room. "I heard the parson was here," he said, glancing around until his gaze landed on Reverend Daniels. "Pardon me, sir, but may we impose upon you for your services as well?"

Hawkins opened the door wider and let Annabella in, rocking her son in her arms. She nodded her greeting to the reverend and he smiled back, a fatherly twinkle in his eye.

Hawkins put his arm around her shoulders. "We would like to be married, sir. If you don't mind. I have a license as well, signed by Colonel Henry Livingston, like Major Taylor's."

Clara gripped Sam's arm excitedly and turned a hopeful face to the clergyman. Reverend Daniels shook his head in amazement. "Should I have a concern that your loyalty in marriage may mirror your loyalty in war, Lieutenant Hawkins?"

Pat choked on a guffaw.

Hawkins was nonplussed. "Sir?" And then he blushed. He searched his pockets, drew out a folded document, and handed it to the reverend.

Reverend Daniels perused the document with a raised brow and a hint of skepticism.

"I'm now Captain Hawkins of the 4th New York Regiment," Hawkins explained. "And Annabella Rogers is my betrothed."

"He's on our side now, reverend, so you don't need to worry about me," Annabella squeaked eagerly. "He'll be raising Redmond's son. A true patriot son."

"As long as you're happy, child." The reverend smiled warmly at her. "You'll bring your son around for baptizing, too, when you're ready."

Annabella curtsied. "Yes, Reverend Daniels."

The reverend turned to Sam and Clara. "Do the major and his lady object?"

"Oh, no, sir!" they said in unison. Clara giggled. Sam was just as anxious as she.

"Very well then, we shall have two couples joined in holy matrimony this afternoon." The reverend waved Hawkins and Annabella over.

With the couples positioned before him, Reverend Daniels began his offices, his baritone voice soothing and melodious. Clara listened to the words just enough to know when it was her turn to say "I do," and when she did, she looked deep into Sam's eyes. Whatever the future held for them in this rebellious country thousands of miles away from her native land, Clara knew that with Samuel Taylor, she was finally home.

About the Author

Regina Kammer is a librarian, an art historian, and an award-winning, international best-selling, multi-published writer of provocative historical romance and contemporary romance with a touch of history. Her short stories and novels make history sexier, whether the era is Roman, Byzantine, Viking, American Revolution, or Victorian. She's even sexed up contemporary settings, Steampunk, and Greco-Roman mythology. She has been published by Cleis Press, Go Deeper Press, Ellora's Cave, House of Erotica, Story Ink, Loose Id, The Naughty Literati, and her own imprint, Viridium Press. She began writing historical fiction with romantic elements during National Novel Writing Month 2006, switching to erotica when all her characters suddenly demanded to have sex.

Keep up with Regina

Check out her website: https://reginakammer.com/
Never miss a new release! Subscribe to *Kammerotica News*:
https://reginakammer.com/newsletter/

Historical erotic romance by Regina

Victorian
The Pleasure Device (Harwell Heirs Book 1)
Disobedience By Design (Harwell Heirs Book 2)
Where Destiny Plays (Harwell Heirs Book 3)
The Westerman Affair (Art & Discipline Book 1)
The Demonstration
The Invitation
Disputed Boundaries (Stories from the San Juan Islands)

American Revolution
The General's Wife: An American Revolutionary Tale
Winter Interlude: An American Revolutionary Novelette
On the Eighteenth of January, '78; or, A Night At Valley Forge

Ancient World
Hadrian and Sabina: A Love Story
Ancient Shorts: An Ancient World Romance Collection

Steampunk
One Cheek Or Two? (Ockham Steam-Works Laboratory Chronicles 1)
Delia's Heartthrob (Ockham Steam-Works Laboratory Chronicles 2)
Swing Follies (Ockham Steam-Works Laboratory Chronicles 3)